CW01642593

WHISPERS AT DAWN

SEAGROVE & RAVEN

BOOK THREE

RACHEL HENKE

RED BALLOON PRESS

DEDICATION

For Greta and Brian. (The best ever!)

BRITISH ENGLISH NOTE

I write in British English, my mother tongue. Most of my stories are set at least partly in England, so it makes sense for an authentic reading experience. I've included a few examples for international readers so you don't think I can't spell or am from another planet!

Common examples of British English spelling and usage:

'Single speech marks' not "double" in dialogue

Colour not color (ou not o for words like this)

Recognise not recognize (s not z)

Travelling not traveling (double ll not single l)

Centre not center (re not er in many words)

Sceptical not skeptical (c not k)

CHAPTER 1

London, May 1941

Lizzie Beaumont's stomach was wound tight as a knot as she paced around Jack's dusty office at the Special Operations Executive on Baker Street. The heels of her shoes tapped on the hard floor as she crossed to the shabby rug by the Victorian antique desk, its expanse of mahogany wood monopolising the space.

Lizzie's fate would be sealed that afternoon, and every minute felt like an hour. She skimmed the leather surface of the desk with her fingers, her mind racing as she considered the possibilities of what might happen next.

The clock on the wall strummed loudly, and Lizzie thought she would burst with anticipation if Jack didn't return soon. And with that agitated thought, she marched towards the door, determined to find something to occupy her, rather than suffer this torturous waiting for one second longer. She would go to the cipher room and make herself useful. Jack would find her when he emerged from the meeting with their superiors.

The door swung open, and Jack—her Jack—his tall frame and broad shoulders dominating the doorway, looked as dashing as ever in his captain's uniform. His presence instantly unravelled the knot in her stomach like a magic spell, and a rush of intense emotion permeated her chest. It was almost a year since they fell madly in love after she arrived in London from Jersey, but somehow, she fell more deeply in love with him every day.

In some ways, one year seemed like a lifetime together.

Lizzie couldn't imagine her life without him, and Jack professed his love for her daily, even though they agreed they must keep their relationship a secret until the war was over. British Military Intelligence frowned upon romantic relationships between agents, and it was generally accepted that falling in love on the job endangered lives and was a strict no-no.

The prelude to every mission followed the same pattern, which was why Lizzie felt so wretched today. She was committed to doing all she could in her clandestine missions with the SOE and French Resistance to stop the Nazis and win the war, but the wrench she and Jack faced each time they were forced to part squeezed the breath out of her. Just the thought of going back undercover in occupied France, unable to see Jack for weeks, perhaps even months, filled her soul with a haunting dread and the exile hadn't even begun.

Perhaps it would be an operation in London, and she wouldn't need to go back into France. She'd heard about agents doing espionage work at home. Lord knew there were enough stories about British traitors and Nazi spies in Britain to keep them all busy.

Lizzie sighed. Her gut assured her this was wishful thinking, and she would soon be on a plane headed for France.

Lizzie stopped abruptly and raised her head to meet the dark eyes of the man she adored who was also her commanding officer. 'Well?' she said, trying to sound cheerful but failing miserably. 'When do I leave?'

Jack clicked the door shut quietly behind him, moved towards Lizzie and swept her into his arms, dropping soft kisses onto her hair and holding her tightly against his beating heart as though he would never let her go. Their proximity and his familiar scent imbued her with a deep yearning to stay locked in his arms forever, and she prayed silently they would have some proper time alone together before they must inevitably say goodbye.

She knew she would do what they asked of her, but she needed time to prepare mentally and rally her courage, which had deserted her for the moment. Lizzie chided herself for behaving like a carefree silly girl hopelessly in love, her emotions all a flutter, when she should be focused on the next deadly mission. Even as the thoughts whirled through her mind, she relished another guilty moment of intoxicating pleasure in Jack's arms, sinking into his hard chest and letting him love her.

Events had come to a head that morning when Val warned her to ready herself. Her next mission would be decided that afternoon in a meeting with the powers that be.

Lizzie's thoughts jerked her back to the present. Jack released his grip on her gently, and she stood in the circle of his arms for a few seconds before they moved apart, and he crossed to his desk and lit a cigarette.

'God, I need this,' he said, inhaling deeply and blowing out the smoke in measured puffs. His shiny black hair had flopped onto his forehead, and he looked as striking as a Hollywood movie star.

'That bad?' Now Jack had arrived, she was scared to hear the news, so she delayed him by remarking on his smoking technique. 'How come you look elegant when you smoke, and I resemble an old farm tractor?'

'Practice, my darling, practice. I much prefer you don't master the art of smoking, though. They say it's terrible for you.'

'So why do you keep doing it, then?'

'It's just so damn pleasurable,' Jack said, pushing his hair out of his eyes with some impatience. 'Besides, I've been smoking so long now, I wouldn't know what to do with my hands if I stopped.'

'I could think of something far more pleasurable for you to do with your hands, Captain King,' Lizzie said, tilting her head to one side, so her lustrous brunette locks coiled over one shoulder.

'I'm sure. You know I am always eager to pleasure you, Miss Beaumont. There's nothing that could ever get in the way of that.' Jack chuckled as he leaned across the desk to stub out his cigarette.

Then his eyes sought Lizzie's, and his expression turned serious.

'What are my orders?' she said. 'We'd better get this over with.'

Jack reached for Lizzie's hand and pulled her gently back towards him. 'It's not what you think.'

'Surely that would depend on what I think. How do you know what I think?'

'It's one of my gifts.' Jack laughed heartily.

His words intrigued her. She knew from experience that if she were flying into occupied France in the next few days, Jack would be sombre and preoccupied, not jolly and laughing. He usually tried to pretend he was focused on the upcoming mission, but she could feel how much the thought of her alone again on enemy soil troubled him.

Predictably, he would make a strong case for going in her place, but young men drew more suspicion than women, so he was just as predictably rebuffed and could only occasionally follow her for backup in an emergency.

Lizzie's heartbeat quickened at the thought of him going without her. Was that why he was so light-hearted today? Suddenly, the proposition of her leaving alone seemed infinitely better. She'd much rather be the agent in action, than be waiting at Baker Street, pining for Jack and fearing the worst as the hours crawled by. She'd experienced that scenario before, when he'd stayed undercover in France, and she'd returned to London. It was awful, and she had no desire to relive it.

'You are altogether too cheerful,' she said. 'What's the mission, exactly?'

Jack raised an eyebrow. 'You read me like a book.'

'It must be one of my gifts, too. Come on, what is it? Do they want you this time?' Lizzie did her best to hide her distress, but she heard her voice crack.

Jack nodded, and Lizzie's stomach lurched.

It was as she suspected, then, so she steeled herself for what was to come.

'When do you fly out?' she asked, her voice low, and her chest tight.

'When do *we* fly out?' Jack replied. 'That's the question you need to ask.'

Lizzie sputtered and her green eyes widened. 'We? Oh, my goodness, I can hardly believe it. Tell me everything.'

Jack pulled out a chair and Lizzie sat down, relief cascading through her.

'I'll grab us some coffee and be back in a minute,' he said.

Lizzie nodded, trying to calm her whirring thoughts. 'Coffee would be good. Thank you.'

Jack strode across the room. The door closed behind him, and Lizzie was alone again with the ticking of the clock and her frantic thoughts.

Could it be true they were finally undertaking a mission together in occupied France?

CHAPTER 2

'I can't believe our good fortune!' Lizzie squealed when Jack told her the plan was for them to go undercover together in an operation in Vichy controlled South of France.

Jack raised his finger to his mouth. 'You'll give us away. I'm certain no one in the history of Military Intelligence has been this excited to venture behind enemy lines indefinitely.'

Lizzie lowered the pitch of her voice so only he could hear. 'You're right. If they suspect us, it'll be called off in a flash, and they'll probably send one of the newer recruits with you.'

Jack's lips tugged into a mischievous smile. 'I did argue for you not to accompany me.'

Lizzie punched his arm lightly. 'Of course you did. I'm sure Val would be suspicious if you didn't try to stop me going. You never want me to have any of the fun.'

Jack held up his hands in a gesture of mock surrender. 'You are a dangerous woman, Seagrove. If going into occupied France is your idea of fun, I confess I'm at a loss how to protect you.'

'You always protect me, Raven,' Lizzie whispered, using his codename. 'But seriously, you must see it's the most perfect opportunity for us to be together like a proper couple. You're always saying we would be married by now if it weren't for the war. Now, we can enjoy all the perks of married life and not be forced to live apart. And with the agency's blessing, too!'

Jack smiled at Lizzie's enthusiasm, which he found contagious. It was just as well they were alone, because anyone would see at a glance how besotted he was with the young woman at his side. 'You really are one of a kind, my darling. Anyone would think we had just won an all-expenses paid trip to the South of France. Have you forgotten there's a bloody war on and we'll be lucky if we get out alive?'

Lizzie shook her head, her red lips curving into a warm smile and her eyes twinkling. 'I haven't forgotten. But I dreaded leaving you again, or even worse, you away without me. Going together is like a gift from the gods. Besides, it *is* an all-expenses paid trip.'

'Only if you don't count the considerable price that will be on our heads the longer we stay.' Jack snorted and slid his arms around Lizzie, and they stood there swaying silently for a while, each lost in their own thoughts.

'I've got to scoot off to an emergency meeting soon. The Dutch section wants me to advise on a situation,' Jack said, breaking the silence.

'You're always in demand. I hope I can be like you one day.' Lizzie was only half joking. Jack was one of the most experienced agents in Military Intelligence, and the fledgeling country-targeted sections of the SOE called on him to share his expertise.

Jack King was a legend in the field and was fast becoming one at Baker Street, too.

He dropped a kiss on Lizzie's pert nose. 'Stay exactly as

you are, please. You are already perfect. Lord, help me if you become a crotchety old spy like me.'

Lizzie glowed under his appreciative gaze, like a cat basking in the sun. 'Will I see you later?'

'You can count on it. Dinner tonight?'

Lizzie nodded. 'I'd love that. I told Ma and Pa I'll be back though, so I'll have to go home after dinner, or they'll worry.'

'No problem. I'll get you back to them safely before the witching hour.' When he reached the door, he turned and winked. 'See you at our usual spot by the station at seven?'

'See you then.'

They spent much of their time dodging other agents, and their personal life was as clandestine as their work. It wasn't easy keeping their relationship secret, but it had to be done.

A joyful smile lingered on Lizzie's face. The implications of their mission unfolded in her mind. They wouldn't have to pretend not to be in love in France. They could live together freely. Clearly, they would need to put some serious thought into their cover as husband and wife so their stories would be bulletproof, but the thought of living openly with Jack made Lizzie's stomach fizz.

Val's face appeared in the doorway, jilting Lizzie out of her romantic reverie. 'I've been looking all over for you,' she said. 'I need you.'

Lizzie was embarrassed to be caught grinning on her own, and she hoped Val hadn't noticed.

'What are you doing mooning around in here, looking like Father Christmas came early?'

Lizzie cleared her throat and forcibly restrained the slow blush threatening to stain her pale cheeks. She was working on controlling her emotions and hiding her reactions, but it was a challenge. 'Oh nothing. I was just thinking about a recent telephone call from a friend, that's all.'

Val looked at her quizzically. 'If I didn't know you barely

have a spare minute for a social life, I would think you were daydreaming about some lucky young man.'

The statement took Lizzie by surprise, and she flicked her hair over her shoulder in an awkward gesture, but somehow kept the blush at bay despite the tingle on her neck. 'Imagine! Wouldn't that be a fine thing? No chance, that will have to wait until after the war, I'm afraid,' she garbled, smiling as she followed Val along the dimly lit corridor to her office. Her heartbeat gradually slowed to its regular pace, and she told herself to be more careful. She was in a hotbed of spies and, despite Jack reassuring her, they were all too obsessed with their work to notice what their fellow agents were doing, Val was astute.

Lizzie fished out the file Val had been searching for and plopped it onto her desk. 'Here it is. Where do you want me today?'

Val pushed her thick-rimmed glasses up her nose and fixed her gaze on Lizzie, reminding her of one of her schoolteachers in Jersey. 'Good question. There's so much going on, we could do with five of you!'

'Shall I take that as a compliment, or as a sign of my inefficiency?' Lizzie smiled.

'Oh, definitely a compliment. I don't know what I'd do without you,' Val said, holding the file. 'Although I'll find out soon enough, unfortunately. Jack told you the news, I suppose?'

Lizzie nodded.

'Thoughts?' Val asked, nibbling the end of her pencil as she studied Lizzie.

'I'm ready for the next mission,' Lizzie said. 'Well, I will be when I know the specifics.'

'Jack's in with the Dutch, but we could make a start without him. Did he brief you at all?'

'No, not really. All I know is we're both off to the South of France.'

'Yes, it's a beautiful time of year for it. Shame you'll have to share it with the bloody Vichy traitors and the Boche tourists.'

'Where will we be based, exactly?' Lizzie asked. She'd visited Antibes as a child with her family and recalled its outstanding beauty, but she wasn't familiar with the South.

'Toulouse.'

'I've never been there,' Lizzie said.

'I have, briefly. *La Ville Rose*, they call it. It's a charming medieval city with pinkish terracotta buildings. The architecture is quite wonderful.'

Val seemed suddenly far away, a soft expression etched onto her usually stern features, and Lizzie wondered what had happened. She didn't know anything about Val's personal life. All she knew was she was a fierce defender of Britain and lived and breathed her job as the right-hand woman to the boss of F Section.

'I'm getting sentimental in my old age,' Val said, shaking her head. 'Anyway, back to the business at hand. We need you and Jack in Toulouse.'

'When will we leave?' Lizzie asked, her pulse racing at the thought of dropping into Vichy France. It would be completely unknown territory for her.

'The sooner the better. But not before you're fully equipped and ready for every eventuality. Pull up a chair and let's get into the details of what we need to do to prep you.'

Stella, the SOE's beloved tea lady, tapped on the door and pushed the rattling trolley into the room, laden with a big urn of tea, mugs, and biscuits.

'How do you always know the perfect time to appear, Stella?' Val asked.

'Well, I have an advantage—it's always the perfect time for

a cuppa and something sweet!' Stella poured two mugs of tea and distributed some biscuits onto a small plate on the desk between them.

'True,' Val agreed, biting into the crunchy biscuit.

Lizzie smiled warmly at Stella, who had been her underground companion when they sheltered from the first London air raid at the start of the Blitz the previous summer. They shared a bond because of the frightening experience and always exchanged a few words when they bumped into each other. 'Heard from your son recently?' she asked the tea lady.

'Last I heard, he's alive and kicking, giving those bastards what for at the Front, God bless him.'

Stella rattled out of the room, closing the door behind her.

'Now where were we?' Val mused, nibbling her biscuit.

'You were saying we should discuss how to prep me,' Lizzie prompted after she took a sip of steaming tea and replaced the mug.

'We urgently need eyes and ears in Vichy France.'

'Understood. Why Toulouse?'

'It's a fair question. The intelligence we intercepted says Toulouse is a melting pot of potential Resistance recruits, so we've identified it as the best location for you to set up camp.'

There was another tap at the door, and Jack's face appeared in the crack. 'Come in,' called Val. 'You've missed Stella, but there are some biscuits left if you're quick.'

Jack pulled up a chair and sat near them before reaching for a biscuit.

'What's the latest from Amsterdam?' Val asked.

'Some agents seem to have got themselves in a bit of a pickle. Nothing that can't be fixed,' he said. 'Gave them a few tips.'

Val knew better than to prod any further. There was a

code of silence between the SOE agents, and it was an honour for Jack to be trusted by D Section.

'We were just discussing Toulouse,' said Val.

Jack dipped his head and hooked a pack of cigarettes from his breast pocket. He lit one and stood before crossing to look out the window. 'You've got the best view in the building,' he remarked, admiring the dome of St. Paul's gleaming in the spring sunshine.

'Yes, and it's staying that way. Don't get designs on my office,' Val quipped.

Jack swivelled to face them, spirals of smoke looping over his head towards the high ceiling. 'I prefer being in the field, anyway. Not cut out for being a desk boffin.'

'Just as well we're releasing you back into the wild, then,' Val said.

Jack smirked. 'Can't say I'm not surprised. I didn't have a chance to ask earlier. How come you and the boss have altered your position? I thought I was too much of a liability in the field unless it's an absolute emergency?'

Val replaced her empty mug on the desk and brushed the crumbs from her lap. 'That's just it. This is an emergency.'

CHAPTER 3

It was a peaceful Saturday afternoon at Jack's flat. Lizzie rested her head on his bare chest, and their limbs lay tangled in the sheet on his big bed after hours of passionate lovemaking. Her cheeks were still flushed, and she basked in the afterglow.

'When did you tell your parents you'll be home?' Jack asked, his deep voice gravelly in her ear.

'I said I wouldn't be home. Thought I'd spend tonight here with you if that's alright?' Lizzie snaked her fingers over his chest. 'You haven't got plans, have you? Sorry, I didn't think to check first.'

'You never have to check. You could move in right now, as far as I'm concerned. I hate it when you're not here, you know that.' Jack twirled a lock of Lizzie's chestnut hair around his thumb as he pondered the curious ways of love. 'It's strange because I used to enjoy living alone.'

Lizzie studied his face. 'You were impenetrable when we first met. I never would have imagined in a million years that we would be together like this. Remember how opposed you were to me joining the SOE?'

Jack released a dramatic sigh. 'Not this again. How many times do I have to explain that I was merely concerned for your safety?'

'Hmm, let me see.' Lizzie raised her eyes to the ceiling and counted on her fingers as if she were trying to figure it out. 'Until the end of days should do it,' she announced, throwing him an impish grin.

'You've got it, then. I will spend every day making up to you for the error of my ways. If it means I get to be with you like this forever, then it's worth swallowing my foolish pride.'

'Did you think you would always be a bachelor?' Lizzie probed, not quite ready to let the line of questioning go.

Jack rubbed his dark stubble. 'I was married to the job. Although I suppose the truth is, I never met the right woman. Not until you came along and beguiled me with your argumentative style of interrogation!'

Jack tickled Lizzie's side, and she squealed as she wriggled and soon, they were kissing again and forgot the serious talk about how they met and fell in love.

As dusk descended, Jack handed her a cup of tea and Lizzie thought about her family at Regent's Park. That morning, she told her mother she had to go into work and would be on the night shift, so she'd catch some sleep at the office and be home on Sunday. Ma rarely questioned her long hours, although Lizzie sometimes wondered that she didn't think it strange her daughter was called to do so many night shifts in the office. But as everyone worked long hours for the war effort, and Lizzie was a FANY, she tried to make it seem normal. Her father never questioned her comings and goings because he knew the truth about her work, which relieved some of the burden of her secret life. When her mother did suspect something wasn't quite as it should be, he would expertly lead her off the scent and wink at Lizzie.

'I don't like lying to Ma,' she murmured against Jack's

chest when he slotted back into the spot next to her. 'But it's that or never stay over with you. I can hardly say you're my lover, can I? She'd be appalled by my wanton behaviour.'

He stroked her hair, and the touch of his comforting large hand calmed her anxious thoughts.

Jack always made her feel safe.

'I know, my love,' his voice soothed, washing away her worries. 'Although you've chosen the wrong line of work if you want to avoid lying. The Official Secrets Act means we lie for a living, or had you not noticed?'

'At least I won't need to lie to them when we're in Toulouse,' she said. 'I know you think it's strange I'm so excited for us to go undercover, but that's one of the main reasons. I live an undercover life here, anyway.'

Jack laughed. 'We'll have to lie to everyone in Toulouse. And there was me thinking, you were so keen because you can't wait to share my bed at night and ravage my body at every opportunity.'

'You're not wrong. I can't think of anything more wonderful than falling asleep and waking up in your arms,' Lizzie said dreamily, her voice overflowing with tenderness.

'Just as well you're staying here tonight, then,' he said, tightening his arm around her shoulders.

'Talking of lies, we need to create a solid cover story for me to tell my family. Have you given it any thought?' Lizzie asked.

Jack shifted, pulling Lizzie up the bed slightly as he repositioned himself against the headboard and lit a cigarette.

'I have.'

'Why am I not in the least surprised? Go on, then. Fill me in. What's the plan?'

'I was thinking you could be called away urgently by the FANYs.'

'What branch?'

Jack's deep voice reverberated. 'We'll make something up. It's a great cover story. Your father knows better than to look for you, and if your mother tries, she won't find any information about the non-existent office. You can say you're working on war records. It's not unlikely the government would keep the exact location under wraps, given the scale and intensity of the bombing around the country.'

Lizzie nodded. 'Nowhere's safe. They blitzed Liverpool to smithereens.'

'Yes, it got a terrible hammering.'

'Alright, so we'll go with that. I'll start thinking about how to break it to my mother. Val said we need to prepare to stay for as long as we can maintain our cover, so we may be there a few months, unless something goes wrong.'

'That sounds about right. We don't know what awaits us over there. By the sounds of it, the Gaullists are recruiting new Resistance members like wildfire and building networks, but we have very little going on.' Jack disentangled himself from Lizzie's warm body. 'I'm going to shave. Tell your parents you may be gone a while, and you will write. We'll have Val arrange to send postcards from you like when you were in Paris.'

'It sounds reasonable enough,' Lizzie said. 'What would have been considered immodest behaviour for an unmarried woman before the war—me being posted across the country on a work assignment—is now just business as usual in wartime. As horrendous as this war is, ironically, it's given women freedom from being chained to the hearth.'

'Wait until you see the château. I promise I won't chain you to the hearth, though. You'll love it.'

Lizzie sucked in her breath and raised her head to search his eyes. 'You never said anything about a château ...'

'Didn't I?'

'No, you didn't.'

'What château is this?'

'It's my uncle's. I haven't been there for years. Henry and I used to help him in the vineyards when we were boys.'

'Vineyards! Gosh, here you go, being a dark horse again. Who forgets to mention they have an uncle ensconced in a château with vineyards in the South of France?'

Jack chuckled. 'He's far from ensconced. Trust me, it's a lot of work and not as fancy as it sounds. And don't forget there's a war on.'

'How many other secrets are you keeping from me?' Lizzie asked as she peered at him.

'It wasn't intentional. It just never came up. Even my mother hasn't seen Uncle Luc in years. She was talking about her brother only the other day. It's a shame I won't be able to tell her we'll be staying with him. We used to see a lot of him, but after my father died, my mother stopped taking us there in the summers and he's not the type to come here. He dislikes the English. Says we have no style.'

'That's too bad. With us going there, I mean. How did he take it?'

'Hard to say.'

Lizzie narrowed her eyes. 'He doesn't know yet, does he?'

Jack shook his head. 'No. In fairness, I only found out myself the other day. I had no intention of going anywhere near Toulouse until Val said we must build networks in Vichy ready for the Allied invasion.'

'What if he's not on our side, given his dislike of the English?'

'Oh, he'll be on our side.'

'How can you be so sure?'

'Because he dislikes the Germans even more! France fought against them in the Great War too, remember.'

Lizzie said, 'He sounds like quite a handful.'

'He's a character, alright.'

'What exactly is the situation with the Vichy region? You'll have to explain it to me, so I understand it properly. I know it's the part of France that's not occupied by the Nazis, but I don't completely understand who is ruling what and why.'

'They call it the *Free Zone*. It's far from free, as you'll see, but it's ruled by the Vichy French administration, who are German collaborators.'

'Hannah is in the South of France, isn't she?'

'Apparently so, but I haven't received a message from her in over a month. Who knows where she is and what she's up to, by now? Taking out enemies at any opportunity, I'd say, if I had to guess.'

'Will we try and see her when we're there?' Lizzie asked.

'It all depends. Not if it risks blowing our cover. We're better establishing separate networks in different regions, rather than putting all our eggs in one basket.'

Lizzie sighed.

'What's wrong?' Jack asked, his deep voice tender.

'Nothing. I miss Hannah, that's all.'

'It's understandable. You two went through an intense time together in Paris. Hopefully, we'll hear from her before we leave and can see her at some point.'

Lizzie's spirits lifted at the thought of being reunited with the courageous Resistance leader. 'And what of Henry? Have they been in touch recently, do you know?'

'Henry is still flying a lot. My mother spoke to him last week and says he claims to be well but sounds fatigued. Then again, she always says that. There were some whispers last week that we may be nearing the end of the Blitz. Word has it Hitler's lost his appetite for it. Tired of us bombing in retaliation.'

'Thank God for that. It seems to have been going on forever. I've grown used to the sounds of bombs dropping and running for shelter at all hours. It's hard to imagine what life will be like when this war is over.'

Jack said, 'That's another good thing about going to Toulouse. It's not being pounded by the Luftwaffe.

Anyway, enough of this war talk for now, my darling. I've got other plans for us before we go to dinner.'

'Have you, now?' Lizzie said, a teasing lilt in her voice, as she caressed his firm muscular body and surrendered to his kisses, shivering beneath his touch.

CHAPTER 4

That evening Lizzie and Jack strolled hand in hand through the war-ravaged streets of London, crumbling buildings now a normal sight, on their way back to Jack's flat after a modest meal. Lizzie pointed to the yellow moon glowing in the darkening sky, littered with twinkling stars. 'What is it they say about a full moon?'

Jack released a deep menacing growl near her ear, and Lizzie jumped and then dissolved into laughter. 'Bloody hell. You scared me, you fool!'

Jack chuckled. 'The werewolves will be on the prowl tonight. Anything could happen.'

'Don't say that. It's such a beautiful evening. The sky looks magical.'

'You're a true romantic, darling,' Jack said, recapturing her hand and pulling her gently along beside him. 'Come on, let's head home for a nightcap.'

They walked on in companionable silence, Lizzie loving the feel of her hand cocooned in his. 'If I'm to pretend to be your wife in Toulouse, I need to know everything about you.'

'I already think of you as my wife,' he said, fixing his dark eyes on hers until she melted beneath the intensity.

Lizzie reached to kiss him, and they stood on the street sheltered in each other's arms, as if there were no one else in war-torn London but them.

A near empty double-decker bus rumbled past, its headlights masked, startling them and they drew apart and resumed walking slowly, not wanting the enchanting evening to end. 'Everyone must be at home already. I don't remember London so quiet on a Saturday night, even since the blackout,' Jack said.

'Let's hope it's not the calm before the storm.' Lizzie stifled a yawn. 'The streets are almost deserted.'

'The Blitz is getting to people. They're worn out with the daily bombardments and I daresay they want to be at home, ready to get the family to a shelter if there's a raid.'

'Where have you been sheltering lately, by the way?' Lizzie asked.

Jack shrugged. 'There's an Anderson shelter down the road, but I prefer the Underground. It's not as cramped.'

'A quiet night would be wonderful,' Lizzie said as they entered the flat, and waves of tiredness crept over her. 'I don't know why I'm so weary. We spent most of the afternoon lounging in bed.'

'I wouldn't call that lounging,' Jack said, his mouth curving into a devilish grin.

'You know what I me—'

A loud haunting sound interrupted Lizzie's sentence, echoing through the flat. 'Oh, my God. I tempted fate.'

Jack grabbed Lizzie's hand and shouted over the din. 'Come on, let's get to the station to be on the safe side. I'm not taking any chances when you're with me.'

'I can't hear you!' shouted Lizzie over the wailing siren.

Still wearing her hat and coat, she turned and exited the

door back into the street, which was already bustling with throngs of people. They milled about, running for shelter. Frightened children clutched onto their mothers' hands and parents scooped up toddlers into their arms so they could run faster.

Lizzie's ears hurt with the shriek of the sirens. They ran to Baker Street station, the Underground swallowing them up like an ancient cave. Streams of people were in front and behind them. 'I thought you said it wasn't as cramped. It's madness in here!'

'Hmm,' Jack said.

'You don't really come here, do you?' Lizzie said when they paused to catch their breath after the frantic run.

'I wouldn't say that exactly. I'm here often to meet you. Come on, this is where I sheltered last time,' Jack said, steering Lizzie into one of the dimly lit passages.

They huddled in a spot on the cold tiled floor, Lizzie leaning against Jack as he propped himself against the wall. Every time they heard a bomb screech and explode in the distance, Lizzie squeezed her eyes shut. She was praying hard that her parents had reached the shelter in the park, and Juliet and Evie were safe with them, and not out gallivanting for the evening, as her mother called it.

Wave after wave of loud blasts shook the foundations of the station until Lizzie muttered in a rare moment of reprieve. 'When is it ever going to end?'

'The Jerries are giving us hell tonight,' he said, shaking his head and drawing on his cigarette. 'Lord knows how much damage there is out there. The bombing hasn't been this heavy in ages.'

A baby whimpered, shifting on its mother's knee. Lizzie could see why many families had taken government advice and evacuated their children to the countryside. She couldn't decide what must be worse for a parent—worrying their children would be struck by a bomb and killed in their beds or being separated from them indefinitely in an effort to keep them alive.

'What time is it?' Lizzie asked, when she awoke from an uncomfortable doze on Jack's shoulder. The dust from the old station glittered on the air and tickled Lizzie's nose, making her sneeze.

'It's after eleven. It's been quiet for a while now. We can leave soon if the bombing doesn't resume. Are you alright?'

Lizzie yawned. 'A bit cold and crumpled, but nothing a hot bath and a few hours' proper sleep won't fix.'

'That's the spirit. Can't let the Boche get us down or they'll have won.'

Lizzie glanced at the rows of exhausted Londoners lining the station floor. There were people of all ages huddled together trying to keep warm, some managing to sleep, whilst others paced nearby. A little girl with black hair, her weary head lolling on her mother's shoulder, caught Lizzie's eye and her heart stirred. This was no life for a small child.

She should be tucked up in bed without a care in the world. The girl reminded her of the Jewish children she and Hannah had sheltered in the farmhouse in Paris. She wondered briefly whether the family had made it to America, and her mind raced with thoughts of all the people she had encountered during her missions and the tragic stories they had shared about their missing family members.

The all-clear siren sounded like a bugle from heaven. 'Let's go home,' Jack said, glancing at his watch and interrupting her reflections.

They unfurled their aching bodies, stood and stretched. It was cold at that time of night, sitting on the floor in the underground station so Lizzie hadn't removed her coat. Jack positioned her hat back on her head, his eyes tender. 'Ready?'

Their movement triggered others to follow and soon they

were leading a chain of tired, but not beaten Londoners in a mass exodus from the station. Further along, others made their way outside. As they emerged onto Baker Street, Lizzie and Jack studied their surroundings cautiously.

'We haven't been bombed here, at least. Let's walk to the SOE and check everything's alright,' Jack said.

They walked for about five minutes until they arrived outside HQ. Jack looked at Lizzie. 'It's fine. Do you want to go in and hear the latest?'

Lizzie shook her head. 'Better not risk it. Us turning up together at this time of night would be a dead giveaway.'

Just as they turned to walk back in the direction of Jack's flat, two ambulances raced up the street, their sirens blaring.

'I wonder what's been hit,' Lizzie said, pointing. 'There's smoke over there.'

As if in a trance, Jack followed Lizzie as she started running after the ambulances and they soon reached a back street, the air thick with smoke. They stared at the sight before them, and for a few seconds they just stood there, mesmerised by the blazing buildings. Then the smoke made Lizzie splutter and cough.

'It's like entering the gates of hell,' she said, the horror reflected in her eyes.

A row of houses had been badly hit, the fire still licking fiercely through the bombed out upper storeys despite vigorous attempts to douse the flames. Fire engines were on site, and a group of grimy faced firemen blasted the burning buildings with water.

A fireman shouted to the gathering crowd, 'Stand back! Stand back. These buildings may collapse at any moment.'

Jack pulled Lizzie away from where she stood transfixed by the terrible scenes of death and destruction unfolding before their eyes.

Auxiliary fire service volunteers were also on site, and

one of them approached Lizzie and Jack. 'If you want to help, grab a pump and blast this.' He pointed to the side of a house that was burning fiercely.

'Are people still inside?' Lizzie asked.

'Hard to say. There was a siren, so hopefully they got out and made it to a shelter before the bombs hit.'

Lizzie and Jack stood side by side with their respective pumps, blasting water at the burning house. The area was in chaos as people stumbled onto the scene searching for loved ones after the all-clear. A woman fell to the ground on her knees, screeching like an injured creature. Lizzie passed her pump to someone else and crossed to her swiftly.

'What can I do?' she asked.

'It's my Joey. He's trapped in the back bedroom. They can't get him out,' she gasped, struggling to speak between choking sobs.

Lizzie tried to console the desperate mother as she gazed at the house she pointed to. It had already partially collapsed, and the thought of the woman's son trapped by the fire upstairs was too much to bear. Lizzie estimated that the density of the smoke alone would be enough to suffocate him.

A few minutes later, a soot covered fireman emerged from the smoke-filled entrance, a small body slung over his burly shoulder.

The woman leapt towards him, making little sounds like a mewling kitten.

'Let's rest him here,' the fireman wheezed, doing his best to keep her at arm's length.

'My Joey,' the mother sobbed, reaching to clutch at her son, but the fireman stopped her again.

'We need a doctor here,' he shouted over the crackling and hissing of the fire, his voice croaky but loud enough to be heard by the medical team.

Lizzie stared at the small unmoving body of the boy on the small patch of grass. His body didn't look injured, but he lay there in his pyjamas as if in a heavy slumber. She desperately hoped she was wrong, but she feared he wasn't breathing. His sooty face bore a peaceful expression.

'Joey, wake up,' sobbed his mother uncontrollably, fighting to reach him. 'Wake up, please.'

They were shuffled out of the way, and a nurse leaned over the boy and worked on him frantically, checking for signs of life. By now, the mother was crying hysterically in Lizzie's arms and all she could do was keep her upright as she sobbed on her shoulder.

The nurse caught Lizzie's eye and shook her head slowly, her eyes full of heartbreak. The boy was dead.

Jack appeared at Lizzie's shoulder and looked at her questioningly over the woman's head. Lizzie moved her chin towards the small inert body on the ground. Jack's eyes met hers in silent understanding just as the woman called out, 'I want to see Joey. Let me see my Joey.'

Lizzie felt a tap on her shoulder, and she turned to see a dishevelled looking giant of a man, his shirt torn, and his clothes covered in soot. Tears trickled onto his dirty cheeks.

'I'm Joey's father.'

Lizzie disentangled herself from the distraught woman and gently transferred her weight to her husband's arms. Then she stood there helplessly, tears streaming down her face, watching them as they clung to each other, rocking back and forth in a desperate lament for the young son they had lost to this devastating night of the Blitz.

CHAPTER 5

Several weeks had passed since that terrible night when Lizzie and Jack stumbled home in a daze through the smoke-filled streets with rage in their hearts.

Thankfully, the members of the Beaumont and King households had reached shelter in time, but others weren't so lucky. Many lost their homes, and over 1400 their lives, in the latest devastating raid of the London Blitz.

The night of the London bombing reinforced Lizzie's commitment to destroy the Nazis and dismantle their murderous regime. It was a timely and shocking reminder of why they risked everything to go on dangerous missions.

The Germans had struck at the heart of government. Westminster Palace had been hit by incendiary bombs and by morning all that remained of the Commons Chamber were smoking ruins.

Fortunately, recent weeks had been quiet with no major raids, and there were cautious whispers they had reached the end of eight months of the Blitz. Intelligence reports confirmed the Luftwaffe was preparing to invade Russia.

Lizzie and Jack were in his office getting organised for the impending mission when Drake, Lizzie's former boss from the War Office, arrived.

'Lizzie, it's been too long. How are you, dear girl? I can't tell you how good it is to see you alive and well with my own eyes.'

Lizzie rose from her chair and shook Drake's hand. 'Thank you, sir. It's good to see you, too.'

'Did this rogue here pass on my regards? I tried to check in on you several times after you transferred, but it was never the right time.'

Drake dropped into the seat Jack pulled out for him after they all exchanged pleasantries, and he immediately lit his pipe. Drake was one of Jack's favourite people. He'd always had a lot of time for Drake, but he was even more grateful to his old mentor for introducing him to Lizzie.

Drake dragged on his pipe and looked from one to the other expectantly. 'So, to what do I owe the honour of being summoned to this noble establishment?'

Jack usually made a point of meeting Drake for a drink at The Ritz, which buzzed with London's elite and was affectionately dubbed, Blitz at the Ritz. Drake used to drop into Jack's old flat unannounced, but Jack had actively discouraged him from visiting his new place, so there would be no risk he'd show up and find Lizzie there. They'd agreed that would be mortifying for all of them, so regular meetings at The Ritz were the norm.

The SOE kept the circle tight and even new recruits weren't allowed in the HQ building anymore. As a founding member, Lizzie was fortunate to be considered one of the inner circle, and to have Val's ear. It helped she was her personal assistant, but even so, she realised it was an honour.

Jack said, 'You were in right at the beginning, Seagrove. It accords some special privileges. The newbies are based in a flat around the corner.'

'Like when Drake brought me to meet you,' Lizzie replied, thinking back to the first time she saw Jack. It often struck her how easily her life could have taken a completely different course if it weren't for that day. If Drake hadn't identified her as suitable agent material, and she hadn't been intrigued enough to accept his unusual invitation, she would probably still be translating mundane documents at the War Office, weathering the war best she could, without any means to do something more significant to defend Britain.

Jack told her after they moved to Baker Street from St. Ermin's Hotel, there were some leaks because they were too complacent about who came and went. They had to introduce stricter protocols.

The SOE had grown exponentially since Lizzie's first day, both with networks in the field overseas and agents on home soil.

Lizzie's attention snapped back to the present as Drake fixed his stare on Jack, waiting to hear why he had been called in.

'Top secret,' said Jack. 'Can't risk flappy ears overhearing our plans at The Ritz.'

'Go on,' Drake said. 'What may I do to help?'

'I remembered you mentioning you spent considerable time in the South of France and are familiar with Toulouse.'

Drake drew on his pipe again and narrowed his eyes as he exhaled. 'Yes, that's correct. Oh, those were the days. They seem like a lifetime ago. A different world.'

'It's a different world alright,' Jack said.

'What's happening in Toulouse?' Drake asked.

'Lizzie and I are going in next week. We need eyes and ears on the ground if we're to have a foothold in the South to prepare the way for an invasion. We've heard repeated whispers for some time now that De Gaulle is establishing Resistance networks in Vichy France.'

'And F Section doesn't want to be left out in the cold,' Drake said, filling in the blanks.

'Correct. It's bad enough we have a rival SOE French group in RF-Section, but we can't have them owning Vichy and us not knowing what the hell's going on. De Gaulle has his own agenda, and it's not the same as ours.'

'Understood,' Drake said, contemplating the smoke lingering in the air.

Jack rose and went to open the window, lighting a cigarette as he surveyed the activity on Baker Street below.

Drake's pipe was a hazard that even Jack, a heavy smoker, didn't bear well.

'I get the hint,' Drake said, resting his pipe on the table with a wry smile.

Jack returned to his seat and Jack asked Drake to tell him all he could about the layout of Toulouse and anything else he could think of that may be useful.

'Of course, this was years ago. I don't know what it's like under the Vichy mob. In my day, it was a genteel place, and I was sorry to have to leave.'

'What took you there?' Jack asked.

Drake touched his nose. 'You know how these things are. Best keep that to myself, old man.'

Jack nodded. 'Say no more. I thought it might have been for personal reasons.'

Lizzie didn't know what Drake's role had been before the war. She knew him only as her former boss at the War Office, and a mentor of Jack's, but his links to Military Intelligence clearly went way back and were more complex than she had realised. Perhaps one day Jack would divulge more about the mystery man, Drake, and how he came to be scouting for suitable recruits for the SOE.

Drake stood to take his leave some time later, but insisted Jack bring Lizzie with him to The Ritz next time. He turned at the door, before Jack escorted him downstairs. 'God bless you both and bring you back safely. Your next cocktail is on me, Lizzie Beaumont.'

'Thank you, sir.'

Drake laughed. It was a joke between them he'd not succeeded in dissuading her from calling him, *sir*.

Lizzie sat there, her heart pounding as she realised the day was fast approaching when they would drop into the South of France by night and once again, she would teeter on the sharp edge between life and death.

She reminded herself she wouldn't be going in alone this time. Jack would be at her side, and the thought calmed her.

'What did you make of that?' Lizzie asked when Jack returned.

'Sounds like it was a lovely city before the war. Hard to know what it will be like now, but we will soon see!' Jack said, pulling Lizzie to her feet. 'You and I are going out.'

'Are we now? Where to, may I ask?'

'It's turned into a beautiful afternoon. I thought we should make the most of it and take a walk in the sun.'

'Sounds good, Captain King,' Lizzie said. She gazed out of the window and saw people below, wearing short sleeves.

They were both in uniform and in the lobby, Jack made a show of them leaving the building on official business.

'It's a lovely afternoon,' the good-natured doorman remarked as they exited onto Baker Street.

Jack shot off at his usual pace and Lizzie did her best to keep up, until he turned and stopped. 'Sorry, am I walking too fast again?'

Lizzie laughed. 'The only way I can keep up with you is by holding onto your arm, but as that's too risky here, I'd better start running.'

Jack slowed, and they walked side by side, arms brushing occasionally, both conscious of how they shouldn't touch in the usual fashion when they were near the SOE.

'Fancy an ice cream?' Jack asked, pointing to a Wall's ice cream vendor.

'What a wonderful idea,' Lizzie replied. 'By the sounds of it, we won't be tasting any ice cream for a while. Val told me rations are just as meagre in Vichy France as in Paris.'

'My thoughts exactly. We'd better make merry whilst the sun shines on us.'

They waited for two small ice creams to be served and took a seat on a wall near Regent's Park.

Lizzie licked the vanilla ice cream with enthusiasm. 'I don't remember when I last had an ice cream. This is delicious.'

Jack laughed and reached over to wipe her face. 'You've got a big smudge of it above your lip like a vanilla moustache.'

Lizzy giggled and for a moment they were like young lovers on their lunch break, without a care.

Jack crunched the last of his cone. 'It's not pre-war quality, but it's edible. Summer is officially here. Come on, darling. Let's take a turn around the park.'

'Lizzie rubbed her hands together and touched her lips. 'All gone?'

'All gone,' Jack said, smiling. 'You're stunning, as usual.'

Lizzie accepted the compliment with grace and countered with one of her own. 'You're attracting your fair share of admiring glances. You cut such a fine figure in that uniform, Captain.'

They entered the park and started walking. 'Gosh, last summer this park was immaculate. Look at it now,' Lizzie said.

Her eyes took in the crushed tulips in the once pristine

flowerbeds. The grass was singed in places and Nissan huts and floating barrage balloons littered the park, making it look more like a war zone than a recreational site.

The sun beamed down on the thick material of Lizzie's uniform, and she was too warm outside for the first time since the previous summer. As she gazed upwards at the pale blue sky, she saw a cluster of fluffy white clouds drift by, as though they had all the time in the world. 'It really is summer. It's been a long old winter, and sometimes I thought the end would never come.'

'This time next week, all going to plan we'll be in Toulouse at my uncle's château.'

'I can barely believe it's happening so soon. It feels surreal,' she said, smiling into Jack's warm eyes.

'We'd better test each other, so we're ready,' Jack said. 'My uncle used to be sharp as a whip, although he's older now, so he might have slowed down.'

'What will we tell him?'

'First, we must pretend he's not my uncle, or it will be a dead giveaway. Some of the older residents of the village may recall he has nephews in London who visited as boys. It only takes one Vichy official or collaborator to mention his sister has lived in London for over thirty years and they'll be onto us before we've found a place to hide our radio.'

'Oh, I see what you mean,' Lizzie said. 'So, what relation will you say you are, then?'

'We'll say I'm a distant cousin who has never visited before. That way, he won't need to remember anything about my fake background. We need to bear in mind, he's elderly, so who knows what state his memory is in. Let's keep things as simple as possible.'

Lizzie's eyes twinkled. 'Talking of which, what do I need to know about you, my darling husband?'

'You know far too much about me already,' Jack said.

'Yes, but I need to know about the imaginary you. If we're to fool everyone into believing we are a married French couple, we must know everything about each other.'

'True. Look how far you've come since last year. Now you're drilling me!'

They walked on exchanging ideas they could use for their cover story, and Lizzie suggested they say they were from Brittany. She had spent a lot of time in St. Malo with her cousins and knew it well. Jack had visited Brittany several times and said he could pull it off. They agreed they would create their exact cover stories over the next few days and would test each other and be word perfect before they flew out the following week.

That night, when Lizzie lay her weary head on her pillow in her cosy bedroom in the Regent's Park house, her mind buzzed with ideas, and she couldn't sleep. When she did finally drift off, she dreamt she was gazing out over lavender fields and sipping wine in a château on the outskirts of Toulouse with her beloved husband.

CHAPTER 6

'It really is grossly unfair. You get to have all the fun,' Lizzie's youngest sister, Evie, complained at breakfast, a scowl distorting her freckled face.

'If only you knew how dull it all is,' Lizzie countered as she spread a thin layer of marmalade on her toast.

'I don't care, Liz, really I don't. I just want to do my bit for the war, like you.'

Evie had blossomed into a beautiful young woman during the past year and Lizzie couldn't treat her like a child any longer, even though she sometimes still behaved like one.

Rose, the girls' mother, hovered near the table. 'You're doing your bit in the sewing circle, darling. I thought you liked that.'

Evie shook her head. 'I do like it Ma, but it's not enough. It's time for me to find a proper job, like Liz and Juliet.'

'Jules could get you something at the MTC, couldn't you, Jules?' Lizzie asked her sister who was reading the paper and sipping tea in a world of her own.

She looked up briefly. 'Pardon?'

Lizzie repeated the question.

'Hmm, yes, I suppose there might be something available. I could ask.'

Evie released a dramatic, long-suffering sigh. 'I don't know the first thing about cars and, frankly, I'm not interested in learning. I want to do something more exciting like Lizzie does with the FANYs.'

'What on earth gave you the idea that what I do is exciting?' Lizzie asked, her stomach jangling nervously. Had she given something away and Evie knew more than she had let on?

'I listened to a programme on the radio about the FANYs and all the different things they get involved in. It sounds like an adventure,' Evie replied.

Lizzie released a measured sigh, and her shoulders relaxed. It was never far from her mind that she'd slip up and, inadvertently, her family would discover the truth about her clandestine life.

Members of the First Aid Nursing Yeomanry, known as the FANYs, performed a variety of duties and the organisation was used as a smokescreen for female members of the SOE. Lizzie had been assigned and issued a uniform the previous year, and Val explained it would serve as the perfect cover. Jack was promoted to the rank of captain, so he would blend into the war effort and not stand out.

Lizzie thought it was a hopeless cause because Jack always stood out, and never more so than when he wore his captain's uniform.

Pa cast a knowing look at Lizzie. It conveyed, *Don't worry, I'll handle it.*

Not for the first time, she thanked God that her father knew the truth and she could trust him to keep her secret.

'Let me see if I can find something administrative for you at the War Office, Evie,' he said.

'That's good of you, Pa, but I want to do something more

active. I know Lizzie's role isn't all that exciting, but I was hoping she might speak to her captain and see if there's something for me, too. I think I'd like to be posted to another city. By the sounds of it on the radio, there are some exciting jobs.'

Rose interjected, 'We have quite enough to worry about, thank you very much. Lizzie's been posted to Oxford. Lord knows where Archie is. We haven't heard from him in over a month, and then there's dear Oliver. When was it you last heard from him, darling?'

Juliet replied she had received a letter from her fiancé two weeks ago.

They all did their best in their own way to quash Evie's enthusiasm for flying the nest. She was the baby of the family and Lizzie thought there was something horribly unsettling about the thought of her little sister not being at home when she returned.

Evie had always been strong-willed, and Lizzie doubted they had succeeded in talking her out of her decision to find an exciting job.

Evie's copper curls bobbed about as she reached across the table to claim a piece of toast. 'Anyway, I must go in a minute, but I'm serious. Lizzie, please will you ask lover boy if there is a position for me in the FANYs? He has contacts, doesn't he?'

Now it was Lizzie's turn to scowl, and her cheeks flushed pale pink. 'Why do you insist on saying things like that? Captain Jack King is my commanding officer, and that's all.'

Evie was the only member of the family who suspected Lizzie was in love with Jack. She'd seen them share a stolen kiss and she never let Lizzie forget it. Lizzie had sworn her to secrecy and threatened all kinds of wrath would rain down on her baby sister's head if she didn't stay silent about what she'd seen. But Evie wasn't easily contained.

Lizzie shot her a warning look, and Evie smiled back mischievously and stood up.

'I'm off now,' she said.

Lizzie stood quickly and followed Evie out of the breakfast room and into the hallway. 'What are you playing at? You promised you would stop that nonsense,' she scolded.

'So find me a job I can get my teeth into, Liz. If I have to sew another bloody button on another bloody blouse, I'm going to go round the twist.'

'Don't let Ma hear you talking like that.'

'Oh, for goodness sake, there's a war on. Who cares if I say bloody? Bloody, bloody, bloody,' she repeated, fixing Lizzie with an impudent glare.

'Oh, do stop being such a child. I was just thinking how you've grown into a mature woman, but I see now I was quite wrong about that. How can I recommend you to the FANYs when you're so silly?'

'Nooo,' Evie shrieked. 'Please Lizzie. I'll behave myself; I promise. Please, please, recommend me. I'm going out of my mind with boredom in this house.'

Lizzie relented. 'All right, I'll see what I can do. In the meantime, behave yourself and not another word about you know who. I'm leaving today so I won't see you for a while. You'll have to wait, I'm afraid, but I'll see what I can do upon my return.'

Evie turned from the mirror where she was rearranging her hat and admiring her reflection. 'Oh, I forgot you are leaving today. Sorry, Liz. Have a safe journey and please send us a postcard like last time.'

Lizzie promised she would, and they hugged before Evie left for her shift at the infamously dull sewing circle.

The thought flitted through Lizzie's mind that there was a possibility she would never see her baby sister again.

Don't think like that, she reprimanded herself. All the

same, she would ask Val if she could find a role to keep Evie out of mischief whilst she was away. Preferably nowhere near Baker Street.

Pa appeared. 'I must leave for the office. I'll say goodbye now, darling girl.'

Lizzie hugged her father, and he squeezed her so tightly, he took her breath away. His eyes were moist, and his voice cracked as he asked her what time she was leaving.

Rose followed Reginald out. 'What on earth has got into you? She's only going to Oxford. It's not dangerous.' She hesitated as she studied her daughter's face. 'Is it, Lizzie?' Fear flashed in her eyes as she looked from her daughter to her husband.

'No, no of course not. No more dangerous than living in London, anyway,' Lizzie assured her.

Lizzie walked her father to the door, and he spoke near her ear, 'Come home to us, Lizzie darling. Please take good care of yourself.'

After one final tight hug, they parted, and Lizzie waved him off from the doorstep. Her eyes were also moist, and she dried them with her sleeve.

Lizzie said goodbye to Juliet and then ran upstairs to pack a small case, as if she were really going to Oxford for an indefinite period. Her mother tapped on the bedroom door and entered. 'May I help you, darling? Have you everything you need?'

Lizzie nodded. 'I'm just about done, Ma. I'll be down in a minute for a cup of tea and then my car should be here.'

'Is the handsome captain picking you up, by any chance?' Rose asked.

Lizzie smiled at her mother. 'No, I don't think so, Ma. Just one of the FANY drivers.'

'That's a shame. I should like to see him again. After your return, invite him to tea, please.'

Lizzie promised she would, thinking if they made it back safely, they would certainly deserve a piece of her mother's delicious apple cake. She lifted her case and cast a final glance around her bedroom. It would never be her childhood home, that was at Seagrove in Jersey, but it was the next best thing. Packing in her bedroom for the next mission always awakened mixed emotions in Lizzie. She still felt like a young girl leaving the protection of her family, but the minute she crossed the threshold and moved into the next stage, she was a fully grown woman and a trained agent.

Lizzie checked her watch repeatedly as her mother chattered about how measly rations were this week, and when a horn sounded, she jumped up from her chair in the front room, pushed back the curtain and peered out the window.

'They're here for me. It's time, Ma.' She was relieved the pretence was over and she could be on her way.

Rose stood on the doorstep waving and Lizzie waved back all the way down the road until the army truck turned the corner and she relaxed against the seat and exhaled.

The first stage of mission preparation was complete.

CHAPTER 7

Just the two of them would fly into France that night. After a day of final preparations, Lizzie passed the evening alone, dozing for a few hours at a safe house after going for a drink with Val in a nearby pub.

'Are you clear on your cover story?' Val asked between sips of gin and tonic. 'This time it's two cover stories to coordinate, so it's vital you memorise every detail of both your backgrounds.'

Lizzie needed to keep a clear head and opted for a fruit drink that didn't taste at all fruity. She wouldn't sleep in a bed until at least the following night in Toulouse, and that was only if things went according to plan. She stopped her thoughts from spiralling into the other grim possibilities. There was no point going there or she would be frozen with fear.

It was difficult to relax at the safe house, which was a cold, sparsely furnished flat in a tall Victorian building. Lizzie wandered about, feeling like she'd broken into a stranger's home, and they might return at any second. She didn't get much rest and was grateful when Jack pulled up outside at midnight and beeped his horn.

Lizzie exited the building, clutching her small French-made case, and Jack jumped out of the car to open the door for her. The summer's night held a chill wind and Lizzie shivered, grateful for her raincoat.

'I'd better not kiss you in case we're being watched,' Lizzie murmured.

'It's unlikely, because we're stretched so thin, but you never know, I suppose. I shall claim my outstanding kiss later.'

Lizzie touched his arm. His presence made her feel better and her nerves settled.

Jack squeezed her hand before pulling away smoothly. 'How was it in there?' he asked after a few minutes of companionable silence as the car navigated the quiet, dark streets.

'Strange,' Lizzie said. 'The waiting is always tough.'

'True. I would much have preferred for you to come back to the flat with me, but Val organised the safe house.'

'Me too. She meant well. Val doesn't know I spend at least three nights a week at your place. I shall have to make sure she never gets the chance to discuss my comings and goings with my mother.'

Jack's deep laugh rumbled through the car, the familiar sound comforting Lizzie. 'There would be some serious gaps in your schedule.'

Jack drove the car out of London and along eerie country lanes towards their departure point.

'Usual airfield?' Lizzie asked.

'Yes.'

Lizzie had flown out of England from the same top-secret airfield on every mission. She still didn't know its official name or location, other than it was somewhere in the Bedfordshire countryside.

'I don't know about confusing the Germans in the event of invasion, but the lack of road signs certainly confuses the heck out of me,' Lizzie remarked.

'That's the idea.'

Jack had drummed it into her during her training, the less agents knew, the better, in case they were captured and interrogated.

'Bloody Hitler has had more than enough success bombing the hell out of us, without pointing him to our airfields used for special operations.'

Soon they turned off the road and stopped at a barrier. The soldier on guard recognised Jack, and he waved them through after a brief security check.

By now, Lizzie's heart was drumming fast, and memories of previous flights swirled around her mind. She knew the drill, she reminded herself.

'You alright?' Jack murmured as they pulled up near a hut.

Lizzie nodded. 'A bit nervous. You?'

'It's only natural. Won't be long now and we'll be on our way.'

Lizzie recalled Jack telling her to greet nerves as an old friend. They were her mind's way of preparing her for potential danger.

The sergeant offered them a cup of tea, which had become something of a pre-flight routine for Lizzie, and she accepted the steaming enamel mug gratefully as she reflected on the day's events.

A costume and props specialist had kitted them out that morning and Lizzie had checked her bag, clothes and pockets repeatedly, almost obsessively. English pocket litter, as they called it in spycraft, could get them killed. If they were caught by the Germans, or even searched by French

Vichy police, something as seemingly innocuous as a London bus ticket would scream British special agent.

Lizzie observed Jack as he chatted amiably with the soldier, as though it was the most normal thing in the world to be hurled from a tiny plane into the French skies in the middle of the night.

Jack was so confident, Lizzie thought. She wished she could be that calm under duress and she took several deep breaths to steady herself. Her hands were clammy, and she wiped them on her raincoat. To distract herself and pass the time, she sipped her tea and thought about the clothes the head seamstress of the SOE French fashion department had kitted her out with.

The clothing was similar to that which she had worn on her virgin mission to Reims the previous summer. The weather would be hot in the South of France in June, and she wore a pale summer dress beneath her summer raincoat. In the early hours of the morning, in a windy airfield in Bedfordshire, it was chilly, and she shivered, partly with cold and partly from apprehension.

Lizzy spotted the pilot entering the cockpit of the Westland Lysander, and her stomach was ablaze with nerves as she looked over at Jack.

'There's our Lizzie,' Jack said as he crossed to her side, and pointed to the plane.

Lizzie was always too nervous to appreciate the significance of the Lysander aircraft's nickname, but Jack found it amusing.

'Shall we?' he said, taking her mug and placing it on a small table in the hut.

Lizzie straightened her back and drew herself up to her full height. Her stomach and chest tingled, and the adrenaline rushed through her body. 'No time like the present,' she said. In her experience, the sooner she boarded, the better.

Standing there thinking about the danger they were about to face would only increase the fear that had already gripped her.

The sergeant accompanied them to the aircraft, where the navigator awaited them and welcomed them aboard, introducing them to the pilot, who called out a friendly hello.

'Alright?' Jack asked once they settled into their seats.

Lizzie nodded. 'Usually, we'd have said goodbye by now and I'd be sitting here pining for you and wishing I didn't have to leave you.'

Jack reached for Lizzie's hand. 'And now you don't. We're together all the way, Madame Dubois.'

Lizzie's eyes glowed with unshed tears. Her emotions were in a tangle, in a mix of terror at what they were about to do, and an intense wave of love for Jack and gratitude that they would face this mission together as husband and wife. It was a surreal adventure, and she squeezed his hand in return and felt the warmth of his fingers cradle hers.

Madame Dubois. She let her mind wander. What would it be like after the war to be Mrs King? Would they be blessed with children? She hoped so. Then her thoughts flickered back to the young boy lying dead on the ground after the night when hell and brimstone rained down on them. She thought of his parents sobbing and remembered the child's name.

Lizzie raised her chin, and fear lessened its grip on her as the memory of Joey filled her mind. If they didn't win this war, it would be far worse in the future. Her colourful imagination painted a future of Hitler and his Nazi mob marching into London. Britain had succeeded in seeing the Boche off in the Battle of Britain, and Hitler had abandoned his invasion plans. The Blitz had taken its toll, but the British people's spirit was strong.

'Safe trip, Seagrove,' Jack whispered in her ear.

The engines roared as they waited for take-off.

'I've got a surprise for you,' Jack said, reaching inside his jacket and pulling out a ball of material like a magician and unfurling it across Lizzie's lap. 'Voila!'

She gasped and her fingers caressed the soft material. 'My lucky yellow scarf! Oh, my goodness, this is wonderful.'

Jack styled the scarf around her neck. 'There, that's where it belongs.'

'But how on earth did you get it back?'

'I did a bit of digging and called in a favour from a fellow in props.'

Lizzie turned to Jack and flung her arms around him. 'Thank you! That was so thoughtful, and I love it.' Her eyes shone as she stared up at him and they drew apart just as the navigator reappeared.

'We're going undercover as husband and wife,' Jack said. 'Practicing so we don't stand out like a sore thumb.'

The navigator inclined his head. 'Best of luck to you, Captain. I hope to have the honour of bringing you both home.'

The navigator returned to his seat, and they were left alone once more. The fuselage was cold, and Lizzie rubbed her arms.

Jack reached down and produced a big wad of padded material. 'Put this over you. The flight will be longer than to northern France, so you can sleep a bit if you want.'

Jack smiled into Lizzie's eyes as he covered her with the jumpsuit. 'I'll wake you up when it's time to get into our gear. No point doing it for a while yet. You'll be more comfortable like this.'

The plane shuddered and groaned as it lifted off the ground, and soon they were airborne. As the tiny aircraft braved the dark sky, transporting its indomitable team, Lizzie looked out the window. The whole country was under blackout, so she could only make out a few sporadic lights in the distance. She was in awe of the pilots and crews who flew into enemy territory as a routine part of their job.

Lizzie was terrified when she had to parachute in, and months passed between missions. The RAF stared death in the face every day, and as the plane darted over England towards the North Sea, Lizzie thought of Jack's brother Henry and prayed he was safe. Her thoughts inevitably turned to Hannah, who was Henry's fiancée, and her trusted friend and partner in the French Resistance.

Lizzie couldn't drift off to sleep, she was far too on edge, but she kept her eyes closed and relished the feel of Jack's hand on hers as she rested. Usually, she felt so alone as she waited for the moment when she must say goodbye to her one connection to Britain and launch herself into the French skies.

The navigator called out to them when they were thirty minutes from the drop zone.

Lizzie stretched before standing and climbing into the jumpsuit, one hand gripping Jack's shoulder. He bent to close the parallel zips. 'You look great in a striptease suit!'

Lizzie remembered how funny she thought it was when she prepared for her first mission and learnt the jumpsuit was called a striptease suit. 'I hope the only striptease I'll be doing is taking this bloody thing off after we jump,' she said.

'Don't be a spoilsport, darling. I'm sure we'll have time for a proper striptease in Toulouse.'

'You're remarkably confident about us being welcome to stay at the château, considering your uncle doesn't even know we're coming, and he dislikes the English.'

'It'll be fine. He'll be happy to have the company. You'll see.'

The navigator's voice rang out through the cool night air. 'Ten minutes to the drop zone.'

'That went quickly,' Lizzie said.

'We're flying over the South of France now. It's nearly time. You ready?'

Lizzie nodded, and she kissed Jack quickly, her expression sombre. 'Good luck, Raven.'

'Good luck, Seagrove. Do you want to go first or second?'

Lizzie replied without hesitation. 'First, definitely first.'

They donned their helmets, and the navigator entered the small cabin to attach the ripcords ready for them to jump. Then he addressed them both. 'It's almost time.'

They moved into position as the hatch flipped open.

Wind whirled into their faces and Lizzie's eyes watered. Her heart pounded, and she stood there trying to calm herself, feeling like she was in a dream.

'10, 9, 8 …' The navigator counted.

CHAPTER 8

Toulouse, June 1941

Jack watched Lizzie prepare to jump. He'd watched her hurl herself into the night once before, and now his heart buffeted in his chest as fiercely as the wind hit the aircraft.

It would be the usual procedure, for him, the captain, to take the lead, but Lizzie was not the usual kind of woman, and if she preferred to jump first, then jump first she would.

Jack wasn't typically a praying man, but beseeching words flooded his consciousness, and his lips moved silently as she jumped. If anyone had heard the noise of the engine and was waiting below, it would all be over for them before it begun.

There would be no reception committee to welcome them, like in Reims. Toulouse was virgin territory for the SOE, and they had no established network to pave the way.

All that would change if the mission was successful. Reims Resistance Network was still fully operational, but unfortunately, The Liberty Network they had set up in Paris was out of action for the time being. It was too dangerous for Hannah or Lizzie to show their faces in Paris after their last deadly operation, so they had alerted all contacts to go dark until further notice. They were here now because the South of France was wide open for recruitment.

Jack looked downwards, and the breath snagged in his chest as he watched Lizzie's silk chute open.

Thank God. He could breathe again, and he inhaled deeply several times. The moon was full, and its silver light bleached the inky sky so he could glimpse Lizzie below as the plane hovered, ready for him to join her.

And then he took the leap and felt his weight sail through the air until mercifully his chute opened, and his feet bounced several times before he tumbled onto the hard ground, his limbs tangled in the material.

Lizzie appeared, looking down at him, and she offered him her hand to help him to his feet and he took it gratefully.

'How was it?' he whispered.

'Fine,' she said. 'I'm glad you're with me. This is the really hard bit when you don't know where to go.'

Jack raised her hand to his lips and kissed her cold flesh. 'I told you, we're together all the way.'

Lizzie had already removed her jumpsuit, and Jack hastily stepped out of his. 'We need to bury them,' she said.

They poked around the outskirts of the field and found a wooded area. 'Here looks good,' said Jack.

Lizzie extracted her torch, and a little spade from her jumpsuit pockets and started digging. Jack did the same, and soon they'd hidden the incriminating outfits. Jack produced his torch, and they huddled beneath the dense foliage and found a spot to sit. The light illuminated their map, and they pored over it to check their bearings with a mini compass.

Jack said, 'If we landed in the right spot, there should be a church a couple of fields further south, and we can follow the path into the village from there.'

They clambered across the lumpy earth and reached the field, each retrieving their case they had thrown clear before hitting the ground.

'Is it my imagination or does the moon look blue?' Lizzie asked.

'Yes, it is a blue moon tonight.'

It gave the landscape lit only by the blue-tinged moon, an eerie feel and Lizzie shivered in the chill breeze and clutched her thin raincoat around her.

Jack said, 'Come on, let's speed up so we can be off the path and out of sight before the labourers start work.'

They hurried across the bumpy terrain and after a while, they glimpsed a church spire in the distance. It was topped by a *girouette*—a weathercock in the shape of a rooster—gleaming against the pink sky that proclaimed the imminent arrival of a new dawn.

Sometime later, Lizzie pointed ahead. 'That looks like the churchyard. I think we've made it.'

As they crept beside an ancient wall, they saw a charming little medieval church and Jack stopped when he reached a wooden gate. Gently pushing it open, its old hinges emitted a creaky whine and Jack beckoned to Lizzie to enter before he closed it behind him.

Rows of uneven, craggy headstones lined the sloping churchyard, and the light glinted on the pale stone.

'It's beautiful. Even the headstones are pink,' Lizzie said with a touch of awe. 'I've never seen a coloured graveyard before. It seems like a good omen that even the graves are pretty in the South of France.'

'They don't call Toulouse La Ville Rose for nothing,' Jack said. 'Come on, I know the way to the château from here and we can hide in the grounds.'

They climbed a steep, winding hill, and Lizzie's foot kicked some small stones that skirted across the mossy ground. The residue of smudgy darkness still lingered in the sky, and Jack strode up the hill at such a pace, Lizzie panted as she fought to keep up with him.

'Nearly there,' he mouthed, turning to face her.

She chased after him, and he left the hilly path that wound into another grassy field. He pointed, 'Can you see the vineyards?'

Lizzie narrowed her eyes and made out the faint silhouette of the vines in the pale dawn shadows.

The chill of the night air had vanished, and Jack could tell it was going to be a scorching day. He loved watching Lizzie, as her gaze swept about her, and she gasped with delight. In the distance, rows of neat lavender swayed in the gentle breeze.

'It's breathtaking,' she said. 'I still can't believe you didn't tell me about this place.'

The sky now formed a pink and blue cape as though they had entered a magical fantasy world.

Jack said, 'Come on.' He took Lizzie's hand, and she weaved along the hillside beside him, careful not to lose her footing in the partial light, still clutching her small case in one hand.

'Where are we going?' she asked

Jack stopped and pointed ahead. 'I wanted to show you this view.'

Far below was a sweeping valley with a maze of buildings clustered around a river. 'Is that Toulouse?' asked Lizzie.

'Yes, we're in the Garonne Valley. I remember this view well. Henry and I used to watch the city from up here when we were boys. He used to say, one day he'd own a big mansion in the centre of the city instead of being stuck up here on the hill.'

'I'm happy we're up here,' Lizzie said. 'That way, we'll get the best of both worlds.'

Jack looked at Lizzie and thought she had never been more beautiful. 'I love you, Madame Dubois.' He tilted his head to kiss her lips softly.

'I love you, Monsieur Dubois,' she said, and then her stomach growled so loudly they both laughed.

'I think that's a sign to introduce you to my uncle and get some well-earned breakfast.'

They sat observing the château as daylight broke and the pale edges of the old house were etched in sharp relief against the colourful backdrop of the sky.

'It's actually got turrets like a fairytale castle!' Lizzie said.

The shutters were opened at 6 a.m. sharp and a woman's head bobbed around inside one room on the upper floor of the château.

'Last I heard, my uncle lives alone, apart from a housekeeper and a small household staff. That must be her.'

Lizzie smoothed out the skirt of her dress as they readied themselves to approach the stately building, speaking only in French.

'Do I look presentable?' asked Lizzie.

'You look incredible.'

Lizzie said, 'Now, I know you're fibbing, but thank you all the same.'

They walked around to the back of the château, and Jack tapped on the door with the brass knocker.

They heard a dog bark and the scurry of footsteps. The door opened slowly, and a woman's face appeared in the crack.

'Oui?'

Jack apologised for the early morning intrusion and launched into an explanation.

The woman's expression switched from one of guarded

suspicion to keen interest, and she stepped back slightly, opening the door wider. A big dog shot out and licked Lizzie's hand.

'Some guard dog, that one,' said the woman, rolling her eyes and permitting her face to break into a small smile. 'Unless he takes against you, he's hopeless.'

Lizzie stroked the dog, who made little yelps of pleasure.

'Well, Monsieur Saint-Clair is on the terrace. Excuse me, whilst I tell him you're here.' The woman beckoned to a table and chairs in the courtyard. 'Please take a seat and I'll be back soon. Beau will keep you company, by the looks of it,' she said, pointing to the enthusiastic dog.

They sat down and Lizzie continued playing with the dog, stroking his big black and tan head and silky ears. 'What breed is he, do you think?' she asked Jack.

'He's a Beauceron, a French herding dog, who's obviously smitten with you. Can't say I blame him.'

Five minutes passed before the woman returned. 'Monsieur says he will see you now.' She extended her hand to Jack and then Lizzie. 'I am Suzanne, the housekeeper, here for ten years. I must say, I've never heard him mention you before. Didn't know he had any family in Brittany. Mind you, he keeps himself to himself.'

'I'm a distant cousin,' Jack reiterated. 'It's been some time since my father was in touch with Monsieur Saint-Clair. Perhaps my letter notifying him of our visit went astray.'

'The mail is unreliable, so that would make sense,' she said, hurrying through the wide entrance hall and beckoning them to follow. 'This way.'

Jack and Lizzie exchanged a look. The success of their mission depended on Jack's uncle recognising him immediately and playing along with their cover story without question. It would only take one wrong word in the housekeeper's presence, and all could be lost.

They followed her into an elegant drawing room with an enormous chandelier and an exquisite parquet floor, through one of the tall double doors and out onto a stone terrace that overlooked a vista of vineyards and lavender fields. The sun had risen and chased away the eerie shadows of the night. The air was warm and white puffy clouds adorned the pale blue sky.

Jack gazed at the familiar view and for a moment it was as though he were still a boy and there was no war. Just a fun-filled adventure to his uncle's château in the South of France.

An old man with a shock of silver hair and dark eyes, just like Jack's, stood to greet them. 'Thank you, that will be all, Suzanne.'

The woman left the room, calling the affectionate big dog who had followed them, to heel, promising him breakfast.

Jack clasped his uncle's hand, and his voice was low. 'Uncle Luc, thank you for seeing us and apologies for the sudden unannounced visit. I told your housekeeper I had sent a letter, but the truth is there wasn't time. May I present my wife, Isabelle Dubois. We are here on a serious matter, and I must ask you to promise to keep our secret, or it could mean death for us all.'

Luc studied Jack and moved his hand in a sweeping gesture. 'How very thrilling. I've been slowly going out of my mind with boredom during this war. You must tell me everything, but first let me order you breakfast. You look as though you've been travelling all night.'

He rang the bell and Suzanne reappeared a few minutes later like a genie.

The door closed behind her once more. 'Now begin at the beginning and leave nothing out,' the old man said, fixing Jack with a steely stare. 'The last person I expected to see was my nephew from London.'

CHAPTER 9

Lizzie immediately liked Jack's uncle and could see he was a forceful character with a sense of humour. A maid tapped on the door and served breakfast, and Lizzie devoured the poached egg on a piece of black bread. Eggs were hard to come by back home, and Lizzie's tastebuds sang a symphony as she ate the freshly laid egg.

'We have hung onto a few of our own hens,' said Luc.

'How fortunate,' Lizzie said.

'Yes, it is. As long as we can keep the German army at bay, otherwise they will take them all for themselves.'

'Coffee?' Luc asked.

'Thank you,' Lizzie said, sipping the hot, seedy coffee with relish. It didn't seem to matter where she went, the coffee was just as bad, but she'd grown used to the bitter flavour.

Jack told Luc why they had come and asked him to pretend Jack was a distant cousin from Brittany, rather than his sister's son.

'Right, I think I'm grasping the essence of your story. What part do you want me to play?' Luc asked, his eyes gleaming.

'The last thing we mean to do is put you in danger, but clearly there is an element of risk if we are discovered.'

Luc gazed out over his vineyards and his eyes wandered to the lavender haze that cast a riot of glorious colour over the fields in the distance.

'Those Nazi bastards want all this for themselves. I'd rather die than let them have it, so count me in. I'll do whatever it takes to help you.'

'Thank you. I thought you didn't like the English, Uncle,' Jack said in a low murmur, one eyebrow raised.

'The English are the least of my troubles now. We've got our own mini-Hitlers in France who are only too happy to throw in their lot with the Thousand-Year Reich, if it means they line their pockets. They've forgotten where their loyalties lie and have made a pact with the devil.'

Jack listened as he finished his breakfast.

Luc cleared his throat. 'You'd better call me Luc, my boy. Start as we mean to go on. One slip up could cost us dearly.' His eyes moved to Lizzie. 'And you, too. Please call me Luc, and know you are very welcome here. After this dark period in our history is over, you shall call me uncle.'

'Thank you,' said Lizzie, relieved they were off to a smooth start. Things could easily have gone differently if Luc wasn't keen or even willing to cooperate. They had formulated a backup plan, but staying at the château as Luc's family was vastly preferable to fending for themselves in Toulouse. Now they would have a safe base from which to operate and begin building their new network.

Jack and Lizzie exchanged a jubilant look.

'Are you from London too?' Luc asked Lizzie, his voice low, as he refilled their cups.

Lizzie shook her head. 'I moved to London with my family, before the Germans invaded the Channel Islands. I was born in Jersey, actually.'

Luc's eyes registered surprise. 'How wonderful. So, you're a little bit French, one might say.'

'A little bit,' Lizzie agreed, her mouth curving into an indulgent smile. If he wanted her to be French, she would be French. She'd always felt half French, anyway. Her father could trace his ancestors back ten centuries in France.

'You speak our language beautifully,' Luc said.

Jack said, 'That's how we met. Lizzie was a translator at the start of the war. It's probably best we don't tell you more. For now, let us be your distant cousins from Brittany.'

'Well, that's close to Jersey. I see why you picked it for your cover. What a clever pair you are and so well-suited. Are you really married or is that part of the charade?'

Jack answered smoothly without missing a beat and laid his hand on Lizzie's. 'We're really married. It was love at first sight. It just so happens we work well together, too.'

'How romantic,' Luc said, and Lizzie wondered whether he believed them or was just playing along.

They finished breakfast and went back inside. 'Let me show you some of the château.'

They followed behind him as he took them on a tour of the ground floor. 'There is so much to see. We will tour it in parts.'

'What a beautiful home, Luc. You must be very proud,' Lizzie said.

'I am proud, although it's rather big for just me and the small staff I keep these days.'

'Were you never married?' Lizzie asked. Then she hesitated. 'Sorry, I didn't mean to pry.'

'Nonsense, my dear. I'm alone in this grand house so much of the time, it's an absolute pleasure to have you to listen to my ramblings. If I talk too much, you must tell me, yes?' His eyes shone and Lizzie warmed to him further. 'The truth is, I always meant to marry, but it never quite happened. I fell madly in love as a young man, but sadly, my fiancée died from scarlet fever.'

'Oh goodness, I am so sorry to bring up sad memories for you, Luc.'

'Not at all. I think often of my darling Mirabelle. It keeps her alive in my mind. The years have passed, but the memories linger on.'

Lizzie noticed his eyes shone, and she regretted bringing up such a poignant event for the old man. She had only meant to make polite conversation to put him at ease. She was, after all, an absolute stranger in his home, who had thrust herself upon his hospitality with no warning, unlike Jack, who was a blood relation, even if they hadn't seen each other for years.

Luc continued talking softly, as if in a dream, as they meandered from one huge elegant high-ceilinged room to another, taking in the majesty of the old château. 'I never met the right woman after Mirabelle. I would have loved to fill this place with children, but it wasn't meant to be. Fate had different plans.'

Lizzie churned with emotion for Luc's lost love, and she glanced at Jack. How lovely that the old man would have his nephew's company for a while.

The housekeeper reappeared and showed Lizzie and Jack to the rooms she had made up for them, and Lizzie's mouth opened slightly when she showed them inside.

Like in the rooms on the ground floor, an exquisite chandelier hung from the high ceiling of intricate carvings on exposed wooden beams, and the open shuttered windows overlooked the breathtaking view of Toulouse, the pink city, nestled in the curves of the Garonne River. An enormous bed stood on one side of the largest room, and plush upholstery covered the opulent yet dated furniture. It was like stepping back in time to an earlier century.

When the housekeeper left them, Lizzie wandered around the adjoining room and called out to Jack. 'We even have our own private sitting room. Have I died and gone to French heaven? These rooms are breathtaking.'

Jack opened his bag and removed a few items of clothing he had placed strategically around their radio to pad it for the drop.

Lizzie reappeared at his side. 'I don't know how you travel with so few items. I swear if you didn't need to buffer the radio, you wouldn't have even brought a case.'

Jack ran his fingers across the stubble on his face. 'I think you may be right. I prefer to travel light.'

Lizzie opened her own little case, which had several hidden compartments sewn into the lining. 'What will you do for clothing, then?'

'I'll ask Luc if he has any for me. If not, I'll get some in the city. It's a good excuse to get into conversation with the locals.'

Lizzie unpacked and hung her clothes in the antique wardrobe, and placed her few belongings in the rickety drawers of a heavy wooden chest. She left her secret items in the compartments of the case, away from prying eyes.

'Do you think we can trust the housekeeper and maids?' Lizzie asked.

'I don't know, but let's act as though we can't. I'll keep an eye on them, and it will no doubt become apparent in time where their sympathies lie.'

Lizzie agreed that was a sound plan, and she would watch them too.

'Wasn't it a tragic love story about Luc's fiancée dying and leaving him unmarried for his whole life?'

'Tragic indeed. I confess I never heard a word about it until today,' Jack said.

'Well, you know how parents like to keep anything interesting from us when we're young,' Lizzie said.

'Yes, but I'm a grown man in my thirties.'

Lizzie teased, 'You're quite advanced in age and your mother still keeps secrets from you.'

'Not that advanced, thank you very much, you cheeky minx, but yes, it would seem so. Not as many as I keep from her, though,' he chuckled.

'Maybe it's her little slice of revenge,' Lizzie said.

'I'd like you to meet my mother soon. It's odd you met my uncle before you met her.'

'Well, if he's anything to go by, I'm sure I'll love your mother.'

'And she'll love you even more if you tell her your ten centuries of French ancestors' story!'

'It's not a story, it's true. It is rather popular with the French,' Lizzie said. 'May as well play to my strengths, even if Jersey has been part of the British Crown since 1066, and I'm a loyal British citizen.'

'True.'

'I'm going to have a wash,' Lizzie said.

'I'll ask Luc if he's got a change of clothes for me, and then I suggest we find our way into the city.'

Lizzie was excited by the thought of visiting Toulouse for the very first time. How different this mission felt from her previous ones. She could almost pretend it was a real honeymoon, and as she washed, she twiddled the slim gold band on her wedding finger.

Lizzie's heart swelled with love for Jack, and she was determined to make the most of this unusual situation, which she never could have imagined. She was Madame Isabelle Dubois, and they would live as man and wife in the South of France.

Lizzie had a feeling their visit would be one to remember.

CHAPTER 10

Jack returned to their rooms, looking dapper in a borrowed jacket, shirt, and trousers. 'I requisitioned these from Luc, in the name of the war effort,' he smirked.

'And very handsome you look, darling.'

'Thank you, my gorgeous wife.'

Lizzie moved into Jack's arms, and they kissed, swaying in the deliciousness of their newfound freedom. Jack's solid frame gave Lizzie comfort as she rested against him.

'Ready for our first adventure in Toulouse?' Lizzie asked when they drew apart.

Jack reached over and straightened Lizzie's lucky yellow scarf. 'Ready now, yes. Let's go.'

They descended the winding marble staircase and arrived in the great hall on the ground floor.

'Where is everyone in this fairytale castle?' Lizzie whispered.

'Luc said he was going to see the workers in the vineyard. I don't know about the others. I managed to arrange us some transport. Let's go and see what we have at our disposal.'

They exited the château the way they had entered, through the main back entrance and down the stone steps.

'That sounds promising,' Lizzie said. 'The most I'd expected was a battered bicycle. That's my usual mode of transport.'

'Luc said there's an old car we can use in the garage.'

'How on earth does he get fuel, or are there not the same shortages here, as in Paris?' Lizzie asked, her eyes wide.

'Luc said they keep a small amount of fuel for the château vehicles, and an old friend of his in the Vichy police turns a blind eye.'

'That's fortunate,' Lizzie said.

'Yes, but it comes at a ferocious price. The vineyard uses half the wine harvest to distil into industrial alcohol by order of the Vichy government for the Nazis. Luc said the Boche use it to make explosives, so he decided a bit of fuel for his car was fair game.'

Lizzie said, 'I'd not thought of how they make fuel before. In Reims, the Nazis stole much of the champagne and wine, so I can't say I'm shocked they're bleeding the château dry too.'

The heat of the day hit Lizzie in the face as she walked with Jack around the courtyard in search of the promised car. Souffle like clouds floated across the deep blue sky and she admired the far-reaching views of the countryside. 'What a gorgeous day,' she said. 'I'm glad I wore my light dress and didn't bring my raincoat.'

'You shouldn't need that today,' Jack agreed.

'I wore my raincoat a lot in Reims, even though it was summer, because it was handy to hide things in the pockets.'

'I think it would be more conspicuous to wear one here when it's so blisteringly hot, but there are bound to be some rainy days. Let's hope they coincide with our more clandestine operations,' Jack said with a wry smile.

They turned the corner and saw a stone outbuilding covered in ivy. Lizzie followed Jack in and a strong smell she couldn't quite place, permeated her nose. He whistled as she caught up to him.

'What?' Lizzie asked, staring at two cars parked next to each other. One was black with a dirty roof, whilst the other shone bright red like an exhibit that had never left the museum.

'That's a Bugatti. What a beauty. I remember Luc driving us around in it when I was a young boy.'

'Gosh, that must be an old classic.'

'Thank you,' Jack said, a twinkle in his eye as he turned to her.

'Oh, you know what I mean. It's been years since you visited.'

'Your point is made! I'm as old, or possibly even older than the Bugatti, but you were still toddling about at the time. Need, I point out, that's why it's called a classic?'

'Fair enough. You're definitely a classic.' She loved teasing Jack about their age gap, and he took it with good grace.

'You're my wife now, Madame Dubois, so it's too late to regret marrying an old timer.'

'I would never regret it,' Lizzie said, and her heart fluttered as she said the words and thought about the future when they would really get married. Her mind drifted. Would they marry in London or Jersey?

'I'm sorry to break the news, but after all that talk, we must go in this old thing,' Jack said, pointing to the inferior car. 'No point attracting attention in a flash motor. It's old, but Luc clearly keeps it in impeccable condition, and it will turn heads. We may as well broadcast our arrival if we drive into town in that.'

'You have a good point.' Lizzie said.

Jack opened the door of the rusty black Peugeot and

signalled with a flourish for Lizzie to be seated. He raced around to the other door and poked about inside the dusty car for a minute before turning the ignition. It spluttered and died several times, and they looked at each other.

'Did Luc say it runs well?'

'He said it's a bit of an old tractor and isn't used much because the housekeeper prefers to do errands on her bike, but it's in working order.'

Jack tried the ignition again, and the small, clanky engine sprung to life and the smell of fumes assailed them both. 'Heck, so this is the result when you make fuel from grapes.'

'Oh, that's what that overpowering smell was. We'll be drunk soon at this rate,' Lizzie said. 'We might be better off riding bicycles.'

'Shame we can't take the Bugatti and drive with the roof down.'

The car lurched forward into the yard and the car took a wheezy gasp and soon they were on their way.

Jack continued, 'It would be fun on the way down, but remember the steep hill on the trek up here? I don't fancy that on a bicycle, do you?'

'No,' Lizzie said. 'Although, it feels a bit like cheating, having our own car on a mission.'

The drove on the narrow road by the château, and the view of the valley stretched before them like a scene in an oil painting.

'Isn't it exquisite?'

Jack agreed it was. 'Henry and I loved staying here in the school holidays. We'd stay for weeks with my mother, and my father would come and go as business permitted. They were wonderful times.'

Lizzie heard the hint of melancholy in Jack's voice. 'I'm glad you brought me with you,' she said, softly.

Jack glanced at Lizzie before gripping the steering wheel

with both hands to take a sharp bend down the steep hill. 'Me too, darling. I have lots of happy memories of this place. I'd forgotten my father visited when we were little.'

Jack's father had died of a sudden heart attack years earlier, and he had told Lizzie his mother had never regained her spark.

Lizzie caressed Jack's neck, and he smiled at her, and she was relieved to see the sadness had passed.

'We'll be entering the city in a few minutes,' he said.

The car rumbled along the bumpy road and Lizzie shielded her eyes from the sun reflecting off the windshield. Then she spotted a beautifully crafted bridge. 'That must be the *Pont Neuf*,' she said.

'Yes, the New Bridge that was completed in 1632!' Jack replied.

'Whoever named it didn't realise how funny it would be hundreds of years into the future.'

Lizzie counted the arches of the bridge as they drove nearer. 'You'd think they'd have called it Seven Arches,' she said.

Pink-hued buildings encrusted the landscape on both sides of the river. 'And this must be the famous River Garonne. Val and Drake were right. It is a charming city with impressive architecture.'

'Indeed,' Jack replied. 'I don't think I appreciated it fully as a boy.'

A delicate summer breeze wafted in through the open window.

'That feels good,' Jack said. 'Let's park and take a walk to find our bearings, shall we?'

'How exciting, this feels like our first holiday.'

Jack laughed. 'I won't repeat my earlier observation in case of listening ears, but it's just as I said.'

Lizzie knew he referred to their conversation at Baker

Street when he observed that he'd never known anyone to be as excited to go undercover in enemy territory.

'You know why I'm excited,' she said. 'This is our chance to be together every day.'

'True, and you're right. We'd better make the most of it.'

They left the car in a quiet side street, and Jack came around to open the door for Lizzie. She smoothed the skirt of her dress down and checked her summer hat was still in place after the bumpy car journey.

'You look perfect, just like you always do,' Jack said, reading her mind.

'You look pretty good yourself,' she said. 'That jacket suits you and those trousers are the right length.'

'Yes, lucky that. Luc said he's shrunk a bit with age, but he's kept many of his clothes from when he was a younger man, and we're of a similar build.'

'Seems like packing light or should I say, packing nothing to wear, has paid off.' Lizzie threw Jack a mischievous smile, and he touched her cheek fondly.

Lizzie tucked her hand in his arm, and they strolled along the cobbled street just like any married couple. After a few minutes, Lizzie said, 'A coffee would hit the spot.'

'Yes, it would, and sitting at a café is a fabulous way to people watch.'

'Are we watching for anyone in particular?' she said.

'I'll be on the lookout for familiar faces, as that's my biggest concern, but I doubt anyone will recognise me now. Let's watch out for conspicuous types and see where they lead us.'

'Ah, finally I'll be able to learn spycraft in the field from the best there is.'

'I don't know who that might be,' Jack said, winking, 'but I'm happy to teach you what I've picked up over the years.'

'You are too modest, darling. You should hear what the other agents say about you.'

'Oh yes, and what do they say?'

'You can play it down, but you're the legendary Raven in Military Intelligence.'

Jack pooh-poohed the idea with an eye roll and a charming smile.

Lizzie knew Jack didn't like people making a fuss of his accomplishments, but she was excited to shadow him and learn some new tricks. Hannah, the Jewish Resistance agent, had taught her so much, just by being near her and watching how she responded to situations.

'You're a natural. Don't water your abilities down by copying how others do things. You know the basics and you've done an incredible job so far. The fact that you're here, in France once again, is testament to that.'

Lizzie accepted the compliment with grace, and decided she would watch carefully what he did, without making a big deal of it. She still had so much to learn, and she wasn't going to miss the opportunity of becoming a better agent by resting on her laurels. Jack was her undercover husband, but he was also her commanding officer, and he had years of experience in the field from before she had even considered being a secret agent.

'Come on, Madame Dubois, let's find a café to partake of our first hideous coffee in the city.'

Lizzie laughed at the comical face he pulled, and feelings of pure joy bubbled in her chest.

They walked slowly through the narrow winding streets, trying not to stand out like they were new to the city, but keen to observe their surroundings.

It was around noon and the harsh sun beat down on them.

'If my cartography is anything to write home about, we should see the *Place du Capitole* shortly.'

Jack's cartography proved impeccable, and after a few minutes they entered a large square, where the City Hall dominated with its palatial façade.

The Tricolore, as well as the Vichy regime flag, were displayed proudly from the building.

Cafés lined the square, and the place was busy despite the noon sun. 'I imagine people will return home for lunch soon, and it won't be quite so busy,' Lizzie said.

'Perhaps, but I suspect the residents of Toulouse might not be quite as traditional in their habits as in Reims or Paris.'

'Why's that?' Lizzie asked, as they scanned the plaza, searching for the best table to begin their city reconnaissance.

'If the whispers we heard in London are correct, Toulouse is a sea of immigrants and political resistors. Before the war, the city was a haven for thousands of Spanish Republicans who fled the Franco regime, and on the fall of France, the French flooded the South.'

'How fascinating,' Lizzie said as they approached a pretty little café under the shelter of the arcades. 'It's baking hot, I think we'll do well to sit in the shade.'

Jack pulled out a chair for Lizzie, and they took a seat and browsed the menu.

'There's not much selection,' Lizzie remarked.

'Luc said the rationing is severe and there are great shortages of many foodstuffs, despite the armistice and not being officially occupied.'

Just as a waitress arrived to take their order, a small cavalcade drew up in front of City Hall, and more Pétain standard flags fluttered from the vehicles.

The waitress cursed under her breath as she watched the scene.

Jack said, 'We're visiting relatives and have only just arrived. Who is that?'

'That's Pétain's mob, the double-crossing tyrant who waves his flag to promote his fictional Free Zone whilst licking Hitler's boots.' She spat the words out with disdain.

'I take it you're not a fan of the new government,' Jack said, his voice low.

'You could say that,' she replied.

A loud voice called to her from the café door, telling her to hurry.

'Apologies, there isn't much time for talking to customers, I'm afraid. We have our own strict regime under Monsieur Jacques. What may I bring you?'

They ordered coffee, and the waitress continued with her duties.

'Well, that's a promising start. If all the Toulousians are as outspoken and gutsy as her, we're going to have a lot of fun disrupting the Vichy regime.'

After their coffee was served, Jack and Lizzie chinked their cups. '*Santé*.'

CHAPTER 11

Lizzie and Jack sat at a table outside the café talking and surreptitiously watching the comings and goings in the Place du Capitole, which was a hive of bustling activity.

Lizzie sipped her coffee and admired her new wedding band that glinted in the sun. 'It'll be strange not to wear this. I've grown accustomed to it already,' she said, her voice inaudible except to Jack. 'How are you finding yours?'

Jack glanced at his gold French-made wedding band and lit a Gauloises, blowing smoke rings in the air above his head, as if he had nothing more pressing to do than while away the afternoon in a café.

'I don't usually wear jewellery, but I love being married to you, so it feels good,' he said, flashing her a smile that melted her heart.

'Correct answer,' she said, amused. Lizzie watched the shapes of smoke float away on the light summer breeze.

Jack caught the eye of the disgruntled waitress and ordered another round of coffees and then asked casually, 'What is there to do around here in the evenings?'

The waitress, whose thick wavy hair was rolled and secured with grips in an elegant style, was the epitome of a chic young French woman, even in wartime.

'Curfew puts a stop to the fun.'

'What kind of fun would that be?' Jack asked.

'Oh, nothing special. What brings you to Toulouse?' she asked, looking from Lizzie to Jack and back again.

Lizzie had gained a lot of experience in reading people's expressions, and she guessed the waitress was afraid she'd shared too much too soon with a pair of strangers.

'Wine. I'm in the wine business. This is my wife, Isabelle, and I'm Michel.'

The young woman inclined her head. 'Good to meet you, Michel and Isabelle, with the rhyming names.' She collected their empty coffee cups and, as she leant over the table, she said, 'Welcome to Toulouse.'

That afternoon Isabelle and Michel Dubois wandered through the picturesque maze of narrow streets in the medieval town. No matter how much they sought to blend in, they were a handsome couple who drew discreet and not so discreet glances of admiration wherever they went. The saving grace was the city was heaving with people and Lizzie hoped there was some safety in numbers.

'This feels almost wrong,' Lizzie said as they walked. 'I feel guilty for enjoying myself like this. It's so different from being in Northern France, where I couldn't relax for a second.'

'It's a welcome change not to see German soldiers at every turn, that's for certain,' Jack said.

'I wonder what will happen in the South. Do you think they'll occupy here too at some point?'

'It's hard to say. They have the best of both worlds since the invasion. With the Vichy lot collaborating fully, the Germans don't need to deploy troops to control the area. I don't suppose there's any reason to occupy unless something changes.'

'I hope we invade soon,' Lizzie said, lowering her voice, so Jack heard her words, but they drifted away as they stepped onto the windy bridge.

'Me too, but we're not ready.'

Lizzie said, 'It seems like it might be fairly straightforward to operate undercover here. I haven't seen a policeman since the square, and everyone's just going about their business normally.'

'Don't let that fool you, darling. Always be on guard.'

'You're right. I mustn't relax just because there aren't German soldiers goose-stepping about the city.'

They strolled along the bridge, gazing at the slow-moving muddied water. 'It's nice to be in France in the summer again. Do you remember how freezing it was in Paris?' Lizzie said.

'Arrêts!' A menacing voice stopped them in their tracks, and they turned to see a short, angry looking policeman bearing down on them. 'Good afternoon. You must be new to the area. I haven't seen you before,' he said, his words escaping his tight, thin lips.

'Good afternoon,' Jack said, as Lizzie smiled politely and tucked her arm into his like an obedient wife. He continued, 'You are to be commended for your powers of observation. We are indeed new to the area and are visiting my cousin and will be staying for a while on business.'

'What is the nature of your business?' the policeman probed, fixing Jack with a pointed stare.

Lizzie assessed him as he questioned Jack and ignored her. He was dressed in a dark blue uniform: a jacket with brass buttons done up to the collar and the traditional kepi hat the French police usually wore. Lizzie was relieved to see that at least the French police hadn't adopted a German uniform—yet.

'I'm in the wine trade,' Jack said, his deep voice confident.

'Papers, please,' the policeman barked, not wasting time on niceties.

Lizzie realised she had jumped to conclusions and the Free Zone might not be much freer than occupied France, after all. The difference was the oppressor wore a French uniform and spoke the native language. It made the betrayal more insidious, and difficult to spot. She adjusted her yellow silk scarf and prayed it would act as her lucky charm once more.

Jack extracted his identity papers from his breast pocket, which had been expertly forged by the SOE, and Lizzie held her breath as a million terrible scenarios whirled through her mind at a lightning pace.

That would teach her to be so blasé. What had she been thinking, acting as though they were on their honeymoon, without a care in the world?

A thin film of sweat coated her skin, and she shifted her position slightly to try to cool herself down.

Jack handed over the document and the policeman studied it, making little grunting sounds.

Lizzie's pulse raced, and she dared not look at Jack. Surely, they wouldn't be arrested on their first day.

The policeman continued to scrutinise the document as though it were the deed to his family fortune, and finally Jack interceded. 'Everything in order, Monsieur le Gendarme?'

'Do you or your wife have Jewish blood?'

'My God, no,' Jack said, shaking his head, a haughty disdain etched on his features. 'Of course not. Why, what's the latest with those dirty Jews?'

'Marshal Pétain decreed we must remove citizenship

from every Jew living in France. He prides himself on not waiting for the *Führer* to instruct us to cleanse Vichy France, and instead we are leading the way.'

Lizzie thought of Hannah and how the Nazis had arrested her parents in Berlin and persecuted the Jews in Germany in the thirties by stripping away all their civil rights. She had hoped the Vichy government was collaborating only on the surface, to appease Hitler, but wasn't enacting the vile anti-Jewish laws actively.

'And just so I understand, in case we should come across any Jewish vermin during our stay, what happens to them exactly, and what would you like us to do?'

'According to the *Statut de Juifs*, they are to be excluded from the press, commerce and the civil service. The administration would be grateful to you for alerting us to any Jews you suspect have not disclosed their status. You may report them by name and address, or, even better, escort them to our headquarters on la Place du Capitole, where we will deal with them appropriately. We have extensive governmental lists, but it's proving difficult to locate many of them. They change their names and are masters of deception, you know. You might find it hard to believe, but some of our own French citizens are helping and hiding them.'

Sweat rolled down the hot skin of Lizzie's back under her dress as she listened to the policeman condemn a whole segment of the country's population purely because they were Jewish.

His pride in his duties and sense of self-importance was evident, and Lizzie swallowed hard. She had heard the horror stories from Hannah about how Jews were targeted systematically throughout Europe, but she had not witnessed it firsthand in a casual conversation as though eliminating Jews from society, were the most natural thing in the world to discuss on a summer's day.

The policeman continued. 'There are stricter measures coming soon, and they try to fool us in a despicable manner, but never fear, we are dedicated and shall track them all down. The collaborators and all who try to shield them will pay the ultimate price for their betrayal.'

'That is reassuring,' Jack said. 'It is good to know someone so dedicated is in charge of these critical affairs in Toulouse.'

The policeman's chest puffed out visibly at the praise, and he nodded eagerly. 'My name is Maurice Moulin. I work closely with the commissaire. You might say I'm his right-hand man.'

'It's a pleasure to meet you, isn't it, Isabelle?'

Lizzie forced her voice to form words, and a sound emerged from her dry throat. 'Yes.'

It was all she could manage.

'Where are you staying?' the policeman quizzed.

Jack replied, 'At the residence of my distant cousin, Luc Saint-Clair.'

Lizzie saw a look of sheer panic cross the policeman's face. He hastily folded the identity document and pushed it back into Jack's hands as though it might burn his flesh.

'Please forgive me, Monsieur Dubois. My apologies for any inconvenience. If I'd known who you were, I shouldn't have bothered you. Give my regards to Monsieur Saint-Clair.' The policeman hurried away, almost tripping over his own feet.

Lizzie stared at Jack. 'What was that all about? Anyone would think we said we were a houseguest of Hitler himself. What on earth alarmed him about Luc so much, I wonder?'

'No idea, but I shall try and find out this evening. Luc invited us to dine with him, talking of which, we had better make our way back to the car. It wouldn't do to be late for our first dinner with our gracious host.'

The episode left a bitter taste in Lizzie's mouth, and she

was pleased to escape the city she had been so keen to explore. The conversation had made her feel grubby. 'That encounter brought me back down to earth with a bump.'

Jack muttered. 'His responses were shocking. I knew about the Statut from intelligence we received from occupied France, but I didn't think they were equally committed or even more zealous about persecuting Jews in Vichy France. So many fled here when Germany invaded.'

'Every time I hear about the severity of the anti-Jewish laws, I struggle to believe this is happening,' Lizzie said in a shaky voice.

'Hitler has stoked and ignited the worst traits in mankind. You'd think, Pétain would be distrustful of Hitler after seeing how the army plunder the region despite this supposed *Zone Libre* agreement.'

Lizzie fell silent. There was nothing to say in the face of such evil. Only actions would make a difference now. Her resolve to do all she could for those being hunted, whatever the personal sacrifice, was like a steely fist in her belly. A shiver reverberated through her, despite her clammy skin, as she realised this mission would take all they had and could cost them their lives.

They left the city in silence and drove into the hills. All sense of lightness and fun she had felt earlier had evaporated into something more sinister. 'That was a close shave.'

'Yes, it could have gone awfully wrong, but our papers are good. As long as we keep calm, we can outwit any of these petty administrators who preen in the limelight. Their defences aren't high, when they are so focused on their own image.'

Lizzie smiled, relief coursing through her. Jack always knew what to say to make her feel better. When he turned the car into the sweeping drive, and manoeuvred the rusty vehicle into the outbuilding, she touched her lucky scarf.

Her heart slowed to a steady beat. They had made it safely back to the château and survived their first reconnaissance mission.

CHAPTER 12

Anticipating a formal dinner at the château, Lizzie had packed one evening dress in her small case. If Luc invited them to dine with him regularly, she would need to take a shopping trip to Toulouse.

Jack wore a dinner jacket from Luc's vast collection of clothes now at his disposal. 'Help yourself,' Luc said. 'I'm not as slim as I used to be, and even with these measly rations, my waistline will never fit into those trousers again. There's something about growing old that changes your shape.'

Jack offered Lizzie his arm, and they strolled down the imposing staircase together and towards the dining room.

Luc stood to greet them when the butler announced their arrival and showed them into the elegant room, as if they were merely one couple from a huge guest list. 'You two are a sight for sore eyes. How overjoyed I am to have you both here. Come, take a seat near me.' He patted the upholstered wooden chairs.

Lizzie hadn't expected Jack's uncle to be so enthusiastically accommodating, and after the depressing events of the afternoon, it was good to feel welcome.

They sat on either side of Luc at one end of the grand table, which had obviously been the setting for many extravagant dinner parties over the years.

'I hope you will excuse our modest table decor. It's been some time since we've been able to conjure our pre-war level of hospitality, but the housekeeper does her best to keep things ticking over with some semblance of normalcy.'

Lizzie thanked Luc and said she was very grateful for his hospitality.

'It is a pleasure, my dear. I rattle around alone much of the time in this great old house, and it's easy to slip into a state of melancholy. Your company will do me the world of good, especially as the news grows darker and darker.'

Luc instructed the butler to pour the wine, and Jack took a sip from a fine crystal wine glass and nodded his appreciation. 'Hmm, magnificent.'

Lizzie did the same, and the fruity liquid tickled her taste buds. 'I'm not a wine connoisseur. In fact, I've not had the pleasure of tasting many wines, but I can see I've been missing out.'

'What a great shame. I shall make it my mission to remedy that.' Luc's face glowed at her words, and it was obvious he was passionate about his wine.

'Which vintage is this?' Jack asked. 'If I'm to pose as a wine merchant, I had better get up to speed fast.'

'Sadly, wine merchants are not overly in demand. Hitler's mob looted our cellars after the invasion, and the Vichy regime isn't far behind. After they take what they think is their share, it doesn't leave much to sell.'

'Who can you sell to now?' Jack asked, not having considered the details of his new career beyond it being a feasible cover story.

'We are permitted to sell to Germany and Axis countries. The Germans, of course, set the prices. I think it's fair to say we are not in for a profitable year, and last year's harvest was terrible.'

'That is a sad state of affairs,' Jack replied.

'It is. Hopefully, the Nazi war machine will wind down soon, but it doesn't show any signs of doing so yet.'

'No, it doesn't,' Jack agreed. 'If anything, Hitler is ramping up operations.'

Luc pointed to the wine bottle on the table. 'This is one of our finest. A 1920 vintage. It's one of my favourites, and I thought it would be an excellent introduction to our wines for you.'

The men had discussed Jack's cover, and Luc had agreed to teach him whatever he needed to pull off their mission.

The story was that Jack worked in the wine trade in Brittany, but business had ground almost to a halt with the occupation, and he had travelled to Toulouse to assist Luc, who had no children and needed help in running the vineyards and the business.

Lizzie listened as she ate a small but tasty dish and asked the occasional question. Jack understood far more than her about the wine business and she must learn all she could if she were to be successful in her role as the wife of Michel Dubois, the wine merchant from Brittany.

'That was delicious,' Lizzie said. 'Please give my compliments to the chef.'

'I'm afraid the days of having the luxury of an in-house chef are gone, but Suzanne will be delighted to hear you enjoyed her pigeon speciality dish.'

Lizzie almost choked on her mouthful of wine. 'Pigeon?'

Jack chuckled. 'Never eaten pigeon before, darling?'

Lizzie's complexion was pale. 'No, no, I haven't.'

Luc said, an amused expression on his craggy face, 'Don't tell anyone, or it will cause suspicion. We are raised on pigeon meat—it's considered a wonderful delicacy here.'

The slip-up reminded Lizzie; she was always just one tiny step from plummeting off the cliff edge in her deception. One wrong word, gesture, or hesitance about something that came as second nature to a French-born person could reveal her identity as a British agent.

She thought back to the many practice sessions she and Jack had done before the mission, testing each other on their fictional lives, so they would pass as husband and wife. He had also insisted they quiz each other on the intricacies of French life.

Lizzie possessed a sound knowledge of daily minutiae, mostly from the long holidays spent with her St. Malo cousins but still she couldn't match Jack, who had spent long stints in France working undercover for Military Intelligence before the war, and whose parents were both French born. It was the little things, as showed by her reaction to the discovery she had just eaten pigeon. The incident was minor between friends, but it could mean certain death.

Jack told Luc about their unfortunate encounter with the over-zealous policeman and related how he had rushed off when he discovered they were guests of Luc at the château.

Luc chuckled, but grew serious. 'Ah yes, there are a lot of these nasty little bureaucrats rising swiftly through the ranks on the coattails of Marshal Pétain, seizing power they would never have dreamt of having before, and stomping about the city ordering everyone around.'

Lizzie was relieved Luc clearly had no sympathies whatsoever for the Vichy government. How much more difficult it would have been if he were a collaborator and they had to fool him as well as everyone else about the nature of their visit. Jack had predicted his uncle would be on the right side of history, but she had worried nonetheless. It was so long since Jack had seen his uncle, and he was still a boy then.

Before the war, Lizzie knew nothing about politics and

realised now she had lived in comfortable ignorance, oblivious to the hardships so common in the world. During the past year, she'd undergone an intensive induction into world politics, and it occurred to her you could know someone in peacetime, but not know where they would stand in a major conflict. In France, people were pitted against each other as they tried to find their footing in Hitler's Third Reich.

Luc said, 'The police lick Nazi boots at every opportunity to ingratiate themselves into this new world order. And of course, I heard about the *Statut de Juifs,* but admit I had convinced myself they would appease the Germans and not enforce these terrible laws. I didn't realise they were hunting Jews here quite so viciously.'

'Why would you when it doesn't affect you directly?' Lizzie asked as she finished her glass of wine.

Luc said, 'Quite right. You have yourself a warrior on your hands, here, Michel. Your father would be very proud.'

They had agreed to use their cover names at all times so the household staff or any unexpected visitors wouldn't catch them unawares.

'You are correct, Isabelle. Men who you think are good men often reveal themselves to be despicable cowards when it comes to making a stand against evil. The commissaire has been a friend since we were boys at school together, and granted, we're not close like when we were children, but it is heavy news that his so-called right-hand man is carrying out what must be his direct orders.'

Lizzie said, 'I bet many turn a blind eye, when there is so much at stake for their own survival. Even here in the Free Zone, just putting food on the table must be a challenge for most.'

'That's true and many struggle to feed their families, which will be reason enough to prostitute themselves to the new regime. Hunger is a great decider in world affairs and focuses the mind like little else.'

Lizzie was surprised to hear Luc talk like this, when she presumed, he had lived a charmed life of wealth and privilege in his splendid château in the hills.

'Forgive me for asking. I don't mean to be rude, but I've never had the misfortune of not having food on the table, even though, of course, rations are tight in London. Have you ever gone hungry, Luc? Somehow, it sounds like you have experienced such hardships yourself.'

Luc swirled his wine glass in his sun mottled hand, dinner now finished, and his plate pushed to one side. A misty look entered his eyes as he relaxed against his chair and began talking.

Jack and Lizzie exchanged a look. Their stay at the château was proving more fascinating than they had expected.

'You are astute, Isabelle. I have endured the kind of hunger that makes your stomach shrink until you forget what a decent meal is. My men and I were so malnourished, we could barely hold ourselves up.'

Lizzie drew a sharp intake of breath. This was the last thing she had imagined hearing from a wealthy winemaker and landowner.

'You fought in World War I,' she said quietly, her eyes meeting Luc's.

'I did indeed. I was a prisoner of war.'

'Something's coming back to me now,' Jack said, squinting, as though dredging through the annals of his mind for a forgotten memory. 'My mother mentioned you fought in the Great War, but I had forgotten.'

Luc's voice echoed with horror. 'It was a terrible, gruesome war. The war to end all wars, or so we believed.'

Lizzie noticed he looked visibly shaken, so she gave him

time to compose himself. 'I always wonder why it's called the Great War, but never thought to ask.' She addressed Jack and signalled him with her eyes to indulge her chatter.

Jack said, 'It was great only in the sheer scale of the destruction and disaster. There was nothing great about it, other than its size. You're right, it is a strange choice of name, of all the names they could have given it.'

Luc cleared his throat and resumed talking. 'I was an officer at the Western Front. Pétain was there too, you know.'

Lizzie and Jack sat transfixed as Luc told them war stories, and how he and three of his men were captured and interned in a prison camp in Germany. 'I thought we were going to rot to death in there, but we made it through to the end of the war.'

Jack looked stunned.

Lizzie saw a deep sadness in Luc's eyes, as though he were accustomed to hiding it.

The butler appeared with dessert.

Luc shook his head. 'That's enough of that. Let's talk about happier times.'

Lizzie picked up her fork with a little sigh and ate the delicious dessert. Luc told her it was made with apples from the château's orchard.

She longed to hear more, but it was clear he had said all he was going to say on the matter.

CHAPTER 13

After dinner, the men moved outdoors to smoke and drink. Lizzie accepted Luc's offer to join them in a glass of Armagnac, and the spicy spirit set her throat on fire, but she rather liked the taste.

'The war has some minor benefits,' she mused, as they stood on the terrace, watching the sun sink into the river like an orange ball of fire.

'And what might they be?' Luc asked.

'Women can enjoy after-dinner drinks with the men, and not be banished to another room,' she said, her eyes sparkling with mischief.

'It is proving to be an interesting time for women. I never thought I'd see it, but they're running many of the factories in France, what with most of the able-bodied men away. Doing a good job too, by all accounts.'

'It's the same in Brittany,' Lizzie replied, practicing her cover story. In less than one year with the SOE, she had already operated under multiple cover names and stories. It could get confusing, so she made a habit of running her fictional life details through her mind at every opportunity.

Luc puffed on his cigar and the acrid smoke lingered in the warm air before swirling away into the darkening night. 'Talking of which, what happened to you upon the outbreak of war, Michel?' Luc asked, dropping his already low voice another notch.

'I wanted to fight, but my heart is weak. I was rejected for conscription. If anyone asks, it should make me less likely to be rounded up and sent off to work at a camp in Germany.'

Lizzie looked alarmed. She hadn't considered Jack would be targeted for any other reason than if they were found to be agents.

The danger caused her spine to tingle, and anxiety coiled in her stomach. In her enthusiasm for going undercover together, had she underestimated the risks for Jack? Lizzie resolved to be more vigilant and not make any slip-ups. One error could be fatal for them and for Luc, who was harbouring British agents and would be tried for treason if someone discovered the truth.

'And what have you been doing in Brittany, Michel?' Luc continued, probing.

'Until the war, the wine trade was good. Since then, business has slowed because we can only sell to the Germans. All the export trade I managed is obviously impossible now. The business can manage without me, which was why I decided to make myself useful and help you, my dear distant cousin,' Jack said, smiling wryly.

'Not bad,' Luc said. 'We have work to do to develop your knowledge of the wine business, but it's a good start. Occasionally, I must host dinner guests, of shall we say, a highly unsavoury nature?'

'Germans?' Lizzie asked, her heart pumping. It would take only one officer from a past operation to recognise her, and it would all be over.

They had discussed the potential risks of Lizzie being

recognised in pre-mission planning, and Val had concluded they were minimal given they would be in the Vichy region.

Val said, 'There's not a chance in hell we'll send you back to Paris for a while. Reims would be risky enough. We need memories to grow fuzzy, and officers to be posted back to Germany. It'll take time, so it's just as well you're off to Vichy.'

Lizzie wondered whether Hannah had been back to Paris since her last daring operation at German High Command. She wouldn't be surprised if she had because Hannah didn't play by the same rules as other people. Lizzie had observed her in action and knew she was fearless.

Lizzie was in no rush to visit occupied France again after what she had done, and was relieved to be deployed somewhere new where no one would know her.

Luc resumed puffing on his cigar and contemplated for a moment before saying, 'Bureaucrats from the Vichy government, if you can call it that, have been here for dinner several times. The commissaire visits occasionally and brings various guests with him. Last time, he brought a Nazi officer who seemed quite personable. Let's hope they don't repeat it, but we shall do well to be prepared in case they do.'

'They are all quite personable until you cross them,' Lizzie said, her voice laced with steel.

Luc studied Lizzie for a moment. 'Yes, you're right. As I said, we must prepare ourselves for every eventuality. There's little the Nazis enjoy more than being wined and dined on French fayre and consuming the best our French cellars have to offer. They are drinking Paris dry from what I hear, as well as sending all our best vintages to Germany. Did you know, they changed the Franc exchange rate so they as good as steal our wine even when they make a show of paying for it?'

Lizzie saw the plundering of his country deeply troubled Luc.

By now, the last shards of daylight had disappeared, and the dusky sky twinkled with silver stars. It was a glorious summer night, with only a slight chill in the air, but Lizzie shivered. They'd barely begun their mission, but when she thought about how audacious their plan was it was easy to lose faith in their ability to pull it off and get back to London alive.

Luc's solemn reminder that they were surrounded by enemies who could enter their safe haven at any moment shook her to the core for the second time that day. Toulouse was proving to be no less a den of vipers than occupied France. At least you could spot the enemy when they were decorated with Nazi insignia.

They would be playing more of a cunning game, where the wolf was disguised in sheep's clothing. The rot was spreading deep within the gut of France, and the most dangerous enemy was the trusted one within.

After their disturbing first day, a week passed without anything to report, other than Lizzie and Jack exploring the château grounds and taking a couple of trips into the city.

Jack was growing more restless. 'I don't know what we're supposed to be doing. There's been no lead for us to follow so far. I mean, yes, some of the characters in the city look like they could easily be ripe pickings for the Resistance but where do we begin without revealing who we are?'

Lizzie agreed they were off to a slow start, but she was enjoying living with Jack in the comfortable tranquil château. If only they could fully relax, it would be heavenly. Waking up each morning and drifting off to sleep at night in Jack's arms was like a dream come true, and one she had not imagined experiencing until the war was over. Luc was the first member of their families who had seen them living openly as a couple.

'How about we take a trip into the city this afternoon? That café we visited on the first day seemed like a good place to hang out to meet dissidents. But first, come back to bed,' Lizzie said.

Jack who was striding around the room, restless, surrendered to her plea and lowered himself back on the giant bed next to Lizzie. The sun streamed in through the open shutters, warming their faces. 'You make a marvellous case for staying in bed all morning, Wife,' he said, taking her in his arms. 'Sorry, I get so uptight when I don't have a plan.'

'Well now, you have one,' she said coyly, tilting her head until her chestnut waves cascaded over one porcelain shoulder and Jack sucked in his breath, instantly distracted from his problem.

'You're right. The day can wait a while longer to begin. I have more important things to do first,' he said, kissing Lizzie and making love to her until she moaned in delight under his exquisite attentions.

Luc was nowhere in sight when they went out to the terrace where they usually took breakfast, and when Jack enquired after the master of the house, the maid informed him Luc had left to do his rounds of the vineyards several hours earlier.

'I think it will be wise if I take more of an active role in learning how the vineyards and the business operate,' Jack said, between sips of coffee.

Lizzie savoured her portion of baguette and thinly sliced cheese. 'Yes, that sounds like a good idea. If we do get any unwelcome guests asking awkward questions, you will be more believable. Should I join you? I also need to pass muster if I'm quizzed about the wine business. What we need to do seems a bit vague to me, this time.'

'It does,' Jack agreed. 'That's what was getting to me earlier. Building a network from scratch is always going to be a frustrating game, but something will pop soon. We just need to keep paying attention to what's going on.'

After breakfast, they readied themselves to venture into the city for another reconnaissance mission. Lizzie wore her lucky yellow scarf and as it was already blisteringly hot, she dressed in a modest summer dress and sun hat, as befitted a family member of the owner of the most prestigious château in the region.

'I wish it wasn't so hot. I would wear my new raincoat,' Lizzie said.

'Spoken like a true Brit. That's not the first time you've mentioned it. Do you miss the rain already?'

Lizzie whispered in Jack's ear. 'It's not that. It's just they kitted me out with the most fabulous reversible raincoat. It's two different colours and I've been dying to wear it again to try the other side.'

'Oh, I see. Never fear, I'm sure we'll get a summer storm one of these days and you can wear it then. I remember the storms here can be quite sudden and violent. Henry and I used to watch the rain beating down on the vines from the turret room, and we would pretend we lived here.'

'Sounds perfect. I shall pray for some rain soon, then.'

On their way to the car, they saw a labourer busy shifting crates, and Jack called out a greeting. The man waved back and introduced himself as he wiped his shiny forehead with a handkerchief. His name was Pierre, and he said he'd been working in the vineyards for the past five years.

'Can I drive this time?' Lizzie asked as they neared the car.

'Of course,' Jack said. He opened the door for her and then circled the vehicle to the passenger side and jumped in.

Lizzie familiarised herself with the workings of the car and revved the guttural engine. This was good, she needed to be in action, like when she was on her own undercover. It was harder to be scared when she was busy. 'I've never driven in France. When Hannah borrowed a truck in Paris, I decided I would remedy that at the first opportunity.'

'When you say *borrowed*, I take it you mean when she stole that milk truck?'

Lizzie laughed. 'Yes, exactly, she meant no harm though.'

'Hannah really inspired you, didn't she?'

Lizzie glanced at him as she steered around the circular drive. The car nosed its way across the château courtyard and slid onto the narrow country road.

'She's amazing,' Lizzie said.

'How many times must I tell you, you are amazing?'

'Keep on telling me, smooth talker,' Lizzie said.

Lizzie pressed her foot hard on the accelerator and soon they were whizzing down the bendy hillside towards Toulouse.

'Whoa,' called Jack, gripping the dashboard. 'You're not holding back, I see.'

Lizzie's yellow scarf flapped in the wind, whistling through the open windows.

'Why should I, darling? You only live once. I mean to make the most of it ...'

The car raced around the bends and Jack roared with laughter as he watched his gorgeous undercover wife clutch her hat to stop it flying away. Lizzie slowed as they reached the city and passed a row of pink-hued buildings.

'You really are priceless, my love. What on earth would I have done if you hadn't come along to rescue me from my miserable existence?'

Lizzie parked the car in a little back street, and turned to face Jack, her adoration for him illuminated in her green eyes. 'That would never have happened. We were always meant to be together. You are my raven.'

Michel and Isabelle Dubois walked hand in hand across the Place du Capitole, luxuriating in their deep love for each other, unaware they were being watched closely by a man in a café beneath the arcades.

CHAPTER 14

There was only one vacant table outside the café, and it was partially bathed in the sun.

'Where do you want to sit?' Jack asked, poised to whisk out the chair of Lizzie's choice.

'I'll sit in the sunshine for a bit, unless you want to. It was such a long winter; I think I'll enjoy the sun on my face.'

Jack slid into the chair opposite her in the shade, which suited him because he had a perfect view of the plaza.

'What can I get for you today?' asked the rebellious waitress with an enthusiastic smile for Lizzie and Jack. 'Don't tell me, I remember you had rhyming names ...' She clasped her hand to her head for a second and grimaced as though it was painful to extract the information. Then she dropped her hand and beamed at them. 'Michel and Isabelle! Am I right?'

'You are,' Jack said. 'Impressive memory. That must be useful in your line of work.'

The waitress looked momentarily startled but quickly recovered her composure.

'Now you know our names. It's only fair we know yours,' he said.

The waitress's thick, dark hair was rolled into the same elegant hairstyle, and she was dressed in a simple black-and-white uniform, like the other staff. Ordinarily she might blend in, but something about her stood out.

'That seems fair. My name is Marguerite.'

Jack had hoped they would see her today. She had showed all the signs of someone who could lead them to other disgruntled Toulousians, some of whom might already be actively resisting the Vichy regime.

Jack ordered coffee and Lizzie raised her face to the sun and relaxed against the chair, her sun hat shading her pale forehead.

They sat in a companionable silence, and Jack reflected on his good fortune. He found himself doing this frequently and couldn't imagine his life without Lizzie. Sometimes, they would sit together without having to fill the space with idle chatter, which in his experience was a rare gift. They talked a lot, but they were equally at ease with each other in silence, and this was one of those times.

Jack gazed up at the cerulean, blue sky as white candy floss shaped clouds floated by. He reminded himself he was here to build a Resistance network and orchestrate chaos, not relax like a tourist on his annual holiday. He was full of gratitude as he scanned the square, studying the eclectic mix of passers-by.

The waitress returned with their steaming coffee and placed two cups on the small circular table.

'Thank you,' Jack said. 'You may recall we mentioned we are new in town. We're visiting a relative up at the Château de Saint-Clair. Are you familiar with it?'

Like Jack had hoped, the mention of the château caught the waitress's attention, and she paused.

'Of course. Who isn't? I went grape picking there as a child.'

They all agreed the château was idyllic and made polite chit-chat until a grumpy man clicked his fingers at her from another table.

'Duty calls,' she said, rolling her eyes. 'Perhaps I'll have a moment to continue our conversation later, if you're not in a rush.'

Lizzie smiled warmly at Marguerite and said that would be lovely. 'We're feeling rather isolated, missing our friends in Brittany and not knowing anyone our age in Toulouse. It would be lovely to meet some like-minded people.'

Jack noted how cleverly Lizzie emphasised *like-minded.*

Marguerite lingered. 'A few of us sometimes meet at Café de Paris and talk about what we'll do when this damn war is over.'

'Sounds good. Maybe we'll drop in and see you there. Would that be alright?' Lizzie asked.

The impatient customer, dressed in French military uniform, was now puce-faced and clicking his fingers furiously at Marguerite.

'I must go, before he gives himself a heart attack,' she said under her breath. 'But yes, come along around six this evening if you can make it and I'll introduce you to some interesting people.'

Marguerite hurried away, and Jack and Lizzie's eyes locked in jubilant victory. They didn't need words to know exactly what the other was thinking.

Jack lit a cigarette and continued surveying the area casually, as if he was a man of means who didn't need to be anywhere other than enjoying his morning coffee in the square with his beautiful wife seated opposite him.

Jack laid his hand on Lizzie's. 'You're far too beautiful to go unnoticed. We must take this into account, unless you disguise yourself as a frump, Hannah style?'

Lizzie smiled at the memory of Hannah's multiple disguises and how she loved to outwit her enemies.

'Whilst I'm happy you think so, it's unlikely you'd be married to a frump, so unless you disguise yourself too, it won't make sense. We're upper-class relatives of Luc's, after all.'

'That's a good point,' Jack said, taking another puff of his cigarette and narrowing his eyes.

Lizzie said, 'I don't think it's possible for you to make yourself blend in, even if you tried. Your height, build and looks are too eye-catching, so we'd better use your looks to our advantage.'

'Is this your way of saying your husband is the most handsome man you've ever seen?' The rich timbre of his voice was playful.

'You've got me. That's exactly what I meant,' she said, and they were lost in each other as though there were no one else in the world.

That's how it was for them. Jack knew their being together undercover was their greatest strength, but also their greatest liability. It wasn't without good reason, intelligence agencies frowned upon agents becoming romantically involved. It made them vulnerable. Lizzie was Jack's Achilles' heel, and he knew it, for better or worse.

A man sat at a café across the square, his eyes occasionally straying to the beautiful couple. He rose from his chair and limped past their table without looking at them.

Jack wasn't as alert as he might be, but he still noticed the man with a pronounced limp. It was nothing unusual though—there were wounded veterans everywhere, so he thought no more about it.

That evening, they excused themselves from joining Luc for dinner, saying they had to go back into town. After a simple meal in their room, they were back in the car, cruising down the hill at breakneck speed. Jack drove and Lizzie enjoyed the refreshing coolness on her skin as she looked out the window at the countryside streaming by. 'Is that the lavender field we can see from the château?' Lizzie asked, pointing to the swaying purple stems in the distance.

'Yes, it's a lavender farm, if I recall correctly. Perhaps we can have a closer look one day, if you'd like. Most of the lavender farms are in Provence, so it's special to have one here.'

'I'd love that,' Lizzie said. 'It's mesmerizing.'

The sun was slowly setting over the city, and the surface of the river sparkled, and the stone bridge glittered beneath the glow of fading rays.

Before they exited the car, Jack said, 'Remember, share only the minimum about us to create rapport and focus on gathering as much intelligence as possible, alerting no one to your special interest in their activities. We can split up if it seems appropriate and work the room separately. That will probably be much more efficient.'

'Yes, sir,' she said, giving him a mock salute. 'I will obey your orders, Captain.'

Jack belly laughed. 'Well, that will be a first! I look forward to experiencing this unusual phenomenon.'

He was in mission mode and knew that the slightest slip could reveal their true identity. He had far too much to live for to risk careless errors.

They walked the short distance to the Café de Paris, Lizzie elegant with her hair in a glamorous updo and wearing her raincoat even though there was not a drop of rain on the horizon.

'There will be a chill in the air in the evening,' she had told Jack when she slipped it on in their room. 'It also has my knife in the lining. It doesn't feel right to go into the city at night without a secret weapon.'

'I thought I was your secret weapon,' Jack had said, pulling her against his hard body and kissing her until her pulse raced.

'You are darling, but Val warned me never to relax my guard, especially when we are together.'

Lizzie was now a fully fledged agent, and she could take care of herself, he realised. Even so, he considered it his job to protect her. If anything happened to her, he would never forgive himself.

'I love how you protect me,' she had said, reading his mind.

The café heaved with people, some older like Jack and others in their early twenties, like Lizzie or younger. Jack saw at a glance, many were locals, but there were others whom he guessed had flocked to the southern city to escape the Nazi occupation.

They made their way through the crowds until they found a section near the bar where they could stand without being shoved.

Soon Jack caught sight of Marguerite, and she must have felt his eyes on her back because she turned and waved, before rushing over to them.

'How exciting. I didn't think you'd really come,' she said.

'Why?' Jack asked.

'Ah, you know how people are. They say one thing and do another.'

'You're awfully cynical for one so young,' Jack remarked, his voice kind.

'Yes, I suppose I am. I'm a product of my circumstances.'

And with that mysterious remark, as the band struck up a lively tune, she shouted over the music, 'Come, I'll introduce you to some other cynics like me.'

Jack held Lizzie's hand as they pushed through the crowd. 'Ignore what I said earlier about splitting up,' he said.

'It's far too busy, we'll lose each other. Let's stay together this time.'

Lizzie agreed. 'Alright, but if we do lose each other, let's meet outside. We've only got a few hours before curfew sets in, anyway.'

They came to a sudden stop in front of a small group of young men and women who looked them up and down with suspicious eyes.

Jack and Lizzie introduced themselves and shook hands with them all, except for a surly looking man who muttered hello and turned away.

'Don't mind him,' Marguerite said. 'He's just a grump.'

They ordered drinks, and Jack surveyed the large room, taking in the various characters, some of whom had already drunk far too much and danced in a vulgar manner. This war brought out the best and the worst in people, he thought. It made one want to live for the moment, which sometimes was a noble endeavour, but at others spiralled into a debauched lifestyle.

'There's someone I particularly want you to meet,' Marguerite said, interrupting Jack's contemplation.

'Oh, yes?' Jack replied. 'Who?'

Marguerite tugged his sleeve and steered him to the corner towards a tall and wiry, earnest looking man who appeared to be waiting for them.

Jack had lost sight of Lizzie who had been talking to someone on the other side of the group. His eyes worriedly scanned the area trying to locate her amidst the crowd, but he still couldn't see her. He reminded himself she was more than capable of taking care of herself and turned back to the man and introduced himself as Michel Dubois.

'Good evening. I'm Lev Elias. Marguerite said you are new to the city and are looking to meet some like-minded people.'

They shook hands and fell into conversation.

One of the rules of spycraft was to trust no one. Even so, a familiar sensation in Jack's stomach told him the game was on.

Lev was an interesting character and judging by his name he was Jewish, so he had everything to lose in this Vichy governed city if the Resistance didn't derail the regime from its increasingly sinister Nazi agenda.

CHAPTER 15

Armand Abadie sat under the shade of an umbrella in the Place du Capitole, in the café he frequented most afternoons. He had just finished a satisfactory lunch, paid for by *La Legion Francaise des Combattants,* and pushed the empty plate to one side before lighting a cigarette.

Since his recent promotion, he had the authority to sign off on the accounts, so it was easy to slip his own indulgences through as a valid expense. It was the least France could do for him after his great sacrifice. His eyes strayed to his wasted leg, and the familiar feeling of self-pity crept over him.

Some of the organisation members made a habit of lunching together, but he didn't enjoy groups. He liked people watching. Toulouse had become a cesspit of the dregs of society, since thousands of Spanish Republicans piled in, seeking refuge from the civil war and the Franco regime. And there were thousands of Jews, too. They had long been a bitter pill for Armand to swallow. They'd been flooding into France for as long as he could remember, but since the occupation, it had become unbearable. They came from all over, and just the thought of them taking over his beloved city made his stomach churn.

Since Armand tasted a slither of power, he had made it his personal mission to rid the city of such lowlifes. His thoughts flickered back to his arch-nemesis in the army. He was a French born Jew who had been in the same regiment as Armand in WW1 and was a constant irritation. Whatever the Jew did, he excelled, and Armand's jealousy burned with an insatiable rotten fury. It grew so bad; nightmares of Abraham, making him look inferior by contrast, plagued his patchy sleep.

One morning, as he sat on guard duty, he plotted Abraham's murder. At first, he didn't take his fantasies seriously, and merely enjoyed the bloody scenarios that played out in his mind, whilst the minutes dragged, and his stomach growled for the next pitiful meal.

Abraham asked him one day, 'Have I done something to offend you, Armand?'

Armand declined to reply. Everyone knew the Jews were wily. He had watched Abraham closely, and saw he was popular in the regiment. His loyal French citizen act was all a pretence, and Armand would not be duped like the others.

Towards the end of the war, Abraham was awarded a *Croix de Guerre* for bravery, and Armand was overlooked even though he too took part in the Third Battle of the Aisne, and his damaged leg was a result of his own feats of bravery. He told himself it was too much for any proud Frenchman to bear. How could these Jews act as though they belonged in his country? How could the government award a medal to this Jew scum, and not recognise him?

It was shameful enough he'd gone unnoticed in his younger years because he was from a poor family. The

French Republic pretended to be for the working man, but it was obvious they favoured the elite.

Armand had never received any commendation for his WW1 service and resentment fuelled his yearning to be recognised for his patriotism.

He stubbed out his cigarette as his eyes scanned the square until they rested on a glamourous looking young couple. The man was tall, well-built and classically handsome. A truly beautiful specimen and a familiar ache tortured Armand's loins as he gazed at him. Armand could tell he was a native Frenchman by the way he carried himself and wore his clothes. The woman at his side was beautiful too, but held no interest for Armand, so his eyes flickered back to the man striding across the square.

His stomach rarely growled these days, because of his comfortable position, but a different hunger clawed at him. He forced his errant thoughts aside, chastising himself for the weakness he knew they showed. Even so, he couldn't stop his eyes from straying back to the man continuously and he watched him display impeccable French manners as he helped the woman be seated at the table. His thoughts turned to whether they were a married couple or just dating.

Impatiently, he shook himself and lit another cigarette. Indulging his feverish thoughts was a sin—one he daren't confess even to his priest. Abraham had also been good looking for a Jew. His face dominated Armand's mind again, drawing his attention away from the beautiful couple across the square. The thrill of satisfaction always cheered him when he relived the incident he had so cleverly engineered.

Armand settled his bill and thought about the little game of cat and mouse he loved to play. Every day when he sat alone at the café, eating his lunch, he would watch people and decide who was a person of interest. It was the perfect spot for fishing out traitors of every description. The Nazis had sent them intelligence that Resistance groups were spiralling out of control in occupied France, and they were showing signs of gaining traction in Vichy France too.

The Gestapo issued specific orders to the Legion that they must not allow the Resistance in any shape or form to embed itself here in any meaningful way. They were causing chaos in Northern France, and they would not stand for a similar situation in the South.

Armand was doing all he could to ingratiate himself with the Nazis. Any fool could see they would win the war and rule the world. The veteran fantasised about securing a place at the top table. Hitler's table. He admired Hitler enormously, despite the Germans' role in the First War, which had wounded his leg and his delicate self-esteem. Armand could see the Führer's vision of the future clearly, and he was determined not to be overlooked this time.

The game sometimes ended there, but at other times led him to trigger a secret investigation. He didn't share his suspicions and suspect details with fellow members of the organisation and preferred to keep the potential glory for himself. Monitoring the suspected traitors was a pleasure, and he often worked late into the night, after his official duties at the bureau were long finished.

He would run through various scenarios of what a person, couple or group might be doing in the Place du Capitole, and then decide whether they warranted further surveillance. It was a time intensive endeavour, because the administration's records were poor. With so many refugees and displaced French citizens fleeing to Toulouse, they didn't have the systems in place to register them all.

Armand relished the thought of bringing traitors to justice and gaining recognition from Marshal Pétain, even though he also harboured some resentment towards him, and ultimately aimed to work closely with the Germans. The

Nazis understood what needed to be done to cleanse Europe of the nasty virus that had poisoned it.

Armand had every confidence that his day would come, so for now he was committed to rising through the ranks of the Vichy regime and he would be perfectly positioned when the Third Reich ruled the world.

He rose with a sigh. He would have liked to stay a while longer, but his formal duties called, and his passion would have to wait.

Armand neared the table where the beautiful couple sat, and it pleased him to see the man was even more impressive up close. He limped across the square back towards his office and was careful not to look at them.

They didn't seem suspicious, but he hoped he would see the man again soon. His loins still burned, and he decided he would pay a visit to his mistress later that afternoon. It wasn't healthy for a full-bloodied male not to relieve himself and satisfy his appetites.

He entered the Legion and sat down at his desk in his private office. A report lay on his desk about Resistance cells springing up in the South, and Armand reviewed it thoroughly. Many of these traitors were dirty Jews and Communists, and it would be his greatest pleasure to rid his country of them once and for all.

CHAPTER 16

Lizzie indulged in a rare lie-in after Jack kissed her at dawn and slipped out of the bedroom to meet Luc and his vineyard crew. By the time she awoke and stretched like a lazy cat, comatose in the rising heat, the sun was already beating on the shutters and the city below was a hive of activity.

Lizzie wandered over to the window wearing just her slip and threw open the shutters to reveal the breathtaking view. The morning breeze blew in and caressed her warm skin, and she just stood there for a moment appreciating the allure of the South of France.

The river curved through the lush valley like a glittering snake sliding through the countryside and into the city. Terracotta brick roofs topped the pretty houses dotted in clusters like a picture-perfect jigsaw puzzle.

For the briefest of moments, she forgot they were at war and, according to SOE intelligence, were now surrounded by committed Nazi collaborators. Fortunately, intelligence reports had also informed them Toulouse served as a base for thousands of refugees who didn't sympathise with or applaud Nazi ideology. Lizzie and Jack's mission was to find and train a leader who would risk their life to develop a new Resistance cell that would cooperate with the SOE after they returned to London.

The previous evening, they had received a message from Val saying she'd had word that there was a growing number of downed airmen in hiding, desperate to get back to Britain. She used just two words as a code to explain what she wished them to do: *Stern Family.*

Lizzie and Jack, who decoded the message after they returned from their evening meeting in the city, were in the turret room Jack and Henry had used as a lookout den when they were boys. By the time they reached the small room up in the sky, after climbing the steep stone staircase, the light was fading fast. The air in the turret was stifling and Jack threw open the tiny window and only the chirping sounds of crickets preparing for a long night echoed around them.

'I feel like a princess in a fairytale, surveying her kingdom,' Lizzie said.

'And I'm your medieval knight, watching for the approaching enemy and defending his lady,' Jack said, wrapping his arms around her waist as he stood behind her and they gazed out the window across the sweeping vineyards as dusk thickened like a smoky sheet and night descended.

'It's so much more peaceful here than in London,' Lizzie said, resting her head against his shoulder. 'I'm used to hearing the constant hum of aircraft back home and bracing to run to the shelter.'

'Yes, it's a welcome respite from all that,' Jack murmured, kissing the delicate skin of her neck and setting her senses alight. She swivelled in his arms, and they kissed, losing track of time until the radio shuddered and screeched to life. Jack hurriedly closed the small window. 'It won't do for any of the staff to overhear us listening to English radio.'

They sent a hasty reply to Val using the coded system they'd agreed on at Baker Street, confirming they had understood her message and would be in touch when they had something to report.

The Stern Family. Lizzie often thought of the Jewish family she and Hannah had helped escape from Paris when the Gestapo were hunting them down. Mr Stern was a gifted scientist, and the Nazis wanted to get their hands on his research, but he said he'd rather die than let them. Val used their name as a code so they would understand she was ordering them to set up a similar escape route for the downed airmen.

Lizzie turned from the window, washed and dressed quickly, completing her outfit with her lucky yellow scarf, and her wide-brimmed sun hat in hand. She walked down the wide staircase to breakfast.

It was strange she was living like a French aristocrat, which couldn't be more different from her previous missions where she'd spent much of her time riding around on a bicycle and queueing for rations as she gathered intelligence and met with members of the Resistance.

'Suzanne, where do you go for provisions?' Lizzie asked the helpful housekeeper who insisted she call her by her first name. An idea had dawned on her as she sipped her coffee under the pergola, shaded from the hot sun which would toast her pale winter skin if she wasn't careful. A plan formed in her mind, and she thought for a few minutes and concluded it was viable.

Suzanne went into the city every morning and had asked for their ration cards when they arrived. Now Lizzie asked if she would be so kind as to give her the ration cards.

The housekeeper's eyes revealed her confusion. 'You do not wish for me to collect the rations today, madame?'

Lizzie explained she wished to explore the city and make herself useful.

Suzanne looked even more confused, but she nodded hesitantly when Lizzie repeated her request, and she returned a few minutes later with the ration cards and placed them on the table. Lizzie asked if there was anything particular she should get if it was available, and Suzanne gave her a quick rundown of the shop to visit and what to try and get.

Lizzie placed her hat on her head and had just descended the back stairs on her way to look for the spare bicycle Suzanne said she could use when Jack appeared. His white shirt was damp from exertion in the vineyards and his face shone with a thin film of sweat. 'Darling, there you are,' Lizzie said. 'How was your first morning as a *vigneron*?'

'Good morning, beautiful. It was fascinating, if somewhat hot. You look like a woman on a mission. Where are you off to, my love?' Jack ran one hand across his stubble.

'I had a fabulous idea,' Lizzie said, waving the ration cards in the air like a fan. 'I'm just going to pop into the city by bicycle.'

Jack froze as if she'd struck him. 'I'm not sure I like the sound of that,' he said, concern blazing in his eyes. 'I thought I would have a quick wash and then we would plan what to do today.'

'That sounds good. When I return, let's do that.'

Jack's forehead creased. 'Now, I'm certain I don't like the sound of it.'

Lizzie touched his arm; the thin cotton of his shirt was warm and damp. She pulled him out of earshot of the back door. 'Our goal is to meet new people who may be able to help us, correct?'

'Go on, I'm listening,' Jack said, his expression serious.

'Well, it occurred to me over breakfast, we've been going about this the wrong way. It's all very fine us living like royalty up here on the hill, but the reason I was successful in my other missions was because I interacted with regular people every day. Potential contacts are much more likely to be sympathetic to a woman who's new to the city if she's alone, rather than if she's on the arm of her handsome husband who happens to be a relative of the owner of this magnificent château.'

Jack studied Lizzie's face, and she could tell by his expression that he agreed with her, but was uneasy to let her go alone.

He also lowered his voice to a whisper. 'Remember, Val wants us to locate the airmen.'

'I haven't forgotten. Perhaps I will learn something of their whereabouts whilst I'm in the city.'

Jack still looked reluctant.

'I will be fine, Raven,' she said, subtly reminding him they were here as undercover agents, not lovers. 'You don't have to worry. I've done this kind of thing a lot on my own. All I'm going to do is cycle into the city and visit the shop the housekeeper usually gets our provisions from. I'll be able to get a much better idea of what's going on than if I'm closeted up here dining on delicacies and sipping the best vintage from twenty years ago, talking about what may or may not happen in the war.'

Jack didn't like it, but Lizzie convinced him it was for the best, and eventually he agreed. They made a plan to meet back at the house, and he walked her to an iron roofed shed covered in cobwebs and helped her extract the old bicycle.

'I'd feel better if I dropped you off in the car,' he said when she sat on the bike and tested the brakes.

'I'll be absolutely fine,' she assured him again. 'You've seen me off on a bicycle before.'

'Yes, but you weren't my wife then,' he said. 'And it was difficult enough then, but it's terrible now.'

She traced his angular cheekbone gently with her fingers. 'I love you, darling, but you know this is all fiction and we're here to do a job. We mustn't let our feelings for each other distract us. You taught me that. I'm not really your wife, and even if I was, we can't let that compromise our mission.'

Jack's eyes were mournful, and Lizzie's heart throbbed. It was so hard to keep their relationship secret at home, and here, where they were posing as man and wife, they had a whole new set of challenges.

'*Yet*, you're not officially my wife *yet*, but for all intents and purposes, you are my wife, and it's my job to protect you. Please don't forget that.'

Lizzie's voice was tender. 'Nothing will make me happier than the day we officially marry, and I can shout out how much I love you to all the world.'

Undeterred, Jack tried again. 'Seagrove, let me take you to the outskirts of the city by car. I can shove the bicycle in the back, and you can ride alone from there.'

Lizzie looked at him, her eyes dancing.

'You went off this morning, and I didn't stop you, did I?'

'That's different. I was just learning the business in the vineyards with Luc, and besides, you know it's different for men. It's true you might attract more sympathy as a woman alone, but you also risk attracting the wrong kind of attention. When I think back to how close I was to losing you in Reims, it terrifies me.'

'I've grown wiser and tougher since then. I promise at the first hint of danger, I'll leave. All I'm going to do is watch and listen and cultivate new contacts. That's the only way I know how to do this.'

Jack sighed. 'Remember, there's also the fellow from the café last night. I arranged to meet him again today.'

'I know, and maybe he'll be able to help us set up the escape route for the airmen, but I don't think we should rely on one man we know nothing about. He could just as likely be a Vichy sympathiser pretending to be against them to fool resistors into revealing their plans.'

Jack kissed Lizzie and she could tell he was resigned to her going. 'All good points. What a suspicious nature you have, my darling wife.'

Lizzie laughed. 'We'll broaden our opportunities if we go separately and get into conversation with different people.'

'Don't worry about Lev. I will check him out further before revealing any information. I see you are determined to make this solo outing, so I must let you. Take care, Seagrove, and I'll see you back here when we're both finished.'

Jack waved to Lizzie as she set off and quickly found her balance on the old bicycle. She waved back and blew him a kiss before turning the corner and pedalling across the courtyard and out of the château grounds. As she picked up speed, adrenaline flooded through her body, and she felt the thrill of being alive. She raced down the hill, the breathtaking vista spread before her and the sun scorching her arms. There was such freedom in riding a bicycle and she thought of Jersey and how she used to cycle into St. Helier to do errands and visit her Pa at his office.

Lizzie felt at home on a bicycle, and memories of her previous adventures filled her mind as she approached the city on the banks of the Garonne.

Living with Jack as his wife was a fantasy come true, but she couldn't let herself lose sight of why they had been posted here. Her gut told her she must also operate alone, and she would follow her instincts, just as Jack had advised her in her initial training.

CHAPTER 17

Lizzie propped her bicycle against a fence near a bush and hoped it would still be there when she returned. By now, the sun was high in the blue sky, but the city was busy despite the early afternoon heat.

War seemed to have overshadowed even the local's proclivity for a long lunch, although most wouldn't have the rations to indulge in a leisurely meal.

The housekeeper had warned her to hurry to get a place in the queue because it was already later than she usually shopped. As Lizzie walked, she admired the pale green dome on the pink building in the distance, sparkling in the sunshine on the left bank of the river. When she had asked Luc what it was, he told them it was the historic hospital in the Saint-Cyprien quarter.

There were so many places she had never visited in France, despite her competence in the language and knowledge of the culture. A wave of nostalgia washed over her as she soaked up the picturesque view. She regretted taking freedom for granted, as if it was her natural right and no one could ever take it away.

How naive she had been as a young girl in Jersey, assuming life would always be the same and she would swim at Portelet Bay every morning from their beautiful house, Seagrove. They had been lucky to escape before the Germans invaded. Now she pondered whether the islanders were permitted to swim in the sea since the occupation.

An image of her grandparents' faces loomed in her mind. They had received a brief message from them before Christmas, but communications were censored, so it said nothing about what life was like on the island. Her father had sent another message more recently, but they hadn't heard yet. She tried not to dwell on the fact that her grandparents were trapped by the Nazis, but when she went undercover in France, the reality of Jersey being under their control hit her afresh.

The view from her family home rivalled the stunning view before her, and she yearned to travel back in time and swim in the bay as the sun ushered in a new day and the Martello Tower stood over her like a reliable old friend.

Lizzie brought her focus back to the present. She was supposed to be spying, not daydreaming. She crossed a small square and turned down a narrow-cobbled street that sloped gently downhill, carefully following Suzanne's directions.

On her way, she noticed a quaint bookshop to her right, and wondered how a bookshop could survive a long war like this. Lizzie loved to read, but she guessed that in these frugal times, buying a new book would be a frivolous luxury, not an essential covered by the household budget. In London, her mother frequented the library and shared her books with Lizzie, who was the most avid reader of her sisters. Not that she had much time for reading anything other than intelligence reports these days, and often her eyes would close as she read a few pages in bed at night. The book would tumble onto the floor, before she turned her bedside light out.

There was no time to browse in the bookshop, and with regret she pushed on, not lingering to look in its windows, but catching sight of a few exquisitely bound French editions.

Lizzie resumed walking until she reached a row of small shops. Three of which looked abandoned, the windows grimy, and remnants of faded graffiti on the doors. Curiosity propelled Lizzie closer to read the scrawl. On one door it said: *Jews go back to Palestine,* and on the next: *Zionists leave France.* On the windows there were antisemitic posters of hook-nosed Jews crudely depicted as controlling the world. Lizzie continued past the shops; her mood becoming gloomy.

A few days earlier, she read in a French newspaper that the Vichy government had freely adopted Aryanization, a term Hannah had explained to her meant the systematic stripping and seizure of property owned by Jews and its transfer to Aryan or non-Jewish ownership. It was becoming obvious through intelligence received by the SOE that the Nazis were intent on cleansing Europe of the Jewish population and making it impossible for them to live as normal citizens. What had begun as a terror regime raging through Germany was now spreading like wildfire through every country Hitler occupied.

Lizzie realised much of what Hannah had predicted when they were in Paris was now unfolding at an alarming speed.

Dear Hannah. Lizzie desperately hoped she was well and hadn't fallen foul of this vicious regime. The one thing that buoyed her spirits was she couldn't imagine Hannah being anything other than full of life. It didn't seem possible, and her intuition told her she was alive.

Lizzie paused on the cobbles as she stood near the boucherie and assessed the long queue that tailed out of the shop and down the street in the opposite direction. Above the butcher's shop was a private residence with pretty pale blue shutters and an ornate wrought-iron balcony.

As she walked to the end of the queue, her eyes scanned the people who stood in line. Some were immaculately dressed, whilst others were dishevelled, as though they hadn't changed clothes in a week. Lizzie noticed a small, slightly hunched old woman who looked to be struggling to stand in the extreme heat.

Lizzie had the urge to offer to queue for her rations too, but she held back. She couldn't allow herself to get distracted, and besides, she already had too many rations to claim and could end up disappointing the poor woman by not bringing her anything at all. Instead, she greeted her cheerily and made polite conversation.

The woman looked interested when Lizzie told her she was new to the area. 'Where are you staying?' she asked, her blue eyes inquisitive.

Lizzie was relieved that for the first time on a mission, she could be truthful about who she was staying with because it was a major part of her cover. She told the woman she and her husband had come to help a relative with his vineyards, and she segued effortlessly into her fictional story.

The woman scrunched up her weather-beaten forehead that stood testament to a long life in the blistering sun and then reeled off a few names of vineyards.

Lizzie said, 'My husband's relative is Monsieur Luc Saint-Clair at the château on the hill.'

The old woman looked impressed, and they chatted a while longer, but the line barely shifted. Lizzie was thirsty after her bike ride and asked the woman if she would hold her place in the queue so she could get some water. The woman nodded happily, seemingly revived after their conversation. Lizzie thought the war must be difficult for old people, especially those who lived on their own.

Lizzie bought a small bottle of water from a vendor across the street. It was aptly named *Eau de Vichy,* and Lizzie thought back to her operation prep with Jack and Val when they explained the spa town was the seat of the Vichy government.

Lizzie slotted back into her place in the queue after sipping some of the water, and she offered the rest to the old woman. At first, she declined, waving her hand as if to say she shouldn't bother about her, but when Lizzie offered again, she accepted gratefully and drank deeply from the mineral water.

The queue moved a little, but they were still a long way from entering the shop, never mind reaching the counter.

The woman engaged her in further conversation. 'We're going to starve to death at this rate if they don't increase the rations soon. It's bad enough for us old folk, but what of the children? My daughter barely has enough scraps to pull together a meal for them. What will become of the little ones in this dreadful world? We've lost our country to Germany, and our new leaders aren't proving any better.'

Lizzie did her best to console the woman and said to try not to worry about her grandchildren. She couldn't share her own stories of who she worried about, but she recognised the feelings of despair, and she patted the woman's crepey liver-spotted forearm.

If there was one thing she'd learnt during the past year, it was that worrying only helped if you could turn it into action. Otherwise, it just got you down and served no purpose at all. Still, not worrying about your loved ones and what would become of them was easier said than done, and she sometimes found herself sinking into miserable thoughts about her grandparents.

It occurred to Lizzie that perhaps the sympathetic old woman had been sent as a reminder that her own grandparents were as worried about Lizzie as she was about them. The thought eased the tension in her stomach. They were all in this together and like her father said, as terrible as the war was now, they would prevail against Hitler, and peacetime would come again.

When she queried her father on how he could be so certain, when everything was chaotic and the Allies hadn't managed to invade France yet, he said, 'Churchill says we will win the war, and if there was ever a man who I put my trust in, it's him. We must believe we will be successful. The other option would be too catastrophic to bear.'

Lizzie was tempted to reassure the woman that the Allies would save them, it was just taking some time, but she remembered Val's caution to not under any circumstances trust the locals in the Free Zone. It was impossible to know who was in favour of collaborating with the Nazis under the Vichy banner and who supported the Allies.

The country was divided in more than one way, and Lizzie examined the faces in the queue and played a game to pass the time. Who was for the Allies and who was a Vichy supporter? At least in occupied France, she had been able to spot the Germans by their uniforms. Here it was more difficult. Nazism was like a poison spreading through the country and she had no way of knowing who could be trusted, so she trusted no one.

The queue inched forward, and it was already more than an hour since she had arrived, and they hadn't entered the shop yet. The heat of the sun pounded on her back and her dress was damp with perspiration. She adjusted her hat to shade her face, but the sun was relentless, and people were flagging in the harsh heat. Eventually, they reached the door, but there was still no space to enter. Lizzie feared there would be nothing left by the time they made it to the counter.

She turned her head and saw people still joining the queue. A man in a veteran's uniform with a coloured badge on his sleeve limped past. Two people exited the shop, and the old woman and Lizzie entered and took their places in the long queue to the counter.

CHAPTER 18

Lizzie reached the front of the queue. The shopkeeper looked weary, but still had a friendly twinkle in his eye.

'A tough day?' Lizzie asked.

'Every day is a tough day,' he said. 'What can I get you, madame?'

'What do you have left?' Lizzie asked.

'We're low on stock and I'll be closing for the day soon. I've only got some ham left if it's meat you're after. I can also give you some cheese and flour for bread if you've got the right coupons.'

Lizzie checked the ration books. 'Forgive me whilst I get my bearings,' she said. 'I'm new to Toulouse and am filling in for the housekeeper.'

This seemed to intrigue the shopkeeper. 'Which housekeeper would that be?'

'Suzanne, from Château de Saint-Clair.'

'Ah, why didn't you say so before?' He lowered his voice so the other customers wouldn't overhear.

The housekeeper had told her to mention her name.

'I always keep a little extra something in for Suzanne. The Saint Clair family has been buying from us since I was a boy, perhaps longer. So, you are new to the area, you say?'

Lizzie nodded and thanked the shopkeeper as he passed her the food items, and she hastily shoved them in her bag. It wouldn't do to spark jealousy and make the shopkeeper regret his kind deed. She turned to leave. The old woman stood behind her, and Lizzie touched her arm and wished her well.

'You are a good girl,' the woman said. 'It's a shame there aren't more like you around here.'

On impulse, Lizzie reached in her bag and withdrew a small portion of chocolate the shopkeeper had added at the last moment.

'Here, take this,' she said, pressing it into her palm.

The woman looked down at her hand, an expression of utter shock etched on her lined face. 'You would do this for a stranger?' she gasped. Then her eyes grew misty, and Lizzie knew she had done the right thing.

An image of her grandmother entered her mind once more. She hoped her grandparents were also benefiting from some selfless acts of kindness in what must be a brutal existence.

'Of course, madame. *Bon appetite*,' she whispered close to her ear.

The people waiting impatiently in the queue started complaining about the delay. 'Hurry, we're waiting too, you know.'

Lizzie touched the woman's shoulder, and quickly left the shop with her haul, as if she'd just unearthed a sack of buried treasure. She looked at her watch and calculated the errand had taken almost three hours. Lizzie's legs ached from standing for so long in one place, and she decided to visit a café to rest and have a drink before cycling back to the château up the steep hill.

At least she wasn't constantly hungry like on other missions, and wouldn't return home skin and bones, and her mother accuse her employers of starving her on the job. Suzanne was keeping them well fed, and she was pleased to have been able to relieve the housekeeper's duties in some small way. It was a shame she hadn't met any promising contacts. She'd studied each of the customers waiting in line, but most of them looked exhausted and beaten. Not the material they needed to recruit for their new network.

Was it possible the intelligence the SOE had received wasn't accurate and there weren't any budding Resistance fighters in the area? Val said there were small cells springing up in the South and they should look for them and see who was the best fit.

Their strategy was to recruit motivated people who were already committed to support the Allies and cause trouble for the Nazi regime. That was a much quicker route to building an effective team than convincing people to join them. They needed leaders, preferably with existing skills, who were courageous enough to risk their lives, because they had nothing to lose, or they could not stand to witness the evil that was sweeping through Europe.

Apart from the waitress who was clearly disgruntled with the government, which was probably fair to say was true of many right now, there was no sign she was involved in any form of Resistance or would risk her neck to attack the Vichy or German regimes.

There was the fellow, Lev, who Jack was meeting with again, but he must be careful not to share anything that could be construed as treason. The man had divulged nothing tangible, but Jack surmised he might be motivated to join them if he was Jewish, as he suspected. Lizzie worried it was a fragile thread. Few would turn words into action when it endangered their life and that of those they loved.

Lizzie wandered through the streets clutching her bag. Suzanne told her she got vegetables from a different shop but not to stop there today as it would be too late, so Lizzie hurried toward the Place du Capitole, straightening her yellow scarf as she walked. Most of the cafés were in that area and it was the cultural centre of the city, so it was the best place to meet people.

It was odd being there without Jack, after they'd visited several times together, but her resolve to be independent strengthened. She had to do her bit and not rely on him to lead the mission just because he was her commanding officer. She was proud of what she had accomplished undercover during the past year, and the war waged on with no signs of abating, so this was no time to take it easy.

Lizzie decided to be bold and frequent a different café this time, and as she passed the one where they had met the friendly waitress, she saw there was no sign of her today. She passed cafés and restaurants dotted around the outskirts of the square, but none of them appealed to her until she came upon a quaint little establishment in the square's corner with a green awning and sparkling gold umbrellas to keep the sun off the customers in the cordoned off courtyard.

This was the one, so she sat at a small table in the shade, grateful for the rest, and laid her shopping bag on the chair next to her. Luc had told them theft was rampant in the city, where food was now as valuable as gold because of the shortages, and gangs of thieves roamed the city by day and night, even during curfew.

Lizzie saw no one who looked like a potential thief, but she knew looks could be deceptive. She kept her bag close by her side and picked up a crumpled newspaper from the table. She unfolded it and saw it was a copy of *La Gerbe*.

The newspaper was a couple of days old, and Lizzie was scanning the front page when a distinguished looking older gentleman came out to take her order. He was pleasant but reserved, and when he returned with a cup of weak coffee, Lizzie was engrossed in reading the paper.

It was always a shock to read the depth of the lies the Nazi regime went to in their quest to spread the belief they were victorious on all fronts and the Allies were weak and didn't stand a chance. The London newspapers told a very different story, and she wondered if there was a Resistance newspaper in Toulouse yet, like in Paris.

In Northern France, there were printed flyers distributed by brave souls in the Resistance, as well as underground newspapers. These efforts, which were at grave risk to the chain of people who created and distributed them, were the Resistance's attempt to counter the immense flow of propaganda with which the Nazis flooded France. If you were to believe what you read in their newspapers, you'd think the war would end any day and Hitler's vision of a Thousand-Year Reich was guaranteed.

Lizzie tried not to think what would happen if the Allies didn't invade soon and take back control of Europe. The reality of a future governed by the Nazis was too terrible to contemplate, which fuelled Lizzie's fighting spirit. The SOE must continue to follow Churchill's order to 'set Europe ablaze' and create chaos for the Axis powers.

When Lizzie joined the organisation, she hadn't fully understood, the importance of succeeding in such dangerous operations in occupied territory, but as she gained experience and witnessed the enemy in action, she realised her job was to prepare the way for the Allies to invade.

When she discussed her thoughts with Jack, he agreed and said if they failed, they would lose the war. There was only so much that soldiers and pilots could do. They followed their orders to engage in battle, and Lizzie was proud of her brother, Archie and Juliet's fiancée, Oliver, but a different battle was happening underground in secret organisations like in Baker Street.

Military Intelligence, the SOE and the Resistance networks who partnered with them on the ground, fought a secret war and engaged in a distinct set of combat rules. Whoever won the intelligence war would be the ultimate victor, Jack said. The price of losing was one they could not afford to pay.

Lizzie sipped her coffee and resumed reading the newspaper.

An article about Germany's relations with the Soviet Union caught her eye. It said the Treaty of Non-Aggression between Germany and the Union of Soviet Socialist Republics was crumbling. Until now, Stalin and Hitler had been allies, so this shift in Hitler's attitude could change the dynamic of the Axis forces.

Lizzie speculated on what it could mean for the Allies. She was frustrated at her lack of understanding of world politics and since joining the SOE; she had done her best to fill the gaps in her knowledge. Her father, who was a high-ranking official at the War Office, was a credible source, and she often quizzed him on his thoughts and opinions.

In Jersey, Pa had explained to her that war broke out when Germany invaded Poland. He said they invaded with the blessing of the Soviets, who in turn occupied and annexed Eastern Poland shortly after. She remembered him talking about a mutual treaty.

The article cited the Union of Soviet Socialist Republics as the enemy of Nazi Germany. Lizzie lay the newspaper down on the table, her mind ticking over furiously. She must treat anything she read in this propaganda rag with caution, but still, if there was even a hint of truth in it, the Soviets would likely switch sides which could only strengthen the Allies, even if they didn't trust them in the long term.

Lizzie rose from her seat with her cup in hand. She pushed the door open and walked towards the counter, surveying the café interior. There were a few people scattered at the tables in the back.

'Merci, madame,' said the man who had served her. 'All to your liking?'

Lizzie smiled graciously. 'Thank you, the coffee was as good as we may hope in the circumstances. How I long for a touch of milk like the old days when we took it for granted.'

His smile lit up his eyes. He leant closer. 'Visit us again soon, madame, and I'll see what I can do to offer you a *café au lait*.'

Lizzie thanked him, touched by the stranger's friendly attitude. Even in wartime in enemy territory, it comforted her to see there were good people everywhere. She walked back through the now quieter streets and was relieved to find her bicycle still propped against the fence. Lizzie cycled up the slope away from the city, and when she hit the steep incline of the hill, her muscles screamed out and she recalled Jack saying the journey would be tough by bicycle.

Even so, the flush of a successful trip into the city alone, her precious rations stashed in the basket, outweighed the pain and she pressed on, pedalling as hard as she could until she dismounted and wheeled the bike to the summit of the hill, panting and grateful for her hat.

As she pushed the bicycle, a strong floral scent tickled her nostrils and through a gap in the wall, she glimpsed a lavender field. On impulse, she entered, and rows of purplish-pink lavender stretched before her in a blaze of loveliness against the backdrop of the clear sky and the château in the distance. The heady scent and the outstanding beauty of the place permeated her senses, and she stood there breathing it all in.

After a while, she turned back onto the road and cycled slowly until she reached the château, which seemed to welcome her like an old friend. Lizzie cycled through the courtyard, her heart pounding with a combination of physical exertion and excitement that she had completed her first solitary reconnaissance excursion.

CHAPTER 19

Jack entered the garage where the old Peugeot stood next to Luc's pride and joy, which, to his knowledge, had not been driven since they arrived. He admired the smooth lines of the vehicle and wished he could drive it now. One day, they would take it for a spin, but it might need to wait until after the war.

After washing away his toil from the vineyards and eating a lunch Suzanne served for him and Luc, Jack dressed in one of his uncle's suits. It wasn't the height of Paris fashion, but as the war progressed, clothes were shabbier as rations grew sparser and people made do.

Jack parked the rusty old car on a side street near the river and walked to the Café de Paris where they had met Lev the previous evening. In an ideal world, he wouldn't rush their friendship and would let it develop slowly, but nothing about this situation was ideal. The message from Val had been a call to arms that they had to establish an escape route now. The longer the airmen were in hiding, the greater the risk a collaborator would inform on them, and they would be arrested or executed.

Lev waited in the dimly lit bar, which offered a welcome respite from the harsh afternoon sunshine. Jack paused before approaching him, scanning the area and checking they weren't being watched.

Lev was wiry and olive skinned, and his lips curved into the ghost of a smile when he spotted Jack. 'Hello, it's good to see you again. What can I get you?'

He ordered Jack a beer from the barman, who he seemed to know well. When they both had drinks, Lev suggested they move to a table in the corner and Jack followed him.

Lev offered Jack a cigarette, and they smoked in an oddly peaceful silence, considering they barely knew each other.

Jack said, 'Is Marguerite a close friend of yours?'

Lev drew on his cigarette, his sharp cheekbones casting shadows over his face. Jack got the impression Lev hadn't considered the question before.

After a pause, he replied, 'We are colleagues more than close friends. But she's smart and I trust her. Why do you ask?'

Jack took a swig of beer and contemplated Lev. 'I'm curious, that's all. She seemed keen for us to meet, and I wondered why.'

Lev nodded. 'She's a sociable sort. I suppose she thought we might have shared interests.'

'That's what she said. Do you think that might be the case?'

Lev sighed and met Jack's eyes. 'I don't think we have time to waste, so I'll be straight with you, Michel. Marguerite said she made it clear she was against the Vichy regime, and you and your wife seemed sympathetic. That's why she connected us up. She said there was something special about you, and I should get to know you.'

Jack's eyes narrowed as he appraised Lev. 'Ah, I see. And how is getting to know me going so far?'

Lev cleared his throat. 'Pretty good. You seem like a good guy.'

'So, am I to understand you are also against the Vichy regime?'

'You could say that,' Lev said, sweeping his eyes around the bar as if he was used to being permanently on guard.

'What else could I say?'

'You could say we're doing what we can to stop these traitors from completely selling us out to the Nazis, whilst pretending they have France's best interests at heart.'

Jack nodded, encouraged. Lev was saying all the right things, but could he trust him? 'Do you have other contacts who share your convictions?'

'I might,' Lev replied, his tone wary. 'I've told you a lot about me. Now I'd like to know more about you and your wife.'

That was a massive exaggeration, but Jack let it go.

'What would you like to know?' he asked, his voice a low, deep rumble.

'I'd like to know what you're really doing here,' Lev said, grinding the stub of his cigarette in an ashtray until the smoke fizzled out.

'The wine business is difficult in St. Malo with the occupation, so we relocated to the château to assist my relative, Monsieur Saint-Clair.'

'You must know a lot about wine.'

Jack blew a smoke ring above his head and let the comment hang between them. Sometimes, the best counter was to say nothing at all. It had been a while since he'd operated in enemy territory to recruit new agents. Since the war, he'd been largely confined to Baker Street, much to his irritation.

On occasional emergency missions, he had gone into

France to back up Lizzie, but they had worked with existing contacts.

When Hannah left Paris, the Liberty Network was put on hold, and instead Val cultivated fledgeling Resistance cells to gain intelligence via radio transmissions. The SOE was sprouting lots of seeds and growing at an impressive rate throughout the occupied territories. This was when Val declared it was time for them to duplicate their efforts in the South.

The thrill of being in action again instead of stuck at HQ recruiting and training was a heady experience.

'If there's something you want to know, I suggest you be more specific, and I'll do my best to put your mind at ease.'

Lev took a sip of his drink and replaced his glass on the table. He raised his eyes to meet Jack's without hesitation. 'Very well. Are you someone with the resources to help us weaken the enemy, or are you more interested in joining us?'

'I think we may be able to help each other,' Jack replied after a few beats.

'Is there something you can tell me to show I can trust you?' Lev asked, dancing strategically around the target like an expert fencer.

Jack rubbed his fingers over his chin. He hadn't had time to shave before joining Luc for their vineyard tour that morning. 'What sort of information do you want?' He joined the dance with an elegant parry.

Lev knocked back the last of his drink. 'How can you help us?'

Jack leaned forward, and his voice was barely a murmur. 'I belong to an organisation that can help you significantly if you're serious about sabotaging the enemy. I'm talking training, support and equipment to build a formidable Resistance network.'

Lev straightened his shoulders and said, 'I fought in the war, you know. I don't need training.'

'Everybody needs training for this,' Jack said with an air of confidence that wasn't lost on Lev.

'We're a raggle-taggle bunch, but we're serious. Word has it some networks in other cities are better equipped.'

'The word is correct,' Jack said, offering Lev a cigarette and lighting his own.

Lev said. 'I've been on the lookout for someone like you who can work with us to expand. That's why Marguerite sent you my way.'

Jack ran his hand through his thick, black hair. 'Before we go any further, I'd appreciate if you tell me a bit about your background and why you are motivated to weaken the regime?'

Lev nodded and rested against his chair as if he too had decided to trust Jack. Then he began talking and his voice was weighted with melancholy. 'My siblings and I were born here in Toulouse. It's all I've ever known—until the war. My mother and father were born in Toulouse. My mother's family goes back generations in this region. I'm Jewish—both my parents are French Jews who have been loyal to France.'

Jack listened, observing Lev carefully.

Lev shook his head as he continued, as if he couldn't quite believe his own words. 'You've heard of these heinous anti-Jewish laws? My parents' shop was ordered to close by the Vichy government. My mother still clutches onto the hope that it's all a mistake and things will return to normal.'

'What's happening is terrible,' Jack said.

Lev examined his hands. 'My paternal grandparents were driven out of Baghdad by persecution under the Ottoman Empire. They wished to emigrate to the Land of Israel, but that was occupied by the Ottomans, so they settled in France in search of a peaceful life.'

Lev glanced at Jack and continued. 'When I was a boy, they told me wonderful stories about their 'lost paradise', and how they loved to swim in the Tigris River. There was a vibrant Jewish diaspora in Iraq all the way back to the 6th century BCE since the Babylonian exile of my people from Judea.'

Jack nodded, not wanting to interrupt Lev's chain of thought. It was at times like these, Resistance members revealed their true motivations, which was invaluable to the SOE.

'As you may imagine, this new reality devastated my grandparents, most of all because they can predict the outcome if we don't stop these tyrants. They will lose their paradise all over again.'

Jack had assessed Lev twice now, and his instincts told him he was the real deal. He could see and hear his heartfelt story was genuine and, in a way, it reminded Jack of when he recruited Hannah in France before the war. She and Lev were from different countries, but both Jewish, and their stories of persecution had a similar tragic echo.

Jack trusted his instincts more than information, and in that moment, he knew he would trust Lev. This was how he had recruited his best agents for Military Intelligence, and he applied his experience to spotting and recruiting Resistance members in London. Some came from contacts he already had, but that didn't necessarily make them suitable. If anything, it made him more likely to go easy on them, so he always relied on his instincts, and they hadn't been wrong yet.

He thought back to his first meeting with Lizzie, and how he'd turned her away. Even in the beginning, he had wanted to protect her. She was so young and innocent, the thought of dropping her into occupied France had made his stomach churn.

'There are a few of us,' Lev said, interrupting Jack's thoughts.

'Are they reliable?' Jack asked. Now he was in his home territory, and he asked Lev more questions to assess what raw materials they had at their disposal. It turned out there was more to Marguerite than he had been led to believe. He wasn't surprised—she'd been sharp from the start.

'It was Marguerite who approached me first about creating some kind of organised Resistance group. She has a contact who is experienced. Unfortunately, he's no better equipped than us, but he's been helping Jews to escape across the Pyrenees for some time.'

Jack's ears pricked up, and he felt a tingle run down his spine. This mysterious man sounded like exactly the type of agent he wanted to recruit. 'Don't worry about supplies. I can handle that. Who is this contact?' He asked casually, as if it wasn't overly critical, and he was merely curious.

But Lev was shrewd and showed no signs of being a pushover.

'I can't give you more details. I'm already risking our lives telling you all this.'

'You're not risking your lives. You can trust me, but I understand. All in good time. We've made promising progress for today.' Jack glanced at his watch and stood to leave. He'd learnt it was always best to leave first and not be too eager when sounding out a new agent.

Lev looked startled, but stood and shook Jack's hand. 'When shall we meet again? I'm keen to move things forward.'

'Me too. I'll leave a message for you with Marguerite.'

Jack placed some francs on the table in front of Lev. 'For our drinks and get yourself a good meal. You look like you could do with it.'

Lev thanked him and Jack exited casually onto the street as if he hadn't just recruited their first Resistance leader in the Free Zone.

Jack walked across the Place du Capitole, his eyes searching everywhere for Lizzie. He walked around again to be sure she wasn't there. Of course, she could be inside a café sheltering from the sun, but it was unlikely. She enjoyed sitting outside.

Was she still in the city? He was more worried about letting her go alone than he cared to acknowledge, even to himself. It was one thing worrying about her when he was in London and could do little but wait for a message, but here it was a different story. He knew he must give her freedom to follow her own instincts, but God, it was hard to exercise his self-control. It was the hardest thing he had ever had to do. Watching her cycle away from him earlier made his pulse race and crushed his chest until he could barely breathe. The feelings of love he had for her were overwhelming, and the combination of trying to protect her and wanting her to flourish were crippling.

He swung the car into the château grounds, all the while scanning the area for Lizzie. Had she made it back yet? There was no sign of her on the journey up the hill and his mouth was dry at the thought of what might have happened. He decided he would see if she was inside and, if not, he would go back out immediately and look for her. His patience had come to an end for one day.

Jack parked the car and headed towards the château. Then he had a thought and turned around. If she was here, she would have put the bicycle back. With his heart booming in his chest like a schoolboy in love, he strode across the courtyard and stood in front of the shed. Reaching his hand out, fear spiralled through him as he pulled the handle.

There stood the old bicycle. Waves of relief washed over him, and he berated himself for panicking, and for the stupid smile that creased his face.

Knowing Lizzie was safe was the best thing in the world.

CHAPTER 20

Lizzie looked for Suzanne in the kitchen and handed her the bag of hard-won food.

'You did well, madame.'

'Thank you,' Lizzie said, running her fingers over the large dog's head as he clamoured for her attention. 'Is Beau your dog?'

'No, he is Monsieur Luc's dog. He enjoys running around here in the daytime but sleeps upstairs with his master. Not much of a guard dog, really.'

'You are a sweetie, Beau, aren't you?' Lizzie said, tickling his chest as he leaned against her hand and stared up at her lovingly.

'He is adorable,' Suzanne agreed. 'I like having his company down here. It can get lonely in this great old place.'

'May I do something to help in the kitchen?' Lizzie asked.

The look of shock on Suzanne's face made Lizzie smile.

'But no, madame. That wouldn't do at all. Monsieur Luc would be horrified.' She paused, an expression of concern settling on her features. 'Is there something you would like that I haven't provided for you?'

Lizzie shook her head. 'Oh no, not at all. Everything is wonderful. Please don't take my offer of help as a criticism.'

'Thank you,' Suzanne said, relief in her voice.

'It's just that at home we have a much smaller house and since the war we barely have any staff, so I've grown used to helping out.'

'I understand. Please don't feel obliged to work here. We are more than happy to do our duties, but if it's company you would like, feel free to drop in for a chat anytime. By the looks of it, Beau will be very happy to see you, as will I.'

Lizzie thanked Suzanne for her hospitality and kindness. 'Is my husband back yet, do you know?' Referring to Jack as her husband was still a novelty, but she said it casually as though she'd been saying it forever. Every time she called him her husband, she felt a warm fuzzy feeling in her chest. It was like a dress rehearsal of when they would be married.

'I haven't seen him return,' Suzanne said.

Lizzie worried about Jack just as much as he did about her. She was still trying to find her feet on this joint operation and there was no doubt that although she loved how they lived together, it added an extra layer of complexity that she would have to get used to.

When she worked alone on a mission, she followed her instructions from the SOE to a point, but then found her own way of doing things. The benefit was she reported her actions to Jack after she had taken them and rarely asked for permission. It was smoother that way and avoided delays.

Now they were together, she had to run everything by him before doing it. His reaction to her going into the city alone was gut-wrenching. It was hard for them both to balance their feelings for each other with their duties, but they must find a way. The success of this mission depended upon it. Lizzie dreaded to think what Val would say if she discovered the true nature of their relationship.

Lizzie's thoughts flicked back to a conversation she had with Val before they left. 'You realise you'll have to share a bedroom with Jack to pull off your cover story? You'll be newlyweds in the first flush of love.'

Lizzie had fought the heat stealing over her cheeks. 'I understand. We've talked about it.'

Val had narrowed her eyes and appraised Lizzie. 'Jack has something of a reputation. Well, he did before the war, anyway. I must say, he's shown little interest in women since then, as far as I'm aware.'

Lizzie nodded, her heart hammering so hard the beat reverberated through her whole body. 'I'm sure we'll be fine. Jack is a gentleman.'

'Yes, he is. I didn't mean to disparage him in any way. It's just that I've seen the damage that romantic entanglements cause in our line of work. We can't risk it because falling in love affects our judgement.'

'There's nothing to be concerned about. We are co-workers, that's all,' Lizzie said, hating herself for lying to Val, whom she respected. 'We're both committed to the mission.' Lizzie stopped herself from adding anymore reassurances because she was in danger of protesting too much. Jack advised her to use words sparingly when under scrutiny.

The noise of an engine snapped Lizzie back to reality. 'Ah, that could be him. I'll go and see.'

Lizzie hurried out of the kitchen with Beau on her heels, and they both bounded down the exterior staircase and raced to the outbuilding.

The old car was parked in its usual spot and Lizzie wondered where Jack had gone. She walked around the corner searching for him, Beau at her side, wagging his tail and making little snuffling noises.

'What are you so excited about?' Lizzie asked him.

Then she saw Jack coming into view around the corner and she ran towards him, and he scooped her into his arms.

'Where did you go?' Lizzie asked. 'I came to meet you when I heard the car.'

Jack's expression was sheepish. 'I went to check your bicycle was back in the shed.'

Lizzie laughed. 'Oh, ye of little faith!'

'Not at all. It's just I don't like the idea of you roaming around a strange city with no backup, should you need it.'

Lizzie luxuriated in the glow of Jack's tenderness and the comforting circle of his arms. She turned her face up to his. 'And what would you have done if the bicycle wasn't there?'

'I would have gone straight back out to look for you. Anyway, let's forget what a lovesick sap I am …' He rolled his eyes.

'I love you, Michel Dubois. And I love how you look out for me. Honestly, though, it was fine. Uneventful really.' Lizzie sounded disappointed. 'I had hoped for more of a breakthrough, but I met some interesting people, so it's a start.'

'Would you like to take a walk?' Jack asked. The sun's not as hot now and it's a beautiful day.

The sky was bright blue with only the occasional tiny puff of clouds overhead, and the sun had lost its intense heat. The temperature was ideal for a walk.

Lizzie said she would love it, and they set off together with Beau across the courtyard and into the field towards the vineyards. 'How was your meeting?'

'It was fruitful. Lev's family is being persecuted for being Jewish, so he clearly has the motivation. He has a small team, and they have carried out random acts of sabotage. He's hungry to do more and wants to work with us.'

They crossed the field hand in hand and Lizzie said, 'How do you know we can trust him?'

'It's just a feeling, really, although his story is solid. He considered getting out of France to join De Gaulle's Free French Forces, but decided he was better positioned to fight from within.'

'He sounds like the ideal Resistance leader,' Lizzie said.

'Yes, my thoughts exactly. He is a skilled artist and forges documents for people on the run.'

'That's handy! Seems like you had more of a useful afternoon than me.'

'We got lucky meeting Marguerite exactly when the Vichy mob turned up. Otherwise, we might never have got into the conversation which connected us to Lev.'

Jack helped Lizzie across a bumpy patch, and soon they were surrounded by vines. He filled her in on more details as the grapes on the vines rustled gently in the breeze.

'What if he's pretending to be on our side but informs on us? I read accounts in London where people inform on friends in exchange for money and food.'

Jack sighed. 'You always get informants who sell out their own in times of war. It's a chance we must take. It's highly unlikely based on my assessment of Lev, but if for some reason he did tell on us, I could easily throw doubt on his accusations.'

'Do you believe he is Jewish?' Lizzie asked.

'I do. He told me his family on his mother's side have been here for generations and his father's parents fled persecution in Iraq. It's a very elaborate story to concoct on the off chance that a newcomer to town is of any significance.'

'True,' Lizzie agreed.

'The Vichy officials wouldn't trust a Jew, even if he has an ulterior motive,' Jack said.

'But couldn't that be part of his entrapment efforts? Maybe he's not Jewish at all.'

Jack laughed. 'I see my work is done. You suspect

everyone and everything. No wonder you make such a brilliant spy.'

'I'm just playing out the potential scenarios, like you taught me,' Lizzie said. She paused and added, 'Mind you, he looks Jewish.'

'What does a Jew look like?' Jack asked, his tone slightly mocking.

'Olive skin?' she said.

'Next you'll be saying they all have the same nose.'

Lizzie shrugged. 'That's the antisemitic stereotype, isn't it, but Hannah is blonde and blue-eyed with a small nose, so that puts holes in that theory.'

'I recall Hannah saying her ancestors came from somewhere in the Middle East and eventually settled in Germany. Hence, her colouring. It's no secret Jews have endured forced conversion to Christianity and Islam over millennia. Some would have intermarried.'

'We've not talked about our religion before. How well do you know your bible?' Lizzie asked, her eyes searching Jack's as they meandered through the vineyards.

'We used to study it at Sunday school. My parents encouraged us to attend, and we did for years. Are you Catholic or Church of England?'

Lizzie said, 'Roman Catholic. My school was quite religious, and we did a lot of bible study, both the Old and New Testament. I remember belting out in assembly: *Let My People Go*, at the top of my lungs. The hymn about Moses leading the Israelites out of slavery and to Israel, the promised land. I thought little more about it until I met Hannah.'

'At least, we won't need to toss a coin for which church to marry in.'

'That's something we didn't consider. What denomination are Michel and Isabelle Dubois?' Lizzie asked.

'Luc is Catholic, like my parents, although I think it's unlikely anyone will quiz us on that.'

'Anyway, we digress. You seem confident Lev can be trusted.'

'Even in the worst-case scenario, I didn't give him anything tangible to hang an accusation on. And I would just deny it and say he's a crackpot.'

They reached the edge of the vineyards, with Beau still escorting them. Lizzie admired the haze of lavender ahead and told Jack she had entered the field earlier.

'It's stunning around here, that's for sure,' Jack agreed.

'What an absolutely wonderful place,' Lizzie said, raising her face to the soothing sun. 'I could live here forever!'

Jack tugged her gently towards him and they stood there rocking back and forth, enjoying the moment surrounded only by nature. Then Beau barked and pawed at Lizzie's leg.

'The daft mutt is jealous!' Jack said. 'You've got yourself another ardent admirer.'

Lizzie bent to stoke Beau's head. 'Come on boy, I bet it's time for your dinner soon.'

The orange-tinged sun sank lower over the lavender on the horizon, and they turned back to the château, enjoying their new life together, no matter how temporary it proved to be.

CHAPTER 21

A few days later, Jack and Lizzie visited Marguerite in the café. When they sat down, she came over and took their order. Then she looked from Lizzie to Jack expectantly. 'Well?' she said.

Jack raised one dark eyebrow. 'Well, what?'

She leant over to wipe the table and whispered, 'Lev wants to know if you have a message for him.'

'He is keen,' Jack replied, his face cracking into a smile.

'Of course he is. We need your help,' Margarite said. 'We can't just let these lunatics take our country. They're going to hand it over to the Nazis on a silver platter, and our children will be raised speaking German.'

The pain was evident on her face.

Lizzie touched her hand and said in a low voice. 'We understand, but don't say more now.'

Marguerite's eyes shone with gratitude. 'I have a message for you from Lev.'

Jack's head jerked up. 'You've been at our table too long. Continue your duties and when you bring our coffee, give it to us then.'

Marguerite nodded and bustled off to another table.

Lizzie looked at Jack. 'Things are heating up.'

'They are indeed. It always takes a while, but once you find the right people, it moves like lightning.'

'It's exciting to build this from the ground up.'

They spoke in hushed tones and Jack held Lizzie's hand as if they were swearing their devotion to each other, not discussing how to build a deadly network that would outwit the Vichy regime.

Lizzie leant over to kiss Jack, so anyone watching them would think they had nothing on their minds but their mutual obsession. 'I'm beginning to understand why Val said being a married couple is such an effective cover.'

'Good, maybe now you won't insist on ditching me to pursue your solo reconnaissance,' Jack said, his eyes full of amusement.

'I don't know about that,' Lizzie said.

Marguerite returned with two steaming cups of coffee and a small pastry Jack had ordered for Lizzie.

'This is one of my favourites,' he said, placing the plate in front of her. 'What's the message?' he prompted, without looking at Marguerite.

'Lev has been asked to organise the escape of a downed airman,' she said, making a show of tidying her hair, whilst barely moving her lips.

Jack raised his cup to his mouth. 'Where is he?'

'I don't know,' she said, smoothing down her apron. 'He said to meet him at the usual place this afternoon if you can help.'

Marguerite took off without looking back and that was the last they saw of her that day. She'd accomplished her task, and the other patrons kept her busy until they left.

'What a mysterious one she is,' Jack said.

Lizzie murmured in between bites of the pastry. 'This is

delicious, you're right. Here,' she said, holding up her fork for Jack to take a piece.

They stayed at the café a while longer, as if they had nowhere important to rush off to, and when they finished their coffee and cake, they stood in a leisurely fashion and walked away at a measured pace without making eye contact with their messenger.

'Our first agents are in play,' Jack mused, as they walked hand in hand across the Place du Capitole.

'It's a great start,' Lizzie said. 'I find it disconcerting we can move about here as though there isn't a war on. It's very different from Paris or Reims.'

'It is an unusual situation, given our proximity to the occupied zone,' Jack agreed, raising Lizzie's hand to his lips and kissing her palm. 'The whole thing is odd, and I think it might get a lot weirder before we're finished.'

They approached the Café de Paris and entered. It was dimly lit, and the smoke formed an acrid smog. It took a while for Jack to locate Lev, who sat alone in a different corner from last time. Jack steered Lizzie towards the table.

'You remember my wife, Madame Dubois?' Jack asked, indicating Lizzie with a flourish.

Lev stood and shook Lizzie's hand. 'A pleasure to see you again, madame.'

'Oh please, call me Isabelle. There's no need to be formal.'

Jack pulled out a chair for Lizzie and she sat down. 'What will you have?' he asked.

Lizzie said she'd had enough coffee for one day and would have a juice. And Lev asked Jack to tell the barman, the same again, for him.

Jack went to organise the drinks at the bar and Lev turned to face Lizzie.

'How do you like Toulouse?' he asked.

Lizzie said she found it charming and was enjoying it so far.

'It must be quite an experience to live in the château.'

Lizzie agreed it was and told him she'd not lived so grandly before, and it took a bit of getting used to.

Their conversation tailed off until Jack returned and put the drinks on the table. 'I see you two are getting acquainted.'

'Indeed. I take it Marguerite gave you my message, and this isn't a serendipitous meeting,' Lev said, cutting through the small talk.

'You are correct. Whilst serendipity is a miraculous thing, I prefer not to depend on it.'

They chinked their glasses and smiled like old friends meeting for a catch up. 'Santé.'

'Tell me about the man,' Jack said, dropping his voice and looking at Lev.

'Actually, I've now discovered there are two of them. British. They were shot down and are making their way here.' Lev tilted his cigarette pack to Jack, who took one, and Lizzie declined with a gracious smile.

Lev lit his cigarette and exhaled. 'Then we'll need to get them to Marguerite's contact who will arrange to take them across the Pyrenees.'

'That sounds like the beginnings of a plan,' Jack said.

'Every day they stay in the same place, the risk of being discovered increases. It's not as dangerous as in occupied territory, but we have our share of traitors and informants here, too.'

'So I understand,' Jack said, encouraging Lev to continue.

'It's quite a way from where they are now to Toulouse. They will move by night and rest and hide out by day.'

'Alright,' Jack said. 'Makes sense.'

'What do you need from us?' Lizzie said, thinking it was time Lev understood she wasn't just an arm attachment.

Lev cast an admiring glance at Lizzie that wasn't lost on Jack, but he couldn't blame him for being impressed.

'That's a good question, Isabelle. It's the tricky bit, I'm afraid.'

Jack's eyes locked on Lev's. 'Tell us. There's no time to beat around the bush. If we can help, we will.'

'I don't have a suitable place to hide them here. When they arrive, we will need to get them out of the way immediately and have them lie low for a few days, in case anyone spotted and reported them on the way.'

'If someone reports them along the way, we will already have a much greater problem,' Jack said.

Lev shook his head. 'Many of the Vichy police are new to the job and are amateurs. They are keen but lack experience, which plays into our hands. Just because they are seen doesn't mean they'll be arrested. And of course, there are some who will do the right thing and look the other way.'

'Right, so where can we hide them? How about a friend's farmhouse?' Jack asked. 'You must know a lot of locals.'

'Unfortunately, many of my friends have had to leave France, and the others can no longer afford to live where they used to. They don't have houses suitable for hiding anyone. There is a sympathetic farmer who sheltered some Jews the authorities were searching for, but he told me that was the last time. They nearly caught them, and he said it's too dangerous. He won't risk it again.'

Lizzie had a vision of the Sterns on the run and wondered if it may have been them. She shook her head and drank her juice. Thousands of Jews had escaped and were trying to escape France as more harsh statutes were introduced. It could have been any family.

The thought of the Gestapo catching them filled her with dread. Those dear children had stolen Lizzie's heart in Paris. The Jew hunts throughout Europe were like something out of a never-ending nightmare, and each time she went back undercover, and heard the latest developments, she was shocked anew.

Lev knocked back the rest of his drink in one shot and his eyes flickered from Lizzie to Jack.

'There's only one solution I can think of at such short notice.'

'Well, don't keep us in suspense, man,' Jack said. 'What is it?'

They studied their new agent's solemn expression.

Lev cleared his throat, and said quietly, 'The château is the perfect place to hide them whilst I prepare their forged identity papers, and we arrange the details of their escape.'

CHAPTER 22

Armand's chest swelled with pride as he drove the Legion's finest vehicle through the streets of Toulouse. He was excited about tonight.

He tried to make conversation with the commissaire like they were peers, but his illustrious passenger only grunted a few times in reply and then stuck his head in the papers he was reading in the back of the luxury car.

The commissaire eventually slid his papers into a folder and rested it on the back seat to prepare for arrival. The heavy car crawled to the top of the hill, and Armand spun the steering wheel sharply and the tyres bumped over the uneven ground at the entrance to the château.

Armand inhaled when the full splendour of the medieval castle came into full view. He'd never been inside the grounds before, and like most Toulousians, he had only admired the ancient house from afar. He had thanked the commissionaire for assigning him as his driver and was thrilled by the honour.

A tall man dressed in a fine dinner jacket cut from expensive cloth stood waiting in the courtyard and ushered them towards a parking spot. Armand parked carefully, his pulse racing and his throat dry as he realised it was the handsome man from his lunchtime spy games. He must be a resident of the château, because a dinner guest wouldn't officially greet them like this. Armand took a deep breath to steady his nerves as he exited the car. The man wished him a good evening, and Armand opened the door for the commissaire.

The man stepped forward and introduced himself to the commissaire as Michel Dubois, a relative of Luc's from Brittany. His accent was undeniably upper class, and his deep velvet voice drifted on the warm summer air like a caress.

The two men walked ahead without glancing at Armand, who shuffled behind.

Suddenly, the man turned to Armand. 'Sorry, how remiss of me. I should have said, supper will be served for you by the housekeeper in the staff quarters.'

Armand flinched as though he had been punched in the stomach. He had dressed appropriately for dinner, taking special care with his uniform, and brushing his shoes until they shone, thinking that although he had been asked to drive the commissaire, he would also dine with them. He was an esteemed and respected member of the Legion, after all, not some lowly chauffeur relegated to eat with the kitchen staff. Or so he had assumed.

He fought to keep up with the two men who strode ahead, but it was impossible with his limp slowing him down, and he tugged at his tunic, which was suddenly too tight, and his face flushed with mortification.

By the time he turned the corner, the men had already disappeared into the château. Armand released an anguished sigh, and his blue eyes were like angry slits in his salmon-pink puffy face. A woman exited a side door and called over to him. 'Good evening. You must be Monsieur Armand.'

He nodded, unable to construct a suitable reply in his indignation.

'We ate early as there is much to do for our distinguished guest this evening, but I saved some for you, so you may dine in peace whilst we serve in the kitchen.'

The housekeeper spoke to him as though she were doing him a great favour and he had to hold his acidic tongue from slaying her offer with a furious response.

A huge black and tan dog came rushing around the corner, and Armand stiffened and stopped. He was afraid of dogs, especially big ones.

The housekeeper noticed his reaction. 'Come here, Beau, don't bother our guest,' she said, calling him until he nuzzled against her, and she stroked his massive head as he trotted beside her through the door.

How absolutely vile. A dog in the house. Armand would have expected higher standards from the upper classes. He sniffed and resumed walking after the woman. The day would come when he wouldn't be relegated to the kitchens with dogs, and he would dine with the crème de la crème and be party to their innermost secrets.

His vision was clear on how the Vichy government would merge seamlessly with the Nazi regime and he intended to play a vital part in the machinations that would be instrumental in bringing this extraordinary collaboration about.

Armand attempted to conjure a small smile for the housekeeper, who showed him into a pleasant room and poured him a glass of brandy when he said that was his poison of choice. Soon after she brought him a meal, and when he finished eating, he flopped into a comfortable chair by the window and admired the view of his red roofed city below.

Oh, to live like the nobility and look down on his subjects from above. Even in the staff's quarters, the accommodations were far more splendid than his small apartment near the river where he lived alone.

Armand felt the heat of the liquid permeate his throat, and he lit a cigarette and contemplated what would surely be his glorious future, whilst trying not to dwell on the fact he had been relegated to the servant's quarters and not given a seat at the table.

My time is coming, Monsieur Saint-Clair. There will be another revolution and I'll be the one living in your fine château if you're not very, very careful.

He touched his *médaille commémorative française de la guerre,* which was a standard medal awarded to veterans of the First War. It still burned, he'd been overlooked for anything more significant, despite his contributions in two wars.

His thoughts circled back to the attractive young man, Michel Dubois. Now he knew where he was staying, there was no need to waste his precious resources tracking him down as he had intended. He could focus his energies on keeping an eye on him at the château. There was something about the newcomer that intrigued him, and it wasn't just his fine physique.

He puffed on his *Gitanes* and decided he would commence his surveillance as soon as he had a vacancy in his busy schedule.

'If there's more to you than you are saying, Michel Dubois, I will soon know about it,' he said aloud, his voice low and chilling.

Armand planned his petty revenge. If he wasn't who he claimed, the commissaire would be disgraced for falling for the ruse. And if Dubois checked out to be who he said he was, Armand consoled himself: he would have an enjoyable time monitoring him, for he was a delight to the eye. There would be other opportunities to bring the commissaire down. The head of the police was entitled and wouldn't suspect his position was in danger.

Forbidden feelings raced through him, causing him to shudder with the ache of unfulfilled desire as his thoughts swung back to Michel Dubois like a magnet. He had made several visits to his mistress since first laying eyes on the delectable mystery man, but unfortunately, through no fault of her own, she was not equipped to satisfy his needs in anything more than a perfunctory fashion.

This was the curse Armand had lived under since he was an adolescent. He had tried everything he could think of to banish his unnatural carnal desires, but each time he thought he had them under control, they raised their head again like a venomous snake. He blamed his father, who had been an effeminate man. Armand assumed he must have inherited the wicked gene, so there was nothing he could do to stop it, but he would make sure no one ever suspected his unfortunate cravings. His bright future would be over if the truth were ever to get out.

Armand finished his brandy and let his eyes close until he drifted off into a light sleep. He may as well rest whilst the opportunity presented itself.

CHAPTER 23

Jack was nowhere to be seen as Lizzie descended the sweeping staircase in her evening dress and hovered at the entrance to the formal dining room, not sure whether she should knock. Suzanne and her small team had been buzzing in and out of the room all day. The heavy wood door swung open, and the butler announced her arrival and ushered her inside.

Luc was seated alone at the long table, which was decorated with vines and vibrant floral bouquets of summer blooms freshly picked from the gardens.

Lizzie gasped in wonder at the sheer beauty of the scene, which was opulent yet tasteful. She gazed about her in wonder at the paintings on the walls and the high plastered ceiling and glittering chandeliers. She had not dined in a setting as grand as this, even though her parents moved in wealthy circles in Jersey before the war. She was a mere child then and hadn't been invited to regal dinners her parents attended.

Like the rest of the château, the furniture showed signs of slight wear, but if anything; it added to the romantic grace of the room. She imagined the countless glamorous parties and dinners that must have taken place there over hundreds of years.

It was difficult to keep up with repairs since the war broke out and the subsequent austerity. In truth, Lizzie didn't know what sort of access wealthy French people like Luc retained to their pre-war money. He had mentioned it wasn't a time for indulgence when people in the village were struggling to put food in their children's mouths.

Luc seemed like a good man. Jack had told her they regularly sent château produce they could spare, that wasn't taken by the Germans, to be distributed amongst the villagers.

'My dear, here you are,' Luc said, his lined face breaking into a genuine smile as he stood and moved towards Lizzie. He looked dashing in a velvet dinner jacket and cravat and was dressed more formally than for their usual dinners. His silver hair was swept back neatly and added to his distinguished appearance.

They kissed, French style, and he escorted her to sit next to him. 'You look exquisite. I confess it is my fault your usually diligent husband isn't here to meet you. Don't be nervous, my friend has risen to a high rank in the police force, but to me, he is still the fellow with whom I used to play boules.' Then he lowered his voice. 'Remember that, if he asks any difficult questions.'

Just as Lizzie was about to ask where her husband had gone, Jack appeared in the doorway with the commissaire at his side, who proffered a charming smile. Jack introduced them and they were soon all seated and making polite pre-dinner conversation.

Lizzie's heart thudded furiously at the realisation they were having dinner with the head of the Toulouse French police, and one wrong word could prove deadly. She controlled her breathing in the way she had been trained, and after several slow intakes of breath whilst being careful not to show her nerves, she calmed down and her heart rate slowed to a normal speed.

The butler served them several vintages of wine to taste, which Lizzie had grown accustomed to as a routine part of dining in a château with its own vineyards and winery.

The commissaire was ecstatic with the vintage Luc recommended he have with his main course. 'No one makes wine like you,' he said, complimenting Luc profusely, his face flushed after several large glasses. 'You've always had the golden touch.'

Luc raised his glass, and they all followed suit.

The commissaire said, 'That reminds me. I'm afraid I may have attracted some attention to Château de Saint-Clair, my dear friend.'

'Oh, yes?' Luc said, a slight frown on his brow.

'When I was in Paris earlier this week, I was invited to a prestigious event hosted by the Nazis and found myself seated next to a decent sort—a great lover of wine like me. Of course, one thing led to another and before I could stop myself, I was gushing about your wonderful vineyards and the wines you grow and produce here.'

Luc listened to his old friend, and Lizzie glimpsed a shadow cross his face. 'Go on,' he said.

'Well, he has a trip to meet with Marshal Pétain at Vichy HQ booked in the next few days, and he asked whether I might arrange a dinner party for us here so he may visit further south. He's not been to Toulouse, before you see.'

'I do see,' Luc said, his tone somewhat acerbic.

'Oh, don't be like that. He will be a good contact for you. We all need friends in high places, and I wouldn't be surprised if the Germans didn't extend the full occupation to our zone sooner than we envisage.'

Jack looked startled, but recovered instantly. 'Why do you say that if I may be so bold?'

The commissaire turned to Jack. 'I may be wrong, but I have my suspicions, that's all, so it would be a good move to entertain Walter Von Shneider and show him your wines. Perhaps he will even buy from you. They are transporting a lot of French wine to Germany, as I understand it.'

Luc's eyes narrowed. 'You mean well, but the Nazis have crushed our wine trade by lowering the Franc rate to such a degree we may as well give them our wine, not sell it to them.'

This was the first time during the evening, Luc had said anything derogatory about the Nazis, and Lizzie held her breath and waited to see how the commissaire would react.

'I am sorry for that. This is a difficult time, and we must make whatever commerce we can. I advise you to create fruitful ties with the Nazis, because, as I said, I predict they will join us permanently in the South soon.'

Jack remained poker faced throughout the entire exchange.

Luc changed the subject swiftly and told the commissaire that Michel was a much-needed extra pair of hands, now he was growing old and had lost many of his pre-war employees.

'It's not too long before we will be in the picking season again, and I must say we will be grateful for your help, Michel. I do hope you can stay on through the summer.'

The commissaire seemed intrigued and asked Jack what he did exactly.

Luc interjected. 'Michel is experienced in the business side of wine, but he's been helping us prune the vines, and carry out daily maintenance.'

'I suppose the wine trade in St. Malo is not what it was before the war,' the commissaire replied.

'Sadly, it is not. There's not much call for my services, so I'm glad to be of use here for the time being, at least.'

'And what of your beautiful wife?' the commissaire asked, turning to Lizzie, whose heart started thumping again.

She really must grow accustomed to being in the spotlight like this now they were permanent guests at the château. In previous missions she had flitted about in the shadows, working undercover, rarely engaging with the enemy directly. It was a frightening experience, and she found herself lacking.

It was Jack's turn to save her by using some of their concocted cover story. 'We are recently married, and could not bear to be apart, so she accompanied me for that reason. She has no official capacity here but I'm sure she will pass the time admirably.'

'I do not blame you, monsieur. Who would leave such a wife behind by choice? A wife's place is at her husband's side, after all.'

Lizzie assumed her subservient role and smiled graciously, her green eyes setting off her red dress to perfection. Jack always knew what to say, and she was grateful she didn't have to pull this off alone. At moments like this, she realised she was still an amateur.

The rest of the meal passed uneventfully, and the evening dragged on until the commissaire finally rose to leave.

'Would you have someone call my driver, please?' he asked Jack.

'Of course. We'll have him meet you by the car and I'll escort you downstairs.'

The commissaire thanked Luc for dinner and Luc said he was welcome anytime.

'Talking of which, the German I referred to is a member of the Gestapo. When would you like to host him for dinner?'

Lizzie sputtered on the last of her wine when she heard his words and worked quickly to regain her composure.

A Gestapo thug for dinner.

The prospect of the proposed dinner set her nerves on end. The commissaire was dangerous enough, but to dine with a member of the Gestapo. That seemed a step too far, even for them.

She saw Jack raise one eyebrow with his first obvious sign of being disturbed by the evening's events.

Luc frowned and looked troubled, dropping his friend's official title and addressing him by his first name. 'A member of the Gestapo, you say? You might have mentioned it earlier, Robert.'

It was a sharp rebuke, like a rap on the knuckles, but the commissaire was clearly adept at dodging people's wrath and brushed it off smoothly.

'Come along now, Luc, my dear old friend. Don't be inhospitable. I promise you there will be something in it for you.'

'I find that difficult to believe,' Luc replied dryly. 'When do you wish this dinner to take place?'

The commissaire placed his cap on his head and scrunched his eyes up at the ceiling, as if it might provide details of his calendar. He was silent for a moment and then announced, 'Soon. I will be in touch.'

Luc gave a minute shrug. 'Very well, we will make plans to entertain your Gestapo officer and be on our best behaviour.'

The commissaire smiled, pleased with his victory. 'That's a smart move, thank you. I will convey your invitation.'

CHAPTER 24

'Dining with the enemy is more nail-biting than breaking into Nazi High Command!' Lizzie whispered to Jack when everyone had retired for the night, and they were back in their rooms.

Jack chuckled at her outrageous statement. 'I don't think I've ever done anything quite as dangerous as that, and if you'd listened to my orders, you wouldn't have either, Seagrove! It brings me out in a cold sweat just thinking about what you and Hannah got up to.'

'Well, I'm here to tell the tale, so it wasn't that bad. But this sitting down to dinner, hoping the enemy doesn't suspect me every time I raise my fork to my lips, is another level of fear. I struggled to swallow through the whole meal.'

'It's a different game we're playing. You did brilliantly, darling. Espionage comes in many forms and sitting around observing can be the most testing. Action is easier because we fire ourselves up and know what the immediate goal is. You'll grow used to dining room espionage the more we do it, I promise.'

Lizzie's senses were still on overdrive as she relived the

events of the dinner. 'I hope you're right. I thought my heart was going to explode when he said the dinner guest is a Gestapo officer.'

Jack said, 'We'll have time to talk it through with Luc to prepare.'

'It's imminent by the sounds of it,' she said, crossing the room to the window where a veil of darkness had descended over the valley.

'Do you think the commissaire suspects something? It seemed a menacing proposal out of the blue like that.'

'I doubt it, I hear the Nazis love a freeloading dinner with the French elite. To be honest, I'm more concerned about him stealing Luc's best wine and loading it on the train to Germany.'

'What a horrible thought.'

'It's not an ideal scenario,' Jack said, raking his hand through his floppy hair, his expression serious.

'That's putting it mildly. You can say that again!'

'I could, but it will only aggravate you,' he said.

Lizzie picked up an embroidered cushion from a nearby chair and threw it at him playfully, but he caught it like a pro with both hands and grinned at her.

'Smart arse,' she said, hands on hips.

'Better than being called a dumbass, like the Americans say.'

Lizzie perched on Jack's knee. 'Do you think we'll look back on our wartime escapades and it'll all be a blur in years to come, almost as though it never happened?'

Jack tilted his head to one side. 'As long as we defeat the Nazis and we have each other, I don't think I'll care.'

'Ah, you are such a romantic,' Lizzie said, pressing a kiss to his lips and leaning against him, relaxing at last. 'I'm right up there with the Nazis!'

Jack tickled her side, and she gasped, wriggling away from his touch.

'I'd love to take you to bed right now.'

'Oh, and what's stopping you?' she said, a flirtatious sparkle in her eyes.

'One minor detail.'

'Go on.'

'Val is waiting to hear from us.'

Lizzie hit her thigh. 'Ah, of course. I didn't think of that. You see, I relax my guard when we're together.'

Jack eased Lizzie off his knee. 'Come on, let's get it done and then we'll have an early night.'

'I can think of nothing better,' she said, leaning in to kiss him as he drew closer and took her in his arms.

'What's the message?' she whispered.

'All will be revealed. Watch and learn, Seagrove.'

He grabbed a lantern from the dresser, and they slipped quietly out the door, checking both sides of the corridor to make sure no one was watching.

Jack took off his shoes and signalled for Lizzie to do the same. They crept along the dark corridor, shadows casting eerie patterns on the walls as they followed the light of the lantern, their feet padding softly on the cool parquet flooring.

The kitchen area was in darkness, the staff long retired after a busy evening and the prospect of a dawn awakening that would stir them from their beds all too soon.

They put their shoes back on and let themselves out the back door. The sultry night air caressed Lizzie's face, and she breathed it in. A chorus of chirping cicadas echoed on the soft wind, and Jack captured her hand as they crossed to the turret room where they had hidden their radio.

Luc said they had his blessing to operate how they saw fit, but it would be safer for them all if they only told him specifics he had to know. That way, if he was questioned, he wouldn't be able to reveal much, even under interrogation.

Lizzie had shivered when he spoke the words so matter-of-factly, and later she and Jack discussed the conversation. It sounded as though Luc was no stranger to torture after being imprisoned during World War I.

The silver moon was high in the violet sky like a precious jewel set in a glittering crown. It was so beautiful here. Lizzie was reminded how lucky they were to be together instead of separated by miles, not knowing when or even if they would be reunited.

In the turret, Jack rested the lantern on a chair. He retrieved a large ornate key from his pocket and placed it on a shelf hewn into the wall before bending down to brush the heavy rug aside.

'What's the key for?' Lizzie asked.

'It's an old spy trick used to throw intruders off the scent.' Jack tapped on a section of the timber floor and removed a plank with relative ease.

'Do you mean the key is just a decoy?'

'Exactly. I asked Luc for an old key we could borrow.'

'You are shrewd, Monsieur Dubois!'

'Still got a few tricks up my sleeve, Madame Dubois,' Jack said, winking. He extracted the radio set from the compartment in the floor that was one of the secret hiding places passed through the generations by his ancestors. He and Henry had hidden things in it when they were boys.

Then Jack set up the radio, pulled out the slim codebook, and put on the headphones. Lizzie leaned against the desk. There was something seductive about watching a spy at work, and she experienced a surreal moment where she felt she should pinch herself to check this wasn't all a dream. As much as she was terrified through most of dinner, she wouldn't change being here with Jack for anything.

Since embarking on her first overseas operation, she had come alive in ways she hadn't envisaged. Every day undercover was a heady rush and add to that her passionate relationship with Jack, and it made for a thrilling life.

A response came through to go ahead and Jack tapped out his message in Morse, confident it was a secure channel and a radio operator was ready to receive and pass the message to Val.

Jack packed the wireless and codebook away, and turned to Lizzie, ready to leave. 'All done.'

'What did the message say?' she asked, curious and keen to improve her spycraft. Despite their intense relationship, Jack was still her military superior.

'The airmen are getting close.'

Lizzie froze.

'How do you know?'

'Marguerite left a letter for you. Suzanne passed it to me when you'd already gone into dinner.'

'What did it say?' Lizzie asked, her weariness gone and her eyes wide.

'That our delivery should arrive sometime this week.'

'My God, this thing is really happening. We're going to hide British airmen in the château grounds when a Gestapo officer is coming to dinner!'

Jack said, 'We'd better not think too much about it now. Besides, remember we have other plans tonight.'

Lizzie's senses leapt at the promise of a night of love-making with no air raids to disturb them and nowhere to rush to. She pushed the fearful thoughts from her mind as they walked stealth like across the courtyard and back through the maze of corridors by the light of the lantern.

Their bedroom was quiet, apart from the sounds of nature bedding down for the night through the open windows. Jack closed the shutters and turned to Lizzie. 'I think we should make the most of our honeymoon.'

Even Luc didn't know they weren't really married. They had kept it from him so there would be no uncomfortable conversation about them sharing a bed. It was simpler to pretend they were really man and wife, and it felt right.

Jack kissed her feverishly, and she returned his ardour with abandon as they removed each other's clothing in a trance.

All thoughts of airmen and Gestapo were banished as they lost themselves in each other and their desire swept them far away from the dangers of Vichy France.

They were newlyweds—Monsieur and Madame Dubois—and at least for tonight, all was perfect in their world. They made love again and again in the darkness, revelling in the freedom to be together all night in such a peaceful setting instead of sharing snatched hours in Jack's London flat.

Lizzie cried out in ecstasy as Jack's hands played on her senses like a maestro conducting a symphony until she barely remembered who she was. They exchanged words of devotion until first light seeped through the cracks in the shutters and they fell into a deep, satiated sleep, locked in each other's embrace.

CHAPTER 25

Armand Abadie sat in his office, taking meetings with informants. Wednesday was his favourite morning of the week, listening to the secrets confided in him by loyal citizens. He commended himself on his clever idea to establish a weekly clinic for concerned Toulousians to meet with him personally. The idea had come to him during one of his people watching lunches and had led to countless successful raids on Jews and other *undesirables*.

Armand had taken to using the expression after watching a newsreel featuring Hitler at the cinema. It was the perfect catch-all term for the scum that had washed into his city in ever-increasing waves since Marshal Pétain signed the armistice, and Jews, communists, blacks, homosexuals, gypsies, and all the other ugly misfits who in his opinion, like Hitler's, had no place in society.

He checked his pocket watch he still used since the Great War. The beauty of the watch face and the intricate craftsmanship of the gold casing still moved him when he looked at it. He kept it on him at all times during the day and lay it on his bedside cabinet at night. It was his most treasured possession.

'Josette!' he called. When there was no response, he rose from his desk, irritation etched into his every feature. 'Josette!' his voice boomed beyond the door and into the reception area.

A petite, neatly dressed young woman came rushing over. 'Yes, Monsieur Abadie? What may I do for you?'

'You may come quicker when I call,' he snapped.

The secretary apologised and looked downcast, as though she might burst into tears.

He held up his hand and tutted. 'Alright, enough apologies and sad faces. Do better next time and I won't need to scold you.'

He issued his order, and she scurried away. When she returned with his coffee in hand, she told him someone had arrived to see him.

Josette took care not to use the dirty word 'informant' even though she knew only too well, that was what was going on in her boss's office. She would have liked to leave the job, but her salary was all that was between her and her mother falling into poverty, so she shut up and did what he told her. He was not the type to risk insulting.

Privately, she dubbed him 'Little Hitler,' and her secret joke amused her. It was a term she'd heard on a British radio broadcast in the early days of the war. It was growing too dangerous to tune into any, but the official French permitted channels now. But that's what she called Armand, although she didn't share her mockery with anyone else. In wartime, it was best to keep such thoughts to oneself.

. . .

Armand drank his coffee, and it didn't cross his mind for a second to offer refreshments to the informants. After two more trickled in and out to report matters ranging from Jews, they believed should be arrested for flouting the latest statutes, to a discarded weapon left on his desk, wrapped in a muddy handkerchief, and found on the banks of the river. 'I believe one of the Resistance rats dropped this,' the man said, disdain spewing from every syllable.

He noted down the incidents and targets of the informants' venom studiously in his lined blue notebook, which he had procured purely for this purpose. He referred to it often and was pleased with the quality of intelligence he was collating. Sometimes incidents and people cross-referenced when he looked back, and he had a growing number of suspects either under surveillance or in line for surveillance when resources permitted.

Armand assembled his own task force with Vichy head office's blessing, and it was clear, at least to him, he was the only member of the Legion in the Toulouse branch who was making significant progress in rooting out traitors. The rest of his colleagues of similar standing merely wiled away the time in uneventful long-winded meetings and dull lengthy lunches where they patted each other on the back for their performance in WW1 and found ways to exploit the current system. Armand suspected some of them were in De Gaulle's back pocket.

The time would come when Armand would have the ear of the Nazi leadership, and he would know exactly who had to go, so he was playing a game of stealth. Few would pass his loyalty test.

He called out to Josette that he wouldn't be seeing any more informants until next week and she should not disturb him. After closing his door, he pulled on the shutters, so the room was in shade, and put his feet up on his desk. His head nestled comfortably into the back of his chair, which he'd taken from the spoils of a Jew's requisitioned family home, and he drifted into a deep sleep within minutes, mouth open and snoring lightly.

He dreamt he was marching up the Champs-Élysées in full battle dress, his tunic laden with medals glorifying his illustrious past. The Führer sat at the front of the parade and bestowed a new medal on him and thanked him for his service.

Then the dream morphed abruptly, and he saw the injured body of a young man in a trench. The man's eyes rolled back in his head, and he clutched his chest where a knife was embedded deep in his flesh through the material of his uniform.

Armand still remembered the words Abraham muttered to him with his last breath. '*Shema Israel*,' he gasped.

Armand had later found out what the words meant because no matter how he tried to dismiss Abraham's death from his mind, the young Jew's face wracked with pain haunted him.

He discovered that *Shema Israel* was the name of a Hebrew prayer: *Hear O Israel*. It was a plea to God that Jews recited, especially when in danger.

Armand's head lolled to the side, jerking him awake, and his eyes peeled open. He rubbed his sore neck and coughed to clear his dry throat, spluttering.

The vision of Abraham's lifeless staring eyes had forced his nap to an abrupt end. He removed his feet from the desk, straightened his uniform, and left the building without a word to anyone.

It was time for lunch at the Place du Capitole. Today, he would order something particularly delicious. He hoped he might see the man from the château with his lady wife. There was something about those two. He didn't know what, but he would get to the bottom of it. He always did.

It was only a matter of time.

CHAPTER 26

Lizzie stirred and the memory of what they were about to do flooded her consciousness, making her senses race so she was instantly wide awake.

She reached out her hand to pat the sheet next to her, sensing she was alone in the big bed. 'Where are you?' she whispered into the dense darkness.

'Morning, sleeping beauty,' Jack said, crossing into the bedroom and standing over her. She could make out his silhouette in the dim light from the bathroom.

He leaned over Lizzie and kissed her. His skin was warm and damp, and his breath minty fresh.

'It's not morning, is it?' she asked, hitching herself up in the bed.

'It's almost three. I was about to wake you. We must leave in the next ten minutes. All going to plan, Lev should be waiting for us.'

Lizzie jumped out of bed and pulled on the dress she'd laid out.

'Wear your coat, too. There'll be a chill in the air at this time of night,' Jack said, his voice gravelly from lack of sleep.

'We're going on a dangerous operation, and you're concerned I'll catch a chill?' Lizzie laughed softly, careful not to wake the slumbering inhabitants of the château.

'You make a fair point, but I can't stop taking care of you. It's ingrained in me.'

'Don't stop,' she said, reaching up on her bare feet to kiss him. 'It's quite the most romantic thing and I wouldn't change it for the world. Doesn't mean you're not funny, though.'

'Great. Just what I was going for. I've become a buffoon,' he teased.

Sometimes, she couldn't believe how blessed she was to have met Jack. What would she be doing now if Drake hadn't spotted her for the SOE and insisted she meet with the recruiter? She'd probably still be translating dull documents at the War Office, bored out of her mind like Evie.

Instead, she was in the thrilling position to make a real difference to the outcome of the war. Unlike when she went on her first undercover mission, oblivious to the knowledge she was the first woman to be dropped into occupied France by the SOE, now there were hundreds of agents embedded in occupied territories. Some worked in key roles within the Nazi administration, passing intelligence to Baker Street, and orchestrating daily acts of defiance. They were all doing their bit, and she was proud to have been involved since the start.

Every operation counted, no matter how small, and tonight would be their first act of violent sabotage against the joint Vichy and Nazi regimes. Val had instructed them it was time to increase resistance in the Free Zone and replicate the damage the networks were doing across occupied France.

As Lizzie finished getting ready, adrenaline washed away the remaining weariness that clawed at her after only sleeping for a few hours. They stood by the door, shoes in hand, ready to slip into the dark corridors and out into the night.

Outside, their path lit only by streams of moonlight, they cut through the orchard and the smell of ripening fruit tickled Lizzie's nose as she brushed past scented trees. Moving at a fast pace and panting slightly from the sudden exertion, she reached the outskirts of the château, closely on Jack's heels.

'Alright?' he asked.

'Yes, fine.'

'Stay close. I scouted out this route yesterday. We can cut down the hillside to shorten the distance.' He withdrew a small torch from his pocket and handed it to Lizzie. 'Tread carefully, so you don't stumble. There are sharp rocks and bushes along the way, so it's easy to trip. It's only about a mile until we'll join the road near the bottom.'

Lizzie stepped with caution behind Jack, clutching her torch and gradually moving down the hill, side-stepping rocks and picking over gorse.

'Ouch,' she said.

Jack put his hand out to steady her. 'Okay?'

'Yes, I just caught my foot on a rock, that's all. Let's go on.'

The yellow moon was high in the sky, surrounded by a blanket of twinkling stars, and there was no sign of daylight. Lizzie shivered and wrapped her raincoat around her. She wore it with the dark side outwards so she would blend into the night.

A while later, Jack paused. 'This is it.'

Jack went first and then turned and offered Lizzie his hand to help her through the small gap. They emerged close to the bottom of the country road they usually drove along on the way into the city.

All was quiet, except for the eerie screams of foxes in the distance, and an owl hooting in a nearby tree.

They set off at a fast pace, using only one torch to light the ground as they walked. The less attention they drew to themselves, the better, because if they were spotted, there was no reasonable excuse for Michel and Isabelle Dubois to be trailing around the countryside at this hour. Lizzie pushed that frightening thought firmly out of her mind. There was no room for doubt on an operation, only a clear vision of what needed to be accomplished and how.

Before reaching the city, they turned off the road and hurried down a smaller hill and cut through several tracks. Lizzie didn't know where they were exactly and was relieved, she didn't have to do this alone.

'How do you know the way?' Lizzie asked, as she fought to keep up with Jack's long strides.

'Henry and I used to play around here a lot. We'd go off for the day on adventures, with only a sandwich and a flask of water in our knapsacks. My mother always encouraged us to be independent and thought it was a good way to pass our long summer holidays.'

'Sounds like an idyllic childhood,' Lizzie said.

'Yes, it was. I'm not sure how it stacks up against your swimming in the bay of your island, but I can't complain. It was exciting. Sometimes we wouldn't get back until dusk. Mother would pretend she wasn't concerned, but would be calling us and hovering in the courtyard. I could see the relief in her eyes when we showed up, exhausted and ravenous just in time for dinner. Gosh, we slept well in those days.'

'You'll have to tell me more about the time you spent here. It sounds wonderful,' Lizzie said.

'It was. I'm sure Luc would be happy to tell you some stories. You should ask him after dinner one evening.'

Lizzie said she would. 'Not on the day our Gestapo guest comes to dine!'

'No, not on that day,' Jack agreed.

No vehicles passed them on the road between the sleepy village and the entrance to the city, but they knew that would change as soon as the labourers and local tradespeople started their day.

'Remember the plan. Whatever happens, we must be back at the château by dawn, or we'll stand out like sore thumbs. We mustn't be visible in daylight.'

'Understood,' Lizzie said.

Five minutes later, Jack shone his torch ahead and Lizzie saw the train track in the distance. It lay on the outskirts of the city and Lev was waiting for them, just as Jack had predicted. He wore a cap and a leather jacket.

They greeted each other in whispers and Lev told them he had planted the explosives on one section of the track and was about to do the other. Jack said he would do it.

Lev said, 'These are the last of our explosives. If we're to continue attacks and scale up our efforts, we're going to need a steady flow. Did you speak to your people?'

Jack told Lev not to worry. He would arrange supplies. 'They want us to carry out the operation today and then we will get organised.'

'You mean I'm being tested?' Lev said, a slight edge to his voice, his cigarette glowing in the dark as he removed it from his lips.

'I suppose you could say that, but it's a formality.'

The acrid smoke assailed Lizzie's nostrils, and she sneezed uncontrollably.

Lev put his finger to his mouth. 'Shhh.'

'Sorry,' she said. 'It's the smoke. How long until the train is due?'

Jack said, 'About fifteen minutes. I'll plant the other

explosives. You two stay here and keep watch. Have your weapons ready, just in case.'

Lizzy touched her gun that nestled in the lining of her raincoat. It was like having a safety net, and she was surprised by how comfortable she was with carrying a weapon. In the early days, she had been terrified, but wartime had made her a quick study.

'Be careful,' Lizzie whispered to Jack.

She and Lev stood watching and waiting on one side of the track.

'Have you done this before?' Lizzie asked.

'I have. You?'

The temptation to regale him with her past escapades was quelled by the knot in her chest that reminded her never to share more than she absolutely had to. Secrecy was her best friend right now, and the less anyone knew about what she had done in occupied France, the better.

Just the hint of suspicion that she had been involved in acts of sabotage against the Nazi regime was enough to have her thrown in the Saint-Michel fortress-like prison in the centre of Toulouse, where prisoners were interrogated or executed. When Luc told them the name of the prison, the irony wasn't lost on any of them.

The night air was still cool and blended with the tremors of fear that ran through her body, making her shudder. Lizzie saw the light of the torch hovering in the distance near the tracks as Jack meticulously planted the explosives.

Soon, he ran back over to them. 'It's done. Now let's get out of the way and wait.'

They lay flat in the ditch at the side of the railway, waiting for the sound of the train as a signal to ignite the explosives. Each minute crawled by and seemed like an hour until Lizzie wondered whether the train wasn't coming. She knew from past operations that a scheduled train didn't mean it would arrive on time, or even at all. She shifted on the hard ground as she watched the track, mouthing a silent prayer that soon they would hear the approaching train.

'There it is,' Jack said. 'Lights, camera, action! You know what to do.'

The train rumbled along the track, and they saw a hazy shape roll into view with its faint masked headlights.

Lev ignited the explosives and called, 'Get out of the way!'

They scrambled out of the ditch and up onto the bank and disappeared into the thick bushes. Their breathing was a hard and fast chorus as they waited to see if the fruits of their labour would be successful.

The steam train hissed closer like a serpent in the dark, fast approaching the rigged track. Then the familiar crackling sound of the explosives reached Lizzie's ears, followed by several loud booms, and she felt a tremor beneath her feet. The sounds of the track cracking ripped through the night, and alarmed voices rang out.

The train screeched to an emergency stop, and for a few seconds, there was a ghostly silence. Then another loud explosion split the track wide open, and the smell of marzipan permeated the air. No soldiers emerged from the damaged train.

The intelligence they had received told them it would be a train packed with produce and provisions destined for the Reich. The Germans had begun systematically plundering the Free Zone, as well as occupied France. The SOE's order was to frustrate their ability to transport goods.

'Time to go,' Jack said.

They ran through the woods and didn't stop until they reached the edge of the road that led back into the city.

'Good job,' Jack said to Lizzie and Lev. 'We put a spanner in the works. That track won't be back in operation for days, if not weeks.'

He patted Lev on the back. 'Now, get home without anyone seeing you. We'll be in touch in the usual way.'

Lev nodded and disappeared onto the dark road.

'We must go quickly, or it'll be light before we get back,' Jack said. 'Can you run?'

'Of course I can. Let's go.'

The wind blew in Lizzie's face, and she ran as fast as she could by the light of the torch. Jack measured himself to her pace and soon they were panting, but back on the hillside and approaching the edge of the château grounds.

Dawn was breaking as twilight seeped through the ether and light triumphed over darkness for one more day.

The saboteurs let themselves into the château quietly through the kitchen door and tiptoed upstairs to their rooms. Jack closed the door behind them and Lizzie rested her back against the cool wall. Her heart was still hammering, and it took a few minutes for her to settle and catch her breath. The thrill of escaping danger was like nothing she'd experienced before the war.

Just as dawn proclaimed its arrival, shimmering across the Garonne Valley with shards of pale light splintering through the shutters, Lizzie turned to Jack with a triumphant gleam in her eyes, and whispered, 'We did it.'

CHAPTER 27

Jack and Lizzie sat in the shade on a blanket with a picnic of baguette and cheese, freshly picked fruit from the orchard, and a bottle of Luc's finest white wine.

Jack had positioned the blanket in their favourite viewing spot. The pink city spread before them, melded in the sparkling valley. Lizzie thought early summer was the best time of year to be in France. The countryside was in full bloom and the landscape was adorned in vibrant colours. To one side, pink-hued lavender waved at them in the soft wind, and to the other was a lush carpet of vines laden with the promise of the new wine season.

'Luc is very generous to us,' Lizzie said, finishing a delicious chunk of cheese and wiping her hands on a tea towel.

'He is. We couldn't ask for a more considerate host, especially when you think what baggage we brought with us.'

Jack opened the bottle of wine, the familiar Château de Saint-Clair label on the front, and poured the crisp, fruity white wine into two small flutes from their picnic basket. He passed one to Lizzie. 'Santé.'

They talked in French, just in case anyone overheard them. They were always careful to keep their voices low, but one word in a foreign language, especially English, would stand out even if the listener couldn't make out exactly what they said.

'The only downside of our arrangement is I feel doubly responsible for keeping Luc safe and protecting the château.'

Lizzie said, 'I know what you mean. It's making us more cautious than usual.'

'Ahh, drink your wine, it's delicious.'

They sat there for a while, savouring the wine and appreciating the breathtaking view.

'We'll tell our children about this one day,' Jack said.

His words startled Lizzie. Of course, she'd daydreamed about having children together in some mythical future, but they'd never discussed anything tangible beyond getting married after the war. Everything had to be on hold until the war was over and there was never time to think about much else. Winning the war dominated every part of their lives.

'How lovely. We've not talked about having children,' she said, touching his hand.

'I know, but I've thought about it a lot. I can just see a little Isabelle playing in the park, eating ice cream.'

Emotion rushed through Lizzie. 'And I can just see a little dark-eyed Michel running around, causing mischief.'

Jack grazed Lizzie's lips, and she rested her head against his chest, and they lay on the blanket, both imagining their future children in a peaceful world.

'Do you find it difficult to envision the war being over?' Lizzie said.

Jack lit a cigarette and pondered as a hazy hoop of smoke drifted away towards the sky. 'I find it's best to live in the moment in our line of work, but I think it's important we visualise a future beyond this crazy war. It will pull us forward.'

Lizzie agreed. 'You are wise, Raven.'

'I'm not sure about that, but whatever wisdom I've gained was won the hard way. And of course, I'm so very old. You will be as wise as me when you reach the grand old age of thirty-four.'

Lizzie dissolved into laughter when he tickled her side, and she did the same to him, but with no reaction. 'How are you immune to tickling?'

'It's a mind game. One day when I was a kid, I just decided I wouldn't be ticklish.'

'Well, I know you can be stubborn! As simple as that, aye?'

'As simple as that.'

They tidied their picnic remnants away in the basket and sipped another glass of wine. Even in the shade, Lizzie could feel the intense heat on her skin.

'We'd better get down to business,' she said.

You are a hard taskmaster,' Jack sighed, shaking his head.

'I promised to help Suzanne make jam later this afternoon. She works so hard, and I like to give her a hand.'

'You have quite the sweetest nature, darling. It's just one of the many, many things I adore about you.'

Jack never failed to build her up, and if she'd had any doubts about herself before they met, his constant admiration had chased away the shadows.

'Thank you for always believing in me,' Lizzie said, a wave of sentimentality overwhelming her.

Jack's eyes shone as he held her tightly to him and for several moments, neither of them spoke. The feeling between them was more powerful than any words could ever be.

When they pulled away, Jack asked what she thought they should do about the airmen. 'Shall we tell Luc or not?'

They ran through the pros and cons. If Luc knew, he was

better equipped to help them hide the airmen, and he would be prepared in case anything went wrong.

On the other hand, if they didn't tell him, he wouldn't be compromised. If their operation was exposed, and the airmen discovered, Luc could genuinely claim he knew nothing about it and that might go some considerable way with his friend, the commissaire.

Jack picked a blade of grass and trailed it across his chin as he peered into the distance, seeking the answer.

'What does your gut say?' he asked, eventually.

Lizzie stayed quiet for a moment. She had learnt to listen to her gut under Jack's mentoring. At first, she had thought it a strange thing to do, but she had trusted him, and it had never led her wrong.

'My instincts say we should tell him. He deserves to know the risks we're taking in his home.'

'I'm inclined to agree, but what if he refuses to let us do it?'

'Do you think that's likely?'

Jack shook his head. 'No, but it's a possibility. This château and the vineyards have been in the family for generations. He may not be willing to risk everything for two British airmen, especially when he's so friendly with the commissaire. It's a lot to ask.'

'Well, we'd have to get Lev to take them somewhere else. If we weren't staying at the château, we would still be involved in helping them. People find a way when they have no choice.'

'Now, who's showing their wisdom?' Jack said, impressed.

'It's true though, isn't it? Under pressure, I've done things I would never have imagined I could do. Imminent capture by the enemy has an incredible way of focusing the mind and making you come up with alternatives.'

They discussed it a bit more, and concluded they would

tell Luc that evening after dinner, so he could give them his blessing to shelter the airmen, or they would arrange a different safe house.

After dinner, as usual, they went out to the terrace. Lizzie joined them most evenings and drank a tipple of Armagnac, which she'd come to appreciate. She liked to gaze out over the valley and watch the sun set on the horizon, but tonight she was tense, knowing the next moments could mean everything was about to change. If Luc didn't support their mission, they would have to figure out a place to move to where they could hide the airmen. To be effective, they needed a base they could use as a safe house.

They had planned that Jack would tell Luc, and the men stood looking over the wall, smoking. Lizzie heard their muttered exchange but couldn't make out what they were saying.

Then Luc turned to face her and smiled. 'It seems you two are even more resourceful than I realised.'

They didn't say anymore. The staff were likely to arrive at any moment to clear away the dessert dishes, and they were all aware of what was at stake. The fewer people in their tightly knit circle, the safer they would all be.

As if on cue, Suzanne appeared to ask if they would like anything else, and Lizzie thanked her for the delicious apple pie. When she left, silence fell over the terrace as if they all knew this was a turning point and there was no going back.

Jack winked at Lizzie to confirm all was well. Lizzie exhaled slowly, the tension gradually leaving her body.

Luc poured them another round, and they went inside to sit at the table. He pulled out an atlas and pointed to the Pyrenees region.

'Where do you plan to smuggle them out?' he asked.

Jack replied, 'The contact who gets them into Spain is based in St. Girons.'

'I know the area quite well from my younger days. It's at the foot of the mountains.' Luc pointed to the map and ran his finger along the page. 'It's about 100 km from here to there.'

Jack said, 'God willing they make it safely here. Let's hope they are in a fit state to resume their journey soon.'

They looked at the map and Jack asked Luc some questions about St. Girons. Then they talked about possible places to hide the airmen.

After some deliberation, Luc said, 'The safest place is undoubtedly the cellars in the vineyards. That way they're some distance from the château. Occasionally we have visitors, but we must orchestrate it, so no one goes down there whilst they're here.'

When they returned to their rooms, Lizzie and Jack readied themselves for bed, exhaustion creeping over them. They lay on the large mattress, curled into each other's arms, and fell into a sound sleep.

CHAPTER 28

A hand-delivered letter arrived for Lizzie on the breakfast tray. Jack and Lizzie had agreed it was less suspicious if a woman sent notes to her as if they were friends arranging to meet, in case a letter was intercepted. One never knew in wartime who might be monitoring the mail, even if a boy from the village delivered it.

After the housekeeper left the dining room, Lizzie slit it open with Luc's correspondence knife, and after she scanned the brief note, she raised her eyes to Jack.

'Our friend is in the woods,' she said carefully, referring to Lev but not saying his name in front of Luc.

'It's time, then,' said Luc, lowering his newspaper. 'How do you want to handle it?'

Jack drained his coffee and turned to face his uncle. 'Well, we can't risk smuggling them in during the day. We'll have to wait until tonight under cover of darkness.'

Luc agreed, 'There are too many workers from the village roaming around the vineyards at this time of year.'

'What else does the note say?' Jack asked Lizzie.

She passed it to him. 'Some kind of coded message which I presume is to tell us where they are hiding exactly.'

Jack read Marguerite's note aloud. 'I'll meet you in the house in the woods.'

A puzzled expression clouded Jack's face as he read the words again so Luc could hear. 'Mean anything to you?' he asked. 'How can we know which house?'

Luc nodded. 'Yes, of course. There are no houses in the woods except for a derelict shack. Only locals would know that, so whoever sent you the note is counting on you asking someone who knows the terrain.'

'Makes sense,' Lizzie said. 'Our contact knows we're your relatives, so it's not a terribly big stretch for us to ask you a question like that.'

'You'd better organise some food to keep them going until we can bring them in tonight. Ask Suzanne for a picnic basket for four. Tell her you're meeting some friends.'

They thanked Luc and excused themselves from the table, going straight upstairs to the privacy of their rooms to discuss their next move.

'What else do we need to take for them, apart from food and drink?' Lizzie asked.

'There's no point taking them a change of clothes without knowing their size, and they won't be cold in this weather. They'll be wanting to sleep, I imagine, after walking through the night.'

Suzanne prepared them a basket which had become something of a habit lately, so it wasn't suspicious at all. When Jack returned from working in the vineyards, they often explored areas of the vast estate and took a picnic for lunch.

Most mornings before the blistering heat of the day bore down on them, Lizzie rose early and accompanied Jack or stayed at the house and helped Suzanne. She was delighted to discover they grew abundant crops of fruits in the fields surrounding the vineyards. There were cherries, peaches, plums, apricots, melons, raspberries and strawberries which needed picking. There was plenty to do at the château and although it wasn't intelligence work, it passed the time in between operations and gave weight to her cover story of being a new wife who had come along to keep her husband company.

The fruit on the trees in the fragrant orchard wouldn't be ripe until later in the summer, but Suzanne showed her how to make jams from the buckets of fruits they picked in the fields. Lizzie also spent time in the large kitchen, making pies just like she had loved to do with her grandmother in Jersey. Rolling the pastry made her nostalgic for her childhood, when she would stand on a box next to her nan and help her fill pies and crumbles with summer fruits mixture.

A shadow crossed her mind when she thought of her grandparents in Jersey. She wondered if her parents had received another message from them yet. Lizzie felt helpless when she thought of them, and she pushed the thoughts away. She would focus on what she could do right now. Anything else only made her sad and afraid.

Jack and Lizzie crossed the courtyard and cut through the field that was the quickest way to the woods. They decided to give the airmen some time to rest, and it wasn't until almost 4 p.m. they glimpsed the outline of a small shack through the trees. They followed the directions of Luc's hand-drawn map, and after crossing a small brook by stepping across large uneven stones, they approached the shack.

Before they could reach the door, Lev appeared from around the back, brandishing a rifle.

Jack whistled to him. 'We come in peace, friend.'

Lev lowered the rifle and something akin to a smile crossed his mouth. He was a serious man, and Lizzie noticed he rarely smiled or showed emotion. She wondered if he was so reserved because of the horrors he had witnessed in recent years, or if that was his nature.

They stood in a sun dappled spot beneath a patchy canopy of trees. Lev confirmed there were two airmen, and they were sleeping.

'One of them is injured. I went home to get some medical stuff and patched him up as best I could, but he needs a doctor.'

'What type of injury?' Jack asked.

'Gunshot wound. A farmer shot him after he disturbed them sleeping in his barn. They escaped, but he was hit. He's been bleeding and is hot and delirious, so my guess is he has an infection.'

'He will need proper treatment,' Jack said. 'We can't take him to the hospital, or the authorities will be onto us in no time.'

'They only had one safe house on the way, so they had to hide in fields or take a chance in someone's barn for most of the journey.'

'Let's see what we can do about that for the next round. There must be more sympathetic farmers we can prevail upon, even if we must make it worth their while.'

Lev said, 'I'll speak to the others and see who we can contact.'

Lev and Lizzie stayed under the shelter of the trees, and she offered him a sandwich, which he accepted gratefully and devoured.

'We brought food for the airmen,' she said, passing the picnic basket to Lev.

'Thank you. I don't think the injured one will be able to eat, but the other is hungry. What's the plan for taking them to the château?'

They spoke in whispers, constantly aware that even the

trees might have ears. The summer winds snatched their words so they could barely hear each other. Lizzie told Lev what they had planned. He was to escort the airmen to a meeting point near the château at an agreed time that night, and they would be there to meet them and smuggle them into the cellars.

'He's too badly hurt to walk alone, but I think we can manage his weight and pull him along between us.'

Jack reappeared and said to Lizzie, 'They are both British. One's from London and the other from Scotland. Lev's right though, the Scot is in a bad way. I'll have to speak to Luc about finding a doctor we can trust.'

They left as suddenly as they had come and slipped back into the grounds of the château with the picnic basket that Lev had emptied and returned to them.

They found Luc reading in the library.

After pondering briefly, glasses in hand, he said, 'I have a good doctor in the village. I'll get a message to him this afternoon and see if he will help us.'

'Do you trust him?' Jack asked.

Luc nodded. 'I do. My only hesitation is that he may be under surveillance, or perhaps not even be living at home anymore.'

'Why would that be?' Lizzie asked, screwing up her forehead.

'He's a Jew,' Luc said. 'Like you heard when you were questioned by the policeman soon after you arrived, the Jews never quite know who is going to be under suspicion next. He's been our family doctor for years, but he likely has had his licence revoked under the latest statutes.'

'How awful,' Lizzie said. 'You'd think they'd want all the experienced doctors they could get in wartime.'

'You would, but unfortunately prejudice has no logic, and the authorities here are hellbent on doing the Nazis' bidding, which, as you pointed out, involves destroying Jewish livelihoods and driving them away until France is 'cleansed'.

The ominous statement rang in the air like a death toll, and Lizzie immediately thought of Hannah and Lev. How long would these brave souls keep risking their lives to get others out, instead of escaping themselves and getting to safety?

Lizzie was subdued as she sat in the shade of the orchard, trying to read a French novel after Jack had gone to inspect the cellars. They had agreed it was best not to attract attention by both going, so she had stayed behind, but her mind wouldn't focus on the story, and she kept reading the same words over again, until she gave up and put the book down. She lay back on the blanket and closed her eyes, trying to rest, but her mind whirled with frantic thoughts.

What if the airmen were intercepted before they reached the château tonight? What if they were caught as they went to meet them? Lizzie knew there were informants all around, and just because they hadn't met anyone on the way to the shack didn't mean no one had watched Lev and the airmen make their way to the woods.

Lev had explained how he'd got them there. They were dressed in civilian clothes, so they blended in well enough, disguised as casual labourers. They had skirted around the city and the village and come the back way to the woods. The chances were they hadn't been spotted, and they had seen no one.

The Free Zone was an eclectic mix of families, wounded veterans, Frenchmen trying to rebuild their lives after returning from the war, fleeing Jews, communists, and other races and minorities who weren't welcome in Nazi-occupied Europe. Lev told her a lot were making plans to leave France before it was too late. Their contact had helped many escapees cross the Pyrenees during the past few months.

Lizzie enquired whether Lev had met the mysterious man in St. Girons. He said he hadn't, but Marguerite had made arrangements for some of his friends to leave via that route.

'What about your parents and siblings, Lev?' Lizzie asked. 'Don't they wish to leave?'

Lev sighed. 'I'm working on it. My parents are as stubborn as mules and won't leave without me. I have told them I cannot leave now. There is too much to do here. My siblings are considering it, but can't bring themselves to abandon our parents, so it's a knock-on effect. I have papers ready for them as soon as they give me the nod.'

Lizzie's chest tightened as he told her about his family. Would it really be a matter of life or death if they didn't leave, or would the Allies invade in time to stop this madness before it went any further?

She lay on the blanket, still trying to drift off to sleep because they would have a late night, but her mind was too full.

They received reports at the SOE and repeatedly discussed a possible invasion, but it was never the right time and was always pushed into the future. It was approaching two years since Germany invaded Poland and Britain declared war. What had seemed initially like something that would be over in no time, had dragged on much longer than anyone had predicted.

Lizzie sat bolt upright when she heard the crack of a twig.

Jack appeared beneath an apple tree and waved to her before crossing the orchard and sitting next to her in the shade.

'How did it go?' she asked.

'Good. Luc was in there waiting for me and showed me a hidden cellar at the back where they can hide. He said when the Germans first invaded, many of the vintners built false walls to hide their best wines from Nazi plundering. We've arranged a place for them to sleep and will take some stuff in for them.'

Dinner time came quickly, but Lizzie could barely swallow the food. Such was the tension at the table. Luc kept glancing at the clock, and when they retired outside as usual to the terrace, Jack chain-smoked until Lizzie had to move away so she could catch her breath.

She prayed that by tonight, the airmen would be safely hidden in the secret cellar.

But a voice kept taunting her. *What if it all goes wrong?*

They could find themselves spending the night in a Vichy jail, not in their comfortable bedroom overlooking the Garonne valley.

CHAPTER 29

The rest of the evening crawled by until it was time to retire for the night. Luc wished them luck and went to his rooms as usual around 10 p.m. Lizzie and Jack followed closely on his heels and bid goodnight to Suzanne as she went around the ground floor performing her nightly bedtime ritual, closing shutters and checking doors were locked. The château fell quiet, and everyone was in their quarters ready for a peaceful night's sleep, but Jack and Lizzie paced about like wildcats, watching and waiting for a sign.

'The waiting is the killer,' Lizzie said when Jack handed her a snifter of Armagnac to calm her nerves. She took a sip. 'It's so strong, but with a hint of a chocolate taste. Could that be right or am I imagining it?'

'You have a good palate. It has a note of chocolate.'

They chatted about wine and brandy to pass the time, Jack explaining to Lizzie what he'd learned about training and pruning the vines under Luc's tutelage.

'How Henry and I worked in the vineyards is coming back to me now.'

'Could you see yourself living here one day?'

Jack paused, the balloon glass midpoint from the table to his lips. 'Live here. What makes you ask that?'

'You seem so at home'

'Do I? I didn't realise,' Jack said, pondering Lizzie's observation. 'I suppose I've always felt at home in France, with French parents and so many visits here in my childhood.'

'How about you? Would you like to live in France when the world rids itself of lunatics and we're back on an even keel?'

Jack never spoke of losing the war. It was as if the possibility didn't enter his mind, or if it did, he wouldn't express it. She followed his example, and they only ever made plans for what they would do after winning the war and Europe was liberated from Hitler's yoke of tyranny.

'I'm not sure. I certainly wouldn't be against it, although I imagine I'll be torn between Jersey and London. I've grown to love London in a way I never thought I would.'

'And Jersey, do you miss it terribly?' Jack asked softly.

'I do. Although, I think a big part of that is the nostalgia of my childhood innocence and how it symbolises life before the war.'

'Makes sense. At least we will have options.'

They sat on the sofa in the large bedroom. Lizzie's feet curled beneath her, her head resting on Jack's shoulder and their hands entwined. The clock ticked ominously, and the hour approached eleven.

Jack stood and stretched. 'We had better get organised. We're to meet Lev in half an hour.'

They dressed in dark clothes and crept out of the big old house silently via the warm kitchen, as smooth as cat burglars stealing away in the night. They wound through the estate and towards the back of the château, part of which was bordered by the woods, where they had agreed to meet Lev.

Lizzie's heart hammered fiercely as she raced to keep pace with Jack up and down the slopes, but it was more from fear than exertion. She had always been fit as a girl, riding her bicycle up the steep country lanes in Jersey, and swimming in Portelet Bay, but her fitness had reached a new peak since training with the SOE and undertaking so many missions.

The lead trainer had told the group, 'Sometimes staying alive is as simple as being able to outrun your enemy. You have to be fit.'

She remembered how he had made them run barefoot cross country, and his face appeared in her mind as they approached the edge of the shadowy moonlit woods. An owl hooted loudly, and Lizzie jumped. Panic spiralled through her and her skin felt like it was coated in sharp needles.

Calm down, she told herself, but her pulse raced as random memories flitted through her mind.

Jack stopped abruptly, signalling for her to follow him as he turned. They entered the woods; their path lit only by the small beam of his torch.

Lizzie's senses heightened with every step. They had discussed the possibility this was a trap. The authorities could be lying in wait for them. It would take only one informant to have noticed something out of the ordinary and to have alerted the police.

They continued walking slowly until they came upon a large tree and Jack stopped. 'We're to wait here,' he whispered.

The rustling sounds of the woods were amplified by the stark quiet and dark of the night. Lizzie's eyes slowly adjusted to her surroundings, and she saw wildlife darting through the trees by moonlight.

'How long do we wait?' she asked.

Her question went unanswered because they both heard

footfall on the ground in the distance and reached for their guns. They stood like statues as the sounds approached and they heard the murmur of voices.

This was the moment. They would either see two British airmen with Lev, or they were about to be captured in an elaborate trap. They had made a basic plan to fight back if the latter scenario unfolded, and they had their weapons, but if the authorities caught them, they would be outnumbered. Escaping would be a long shot.

Jack reached for Lizzie's hand and squeezed it. The seconds passed in an agony of sluggishness until Lizzie thought she might explode with the tension.

Then a wiry figure stepped out and joined them in the hazy torchlight beneath the tree.

Lizzie saw it was Lev and sent up a fierce prayer of gratitude.

'Did you bring them?' Jack asked.

'Yes, of course. I wanted to double check you hadn't been compromised.'

'As far as we're aware, all is secure. We need to get them into the château grounds and out of the way quickly,' Jack said.

'Come help us. The wounded one is in a worse state than earlier.'

Jack and Lizzie followed Lev a little way deeper into the woods and found the two airmen waiting. One was leaning against a tree, groaning.

Jack passed him his flask of brandy he had brought specifically for this purpose. It revived the wounded man slightly, and Jack told him he mustn't make a sound when they entered the château grounds, or it would endanger their lives. 'Can I count on you?' Jack asked, his military style taking over and immediately gaining the airman's respect.

He croaked, 'Yes, sir.'

Jack nodded and gave the command. 'Let's go.'

Jack, Lev and the other airman took it in turns to shoulder more of the wounded airman's weight.

Jack turned to him. 'Not a sound, remember.'

They left the safety of the trees and emerged onto the bordering fields of the château. Soon they crossed into the grounds, and Lizzie held her breath. They must be so quiet, none of the staff or Beau would hear them. If they thought they were being burgled, the operation could go horribly wrong in an instant.

Lizzie led the way with her torch shining close to the ground. She raised her eyes to the quarters where the staff slept and was relieved to see no lights shone through the gaps in the shutters.

Foxes whined in the distance, but the more background noise there was, the better to cover the human infiltrators.

Lizzie beckoned to the men, inching along slowly behind her, that all was clear. Eventually, after what seemed like an age, they reached the vineyard cellar entrance. Jack had left it unlocked for easy access. Lizzie pulled the door and the men, panting from the weight of the airman leaning heavily against them down the stone steps, stumbled into the dark cellars.

They eased him down onto the ground and took a few moments to regain their strength. Jack passed the flask around and they all had a sip of brandy.

'Seagrove, light the lantern, please,' Jack said, shining his torch onto a chest by the cavern wall.

Lizzie held the lantern, and the men picked the heavy weight up again. The airman let out a squeal like a wounded animal as they lifted him back onto his feet.

Jack said, 'Shh,' as they moved further into the bowels of the cellars.

'When we are deeper inside, you can make some noise,' he whispered. A few minutes later, he said, 'This is it.'

He ran his hand along a wall and pushed hard in a particular spot. There was a small cracking sound, and the wall creaked and moved.

Lizzie's mouth gaped. She would never have guessed there was an entrance within the thick wall. Jack opened it further, and the men lurched through into a musty smelling room.

'It's not the Ritz, but I'm afraid it's the only place we can keep you safe. There are blankets, pillows, medical supplies, food and drink, so you'll be alright. Try to get some sleep.'

Jack placed the lantern on a crate in the corner, and Lizzie saw the alarm in the eyes of the English airman. 'What about Billy?' he whispered to Jack, loud enough for Lizzie to hear.

'We'll make him as comfortable as we can for tonight. We're working on getting him a doctor.' Jack patted his shoulder.

After they positioned Billy on a mattress on the stone floor, Jack said they would return the following day.

'This is the safest place you can be until we can make arrangements to get you back to Blighty.'

Another grunt of agony resounded in the cavernous space and Lizzie wished they could take the poor man into the château and let him rest on a comfortable bed and have a doctor tend to him properly.

The panic in the airmen's eyes clawed at Lizzie as they locked the door back into place. She prayed Billy would make it through the night and they would soon be on the next leg of their journey to the Pyrenees and into neutral Spain. Once there, the SOE would transport them safely back to England somehow.

Their orders were to set up a reliable system with a fully operational Resistance network, to get as many airmen out as possible. 'There will be many more,' Val had said ominously. 'If we leave them in Vichy France, we may as well issue them a death warrant. They will almost certainly be found and murdered, even if the locals are brave enough to hide them.'

Val told Lizzie the story of an airman who had been captured in a village near the city of Vichy a few weeks earlier. They tortured him and then shot him in the town square and put his head on a spike like in medieval times. They also rounded up the couple who took him in and shot them, too. The message was clear. 'If you help Allied airmen, this is how you will end up.'

Lizzie had been distraught. 'That happened in Vichy France! I thought they were supposed to be neutral.'

Val had quickly dispelled any illusions Lizzie had clung to about the Vichy regime not being as tyrannical as the Nazis.

Outside the cellars, Lev nodded to Lizzie and Jack, then edged silently away.

Lizzie and Jack entered the château through the kitchen door they had left on the latch on their way out.

All was as silent as when they had left, and Lizzie's heartbeat gradually slowed. Despite the acute suffering of the airman, she felt the familiar elation of a successful mission. They had done all they could for tonight.

Exhaustion crept over her, and she looked forward to climbing into bed and snatching a few hours' sleep before the staff woke at daybreak.

Lizzie entered the kitchen first, and Jack locked the door behind him. A blurry shadow by the kitchen table moved, and she jumped. As her eyes adjusted, she made out a hooded, cloaked figure sitting on the bench beside the scarred wooden table where she often drank coffee in between jam and pie making.

Their face wasn't visible, but the barrel of a gun was pointed at them and a gruff voice said, 'You two had better tell me where you've been and what's going on.'

CHAPTER 30

Armand Abadie awoke as the birds chattered noisily outside his window, hopping along the bedroom balcony railing overlooking an apartment building. The stale taste of tobacco and whisky lingered in his throat, and he immediately lit a *Gitanes* as he studied the white plaster ceiling.

Recently, he switched from smoking Gauloises in his efforts to cultivate his image as a man of intellect and style. Briefly he had considered stopping smoking, but a life without one of his greatest pleasures seemed like no life at all.

He thought of the château and what it would be like to wake up and feast his eyes on the view of his city from the hill. One day, God willing, in the not-too-distant future, he would live in such a home. His mind skirted back to the events of the previous evening. The commissaire had sent a note to his office requesting his driving services again. A Gestapo officer would arrive from Paris that evening, and he had assigned Armand to be his personal driver for the duration of his stay.

Despite not enjoying being relegated to the position of chauffeur, he was honoured to have been selected for the role. Armand knew there were many at the Legion who would jump at the chance to ingratiate themselves with the commissaire, not to mention become acquainted with a high-ranking Nazi official. There were constant machinations between Legion members, who tried to figure out ways to get noticed and rise through the ranks of the organisation faster. They worked closely with the police, and all knew the Legion was destined to play a big part in the future of the new France.

Armand brewed some coffee on the stove and laid out a clean shirt to wear under his uniform. He must look his finest today. First impressions were critical, and if he wanted to make a mark on the Gestapo officer, this would be his big opportunity. The commissaire told Armand he would notify him as soon as the date and time for dinner at the château was confirmed, for he would need to be available to drive their guest. Armand wondered whether he would drive them both. Being a fly on the wall for the conversation between the commissaire and his esteemed guest might indeed prove to be fascinating.

It was Saturday, and he decided he wouldn't go into the office this morning. He sat at the table, wearing only his white vest and briefs, and spent a few leisurely hours reviewing his little blue notebook. The lined pages contained scrawled notes of his latest findings on suspected enemies of the state. The list of names was growing fast, and he ran one tobacco-stained finger beneath the recent entry of the couple staying at the château.

Armand hadn't seen the attractive man since the dinner, and decided it was time to escalate his surveillance, if only for the guilty pleasure of watching him. He wouldn't assign the task to one of his team, but would monitor the couple himself. Armand hoped he would see the lithe young man again when he drove the Gestapo officer to dinner.

After smoking several more cigarettes until the room was a thick haze of smog, and draining his pot of coffee, he washed and dressed and walked slowly, his leg dragging slightly as he manoeuvred the fourth-floor stairs. He had applied for ground floor accommodation on account of his disability, but had received no notice from the Legion of an impending award of new housing. It was a disgrace, the way the government treated an illustrious ex-serviceman like himself. All of that would change in the new France.

If they were to live up to the Vichy administration's motto for France: *Travail, Famille, Patrie*—Work, Family, Fatherland, they would need to do better. Armand believed he had been born with a purpose to restore his country to its former glory, and he was now fulfilling his ultimate duty.

His mind bounced over thoughts of his usual grudges and grievances in the familiar, resentful grooves he revisited every day.

'Good morning,' he said to a shabbily dressed man as he passed him on the second flight of stairs.

The man muttered a reply and hurried on without making eye contact.

Ever alert for the enemy, he wondered who he was. Armand had seen him once before, and he looked suspicious. The man must be a new resident, and Armand made a note to check the records of who had moved into the building. He had a swarthy Jewish look about him, and worse still, something of the air of a communist. Being Jewish was dreadful enough, but a Jewish communist was scraping the bottom of the cesspit.

The bile rose in Armand's throat as he considered the scourge that had overtaken his beloved country. The man was already half a flight of stairs ahead of Armand, when it occurred to him, he didn't know his name.

'Monsieur,' he called in a polite tone.

The man paused and swivelled to look up at Armand. 'Yes,' he replied, alarm springing into his brown eyes.

'I don't believe we have met. What is your name? It was rude of me to greet you without welcoming you properly to our building. You are new here, isn't that so?'

Armand thought the man looked shifty, and he studied his face as he stared back at him.

The man coughed and then replied, 'I'm an ex-serviceman like yourself. My name is Azimov. You need not concern yourself, monsieur. I'm only staying in the building temporarily at my sister's apartment until I find permanent accommodation.'

'Are you Russian, by any chance?'

The man now looked terrified as Armand limped down the stairs and grilled him up close.

'No, I was born in France, monsieur,' he said, in perfect French, his voice slightly hoarse.

Armand nodded. 'That is good to hear. One can't be too careful these days, I'm sure you'll agree.' The ominous threat hovered in the stairwell and the man stood there like trapped prey.

Armand switched tack suddenly and smiled as if he were most happy to have made the man's acquaintance. He then dismissed him and continued with his slow, limping gait down the stairs and out into the narrow-cobbled street bathed in late morning sunshine. His stomach rumbled, and he made a beeline for his regular café. He would be an early diner for lunch and get the pick of the spoils.

Armand signalled to the waiter who knew him from his daily patronage, and he rushed to find a table for him outside, ideally positioned to watch the comings and goings of the Saturday lunch crowd.

A group of women and children bustling about beneath the arcades to one side of the square caught Armand's eye after he settled down with a contented sigh, apéritif in hand, under the shade of the awning. They looked like trouble if ever he saw it, and he resolved to watch them closely.

The waiter informed Armand the special was *Moules Marinière,* and he ordered his favourite dish, a rare treat in wartime, without hesitation. Armand ate the delicious meal, mopping up the garlic and wine sauce with the crusty baguette and licking his lips as he cleaned the bowl and forgot about the troublesome women.

He pushed the plates away and relaxed back into his seat, drawing on a newly lit cigarette. Despite his many grievances, life was proving good for him as a Legion employee. He was feeling quite pleased with his lot, when suddenly he noticed the women converging on *Le Capitole,* the city hall. They formed rows and were marching near the building.

Armand's mouth fell open as he witnessed their audacity. Demonstrations were strictly forbidden without prior authorisation, which, of course, wouldn't be granted. The women and some of the older children held handmade signs protesting against food shortages.

Armand squinted to read the script: We need more food to feed our starving children.

They marched up and down in front of the city hall and no one came out to stop them. For once, Armand found himself at a loss for what action to take. Whoever heard of housewives having the gall to protest the government in this manner? They got rations just like everyone else.

He rallied his thoughts and decided he would investigate in person. This was a new phenomenon as far as he was aware, so it would impress his superiors at the Legion if he were first to report it.

Armand paid his bill and took a receipt to claim back his expenses. He would fudge the date, so his meal would be covered even on the weekend. His salary was pitiful and if it weren't for additional benefits, he wouldn't have a spare Franc in his pocket.

Armand straightened his cap and set out with his crooked gait towards the small crowd of protestors. It took him longer than he would have liked to reach them, and he noticed a few of them dispersed as they saw him approach.

One housewife was brazen enough to step forward to meet him and introduce herself as if she were proud of her performance.

He listened, again shocked at the nerve of this woman. Who did she think she was, questioning the authorities in wartime?

Armand introduced himself with all the command he could muster, but to his further irritation, the woman looked unimpressed.

'We are here to speak to whoever is in charge in there,' she said, pointing her chin to city hall. 'We won't be ignored, whilst our children starve to death and Pétain's officials dine like kings.'

Pangs of indigestion rose in Armand's chest, after he was disturbed so rudely, and had to rush across the square. He gathered himself up to his full height, which wasn't significant. 'Madame, I fear you are sadly mistaken in your endeavours, and I urge you to call your gang to attention. I'm afraid this will not end well for you.'

'Is that a threat?' the woman said, a hard edge to her voice, her head the same height as his, and a small snivelling boy at her side.

Armand was taken off guard. He hadn't expected push

back from a mere housewife. He quickly calculated his best move. It didn't seem wise to get heavy with women and children, and there might be unforeseen consequences.

The others continued marching, and the woman snorted in his face. 'I suggest you move out of my way, monsieur, and let me go about my business.'

Rage at her insolent attitude and lack of deference flickered in his gut and he had to hold his hands at his sides to stop himself from grabbing her and showing her who was in charge. He'd like to arrest her, and throw her in jail for treason, but a cautious voice in his head told him this was beyond his remit, and he must step away.

He took a deep breath and reined in his wrath as he glowered at the woman who still showed no signs of fear or remorse. This was an official matter to be handled with delicacy and wasn't worth him risking his good standing, in case the commissaire disproved of him taking it into his own hands.

'Madame, take it as you wish. I shall report you and your gang to the authorities and am advising you to temper your actions. Consider yourself warned.' Armand turned on his heel without waiting for any further response and limped out of the square, his fine lunch experience ruined by the resentment churning in his gut.

The realisation that he still had no power hit him like a cold shower. His resolve deepened and as he exited the square and turned into the cobbled street, he swore he would secure a spot at the table with the top brass in Hitler's Third Reich.

He would do it if it was the last thing he did. Driving the Gestapo officer to the château would be an ideal time to intensify his campaign with renewed enthusiasm.

CHAPTER 31

Lizzie was rooted to the spot in the kitchen. Neither she nor Jack had time to reach for their guns and had been taken wholly unawares. They had made it safely back into the château, and the last thing she'd expected was to have a gun pointed at her on entry into the kitchen.

Jack stepped forward to stand with Lizzie in front of their cloaked and hooded assailant, who had moved from the bench by the table and now stood, still brandishing a gun.

'There must be some mistake. We couldn't sleep and went for a walk around the grounds,' Jack said, holding his hands up.

'Don't move. Stay back,' the low voice barked.

Lizzie suspected one of the male staff. How else could he be inside the château, waiting for them like this?

Lizzie's pulse raced as she stared at the shrouded figure, illuminated only by a candelabra that flickered on a counter in the large kitchen.

'Who are you and what do you want?' Lizzie asked, sounding much calmer than she felt.

'I'll ask the questions,' the voice commanded. 'What were you really doing out there?'

Lizzie cleared her dry throat. Talking with a gun pointed at her head didn't come easily. 'Like Monsieur Dubois said, we couldn't sleep. We were worrying about our family in Brittany and took a stroll to the vineyards.'

'Why are you dressed like that?' the voice questioned.

'Like what?' Jack asked.

'All in dark clothing, as if you have something to hide. Are you spying on us?'

Lizzie calculated whether to draw her gun from her pocket. Not seeing the assailant's face made it difficult to gauge how dangerous he was and how likely to react by shooting.

Jack's voice was steady. 'I don't know about you, but it's been a long night, and I'm tired. I'd like to get to bed. I don't think Monsieur Luc will be impressed by this little hold up of yours.'

The figure remained quiet and seemed to consider Jack's statement.

Jack stretched out his hand. 'Give me the gun. I promise we won't report you and we can all forget this ever happened. We understand these are frightening times and you've let your imagination run away with you.'

Lizzie struggled to breathe. Anything could happen if this man was a loose cannon. If there was one thing she'd learnt in the past year, it was how unpredictable people were.

The three of them stood there and all Lizzie could hear was the methodical tick tock of the kitchen clock on the wall. It was hard to believe they were being held at gunpoint in what she thought of as their safe haven.

No one moved. Lizzie knew whoever backed down first would be the loser. It was imperative they didn't show their fear, and she decided it was too risky to reach for her gun.

Jack had presumably come to the same conclusion and stood at her side.

A sound startled them, and the interior door, which had been closed, creaked slowly open. The man couldn't move without turning his back on them, but Jack and Lizzie's eyes swivelled to the door.

A wave of relief surged through Lizzie when she saw Luc's familiar form, his silk nightgown visible in the candle-light, and his pistol pointed at the assailant.

'Who have we here?' he said, piercing the charged silence as he stepped into the kitchen with Beau at his side.

The figure removed their hood to reveal a pale face.

'Suzanne!' Luc said. 'Why on earth are you holding our guests at gunpoint?' He reached for her gun, and she let him have it with a sigh.

'Suzanne!' Lizzie echoed, astonished to see the friendly housekeeper who was her jam making partner.

'Let's sit down and calm ourselves. Whilst I appreciate your nighttime vigilance, I can't have my relatives accosted by an armed guard, as I'm sure you appreciate. Please explain yourself, Suzanne.'

They all stared at the housekeeper as Beau licked her hand.

'I'm sorry, but our guests are not who they seem. I have heard them sneaking in and out of the house during the past few weeks and until tonight, I told myself it wasn't any of my business. But tonight, I saw from the window, they brought suspicious strangers onto our grounds, and I couldn't ignore their nighttime prowls any longer. We have enemies of the state in our midst, and I wished only to protect you, monsieur.'

Luc smiled at Suzanne, and his voice was filled with tenderness. 'Dear Suzanne, now you have explained the situation to me, I understand why you did what you did. You have lived here for over ten years, and I know how loyal you are, but let me assure you, we have nothing to fear from these two.'

Confusion swept over Suzanne's face. 'You knew about tonight's goings on?'

Luc didn't confirm or deny, but said he must ask her to keep her suspicions to herself and not talk to anyone about what she had seen.

Suzanne looked sheepishly at Lizzie and then at Jack. 'I feel foolish now and must apologise. I did what I did only to protect Monsieur Luc.'

Jack stepped forward and patted Suzanne's arm. 'Think no more of it. You have proven yourself to be loyal and true in the face of what you thought was treachery. I applaud you for it.'

Lizzie met Suzanne's eyes. 'I didn't guess it was you. How did you throw your voice like that?'

'I acted in many plays at the theatre before I worked as a housekeeper. My roles were often of men, and I perfected a male voice. It came in handy tonight.'

Lizzie studied Suzanne, still surprised by the revelation. 'It certainly did. I thought you must be one of the vineyard workers.'

Suzanne removed her long black cloak and hung it on a hook on the door. 'One of my props, from when I played a highwayman in my last performance. I made it myself and kept it as a souvenir to remind me of those days.'

Lizzie was grateful the situation had been diffused. They would need to talk to Luc about Suzanne and make sure he trusted her to keep their secret, but it seemed her loyalty was to her master, and that was what motivated her bizarre behaviour.

Suzanne made hot chocolate to restore their spirits. 'It's the least I can do after making such a terrific blunder. Once again, I must apologise. I didn't know Monsieur Luc was aware of your activities. You can count on me not to say a word to anyone.'

They drank the soothing chocolate and then Suzanne retired to her quarters after apologising repeatedly.

Luc spoke to Lizzie and Jack, merriment twinkling in his eyes. 'What an uproar. I know Suzanne is protective of me, but I didn't expect for one minute to find you held at gunpoint by Claude Duval in the kitchen!'

'Claude Duval?' Lizzie said.

'He's a famous French highwayman,' Jack told her. 'A bit like England's Dick Turpin.'

'Ah,' Lizzie sighed. 'Another hole in my French cultural knowledge. 'Sometimes, I think it's a miracle I've made it this far.'

The tension of the previous days, and the relief they had not been exposed, caught up with them, and they all started laughing, until tears streamed down their faces.

'That must be the most ridiculous situation I've ever found myself in,' Lizzie said, gasping for breath as she wiped her eyes.

Exhaustion was fast on the heels of their mirth. They drained their cups of the dregs of the precious chocolate and tiptoed back to their bedroom through the maze of corridors just as dawn broke over the Garonne Valley.

They had survived another day in enemy territory.

CHAPTER 32

At breakfast, they were all weary from lack of sleep. Suzanne appeared, and none of them mentioned the strange events of the night before. It was a stormy morning, and they took breakfast inside rather than on the terrace.

'Isn't this weather unusual for summer?' Lizzie asked, stifling a yawn.

'The winds are blowing in off the Pyrenees,' Luc replied. 'It'll probably calm down this afternoon.'

The mention of the Pyrenees reminded Lizzie of the airmen and when they could leave for St. Girons. The sooner the better, she reasoned as she bit into her toast covered in a delicious smearing of home-made strawberry jam. Every day the airmen stayed on the grounds would endanger all the residents of the château further.

Luc slit his correspondence open after finishing his meal and groaned as he read.

Suzanne had already left the room and none of the other staff were present.

'Is something wrong?' Lizzie asked.

'I'm afraid so.' Luc removed his reading glasses, and swung them in his hand as he looked at Lizzie. He lay the glasses down on the table and pinched his nose, his brow furrowed.

'You are tired, Luc,' Lizzie said. 'Perhaps you should rest this morning, and we can take over any duties you had planned.'

'That is thoughtful of you,' Luc said, 'and I may indeed do as you suggest. It seems we are going to have an unpleasant evening.'

Jack glanced up from his newspaper. He kept an eye on the classified section in case one of his agents was trying to get a message to him. 'Why, what's happening this evening?'

'The commissaire just informed me we must host the dinner for the visiting Gestapo officer he threatened us with when he was here.'

'And if you refuse?' Jack queried.

Luc shook his head. 'I don't think it's wise to refuse the head of the local police and his Gestapo sidekick, do you?'

Jack sighed and rested the newspaper to one side. 'You make a good point.'

'What time are they coming?' Lizzie asked.

'Eight sharp. He says it doesn't do to keep the Germans waiting.'

'Goodness, it seems rather rude, bossing you around like that,' Lizzie said.

'You're right, my dear, it does. My childhood friend is taking advantage of our relationship and sees the château as an extension of his own hospitality for his Nazi gang.'

Lizzie said, 'Must we all be here, or is it sufficient for you two to dine with them, do you think? I fear I'll make another pigeon faux pas and risk exposing us.'

Luc retrieved the letter and read aloud to Lizzie. 'We look forward to dining with you and your charming relatives. I enjoyed their company so much last time, and Herr Walter Von Schneider is looking forward to making their acquaintance.'

Lizzie sucked in her breath. 'How will we make it through dinner with a Gestapo thug whilst we have two British airmen hidden in the cellars? Do you think your friend suspects us?'

'No, my dear. My guess is the commissaire is looking to impress his visitor, that's all. As long as we all stay calm, everything will be fine,' Luc said, sounding more confident than his expression portrayed.

'Talking of the airmen, we'd better see how they are doing,' Jack said.

Luc replied, 'I told the crew to work on the other side, so you don't run into them.'

'I hate to ask, but can we trust Suzanne?'

Luc nodded. 'I'd trust her with my life. I spoke to her before breakfast and told her there are things it's better she doesn't know for her own safety, but to assist you with anything you need.'

'And did she seem happy with that?'

'She seemed rather thrilled by it all, to be honest. You have nothing to worry about in Suzanne. I told her it's essential she keep this matter to herself, and she swore she would. Actually, she asked if you are in the Resistance and volunteered to help.'

'Good to know,' Jack said. 'That's an interesting development.'

They formulated their plan, and Lizzie went down to the kitchens to find Suzanne and gather fresh supplies for the airmen.

'You are still hungry, madame?' the housekeeper asked when she explained what she needed.

Lizzie said it was for later, and didn't elaborate.

Suzanne stared at her for a second and then hurried to slice some bread and cheese and extract a pot of jam from the pantry. 'Shall I put it in a picnic basket?'

Lizzie shook her head. 'No, thank you. Just wrap it in small packages and I'll grab my raincoat as it's still stormy outside. When Lizzie returned, several neat packages awaited her on the kitchen table with a flask of coffee.

'Thank you so much,' Lizzie said, scooping up the hastily prepared food and slotting it into her pockets.

How quickly things changed on a mission, Lizzie reflected. Only last night, the housekeeper held a gun to their heads. This morning, Suzanne was helping them. What strange times they lived in.

Jack and Luc had already returned to the vineyards, as they often did after breakfast. They all agreed the more normal they could keep their schedules, the less likely they would attract attention to their guests.

When Lizzie stepped out the door and onto the back steps, the high winds lifted her raincoat, and she buttoned it up to the collar. If she had worn a hat, it would have blown off her head, such was the force of the wind. Fortunately, the sideways rain had subsided, but the air was clammy, and the sky was an ominous grey blue. Thunder and lightning were on the horizon, she guessed.

Lizzie scrambled across the fields as fast as she could, clutching the flask, and as she approached the cellar, she saw Jack standing nearby smoking. He hastily extinguished his cigarette and disappeared into the dark recesses. Several minutes later, panting, she followed him in.

'There you are. Everything alright?'

'Seagrove,' he whispered, flicking on his torch. 'All as normal.'

'I've got some food,' she said, and they walked deeper into

the musty cavern until they reached the false wall of the secret cellar.

'Well done. Was Suzanne weird about it?'

'No, she was helpful. Her discovery of our clandestine activities might be for the best. She could be useful.'

Jack tapped several times on the wall, and when they heard a gruff voice, he opened the door. They entered, and he pulled the door closed behind Lizzie.

'How was your night?' Jack asked the airman, who stood to greet them.

'It's always night in here,' he replied.

'True enough. Sorry about that, but this is the only way we can keep you out of sight.'

'I didn't mean to sound ungrateful,' the airman said.

Lizzie passed the flask of coffee to him and then bent down to the wounded airman. 'How are you feeling, Billy?'

He grunted in reply.

'He's been burning up all night and needs medical attention desperately.'

Lizzie rested her palm on his forehead. 'Yes, he has a fever.'

Jack knelt beside her. 'The wound is bleeding through the bandage.'

'Any news on the doctor?' Lizzie muttered to Jack.

He shook his head. 'I'll go and see if he's at home and bring him back with me if he's willing.'

Lizzie worried Jack risked blowing his cover by searching for a Jewish doctor in the village. When they weighed up the risks during mission preparation, Jack decided it was unlikely someone would recognise him after all these years.

The patient writhed and his head jerked from side to side. A pearly coat of perspiration gleamed on his face in the soft light.

Jack stood and signalled to Lizzie to follow him. They

moved away from the wounded airman and talked in low voices. Jack said, 'I'm worried I'll only make it worse if I remove the bandage. He obviously needs medicine. The question is, will the good doctor have any, even if I can find him?'

'The sooner we see if he's there, the better. We'll need to find a different doctor if not. I should go. I'll attract less attention than you,' Lizzie said after a pause.

'In what world is that true?' Jack asked, raising one eyebrow.

'You know what I mean. Suzanne told me she sometimes takes jam and freshly picked fruit to the households with children in the village. Many with big families can barely get by. They're living on starvation rations, so every bit helps.'

'Ah, I see. Yes, that makes sense.' Jack's tone was reluctant, but Lizzie knew he wouldn't fight her on it because it made operational sense.

'I'll ask Suzanne to come with me and we can do the rounds and drop into the doctor's house. That way, we shouldn't raise suspicion.'

The airman's groans grew louder. Lizzie emptied her pockets and put the produce on a small table. 'See if you can get him to drink water,' she told the other airman, who was pacing around the small space.

Outside, the sky had turned gunmetal grey, and the wind had whipped up even further. 'It's not ideal weather for making house calls, but that poor man will not make it if we don't get him help,' Lizzie said.

They agreed the plan was as good as they could manage in the circumstances and as they rushed back to the château, the rain started pelting down like stair rods.

Lizzie bowed her head and pulled her raincoat closer as she shivered from the chilly rain and battering winds.

Jack wore a thin shirt which was already soaked, but he

wrapped his arm around Lizzie and tried to shelter her as they hurried along across the uneven ground. The lavender was like a comforting purple sign in the distance, against the dark threatening sky.

'How different it all looks this morning,' Lizzie gasped as they pushed through the wind at a punishing pace.

Back at the château, they dried off, thankful to be out of the elements.

'What does a benevolent member of the Saint-Clair family wear to make house calls to the needy of the village in the middle of a massive storm?' she asked.

'Wear the outfit we bought you in town last week. That says classy without being over the top.'

Lizzie dressed in the new clothes she'd bought with a combination of coupons and francs. It wasn't smart to flash too much cash around. 'How do I look?' She turned to Jack.

'Beautiful. Like always. But wait,' he said, crossing the room and returning with something behind his back. 'You swapped places to protect me, but endangered yourself. If it wasn't a smart cover story, I wouldn't go along with it.'

Lizzie smiled. She guessed the switch wouldn't go unnoticed. 'What are you hiding behind your back?'

He produced her yellow silk scarf with a flourish. 'Ta-da, you're not going without this.' He tied it around her neck and swivelled her around to admire the effect in the tall mirror. 'Perfect.'

'It goes well with the outfit.' Lizzie touched the scarf. 'I always feel lucky when I wear this. Thank you for bringing it.'

They made final arrangements, and Lizzie reached up to kiss Jack. 'I'll be back before you know it.'

He held her tight against his chest, and she felt his lips brush her hair before he slowly released her. 'Take care, Seagrove. If anything unusual happens, cut your rounds short and come straight back. That's an order from your commanding officer!'

'How will I know what's unusual when I've never been there before?' she queried, a wicked glint in her green eyes.

'You'll know. Watch Suzanne and take her lead.'

Lizzie promised she would be extra careful. 'What will you do whilst I'm gone?'

'I'll sit down with Luc and run through potential avenues of escape for the airmen, so we anticipate any eventuality.'

Downstairs, Jack released Lizzie's hand, and they went in separate directions, both looking back until they could no longer see each other.

Lizzie searched for Suzanne, and Jack went to see if Luc was in his favourite spot in the library. Events were unfolding fast, and the mission was in full swing. Lizzie tried to calm her fears, but she was anxious about the fate of the British airmen, especially Billy, the feverish one.

The timing to host a Gestapo officer for dinner could not be worse.

CHAPTER 33

The violent storm had passed as though it had been a figment of the imagination, and the blooms fluttered on the magnolia trees in the balmy evening air.

Armand found it rude in the extreme that his passenger, Walter Von Schneider, made no effort to engage with him. It was a sign of poor breeding, he decided. When Armand went to Paris for training on how to hunt the enemy in their midst, which took place at the Gestapo's infamous HQ on Avenue Foch, the inferior quality of the newly ranked police officers who attended shocked him. Armand considered himself special, despite his humble upbringing, but most of the attendees were clearly out of their depth, whereas he shone and was proud of his performance.

It was common knowledge that experienced long serving police officers loyal to the pre-war administration had been replaced by sycophants, handpicked by the Vichy government to appease the Nazis. Whilst Armand supported the initiative wholeheartedly when it suited him and was all for a new order, the experience at Gestapo HQ disturbed him.

Von Schneider eventually raised his head from his newspaper and snapped, 'How long until we reach this wretched château? I'm seasick around these bends and up and down these hills.'

Armand bit back what would have been his angry retort if the man wasn't a special guest of the commissaire and an esteemed member of the Gestapo.

'I detest leaving Paris,' Von Schneider complained. 'It's the only civilised city in the whole of this damned country, judging by this provincial backwater.'

Armand seethed with indignation and had to force himself to remain courteous. It was too dangerous to share his real thoughts and wouldn't further his cause. He must put up with these faux leaders on his rise. Just because they were Nazis didn't mean they all possessed Hitler's intelligence and charisma. He consoled himself that every great man faced vicissitudes on his rise to the top, and this was merely a necessary evil he would look back on and laugh.

Unable to silence himself entirely, Armand pointed to the breathtaking view of the golden sun sinking over the Pyrenees in the distance from the top of the hill. 'The medieval city of Toulouse is known as La Ville Rose and is admired the world over.' He paused. 'I'm sure you'll agree that's a stirring scene, Herr Von Schneider.'

His passenger snorted. 'It's not bad, I suppose, but it doesn't compare to the Bavarian Alps,'

Armand clamped his jaw tight. Who was this bully to lecture him and disparage his beautiful city? Everyone knew Germany was a lowly mongrel state. It wasn't all that long ago it was still called Prussia. That was why Hitler had such a monumental task on his hands in his admirable quest to cleanse Europe. Germany had been a big part of the problem, flooded with undesirables, and until the Führer rose to power, wealthy Jews controlled everything.

Armand took several deep, calming breaths. He mustn't lose his temper and ruin his chance to make a useful contact, and so he remained silent until the car swung through the wrought-iron gates of the château. This time, a staff member greeted them. Armand expected Michel Dubois, his prey, to await them and disappointed slithered through him.

The butler was as formal as though he were greeting guests at the Palace of Versailles, and this time Armand harboured no illusions that he would be invited to dine with the police chief and his Gestapo friend.

As if on cue, the commissaire's car rolled into the spot beside them. He had opted to drive himself this evening and instructed Armand to be completely at the beck and call of their elite guest.

Armand opened the door for his passenger, who stepped out of the car and then shrugged his black leather trench coat off and handed it to him as though he were a servant who lived solely for his comfort.

The commissaire greeted Von Schneider enthusiastically, and then the butler ushered them towards the château. Armand glanced around the courtyard and his eyes swept over the medieval building, and he tilted his head back to look up at the charming turret that rivalled a scene from a fairytale. The small window etched into the pink-hued stone was like a porthole in the pale blue sky. What a magnificent view it must be from all the way up there. Armand decided after dinner he would ask the housekeeper if he might walk up there and see it for himself.

The troublesome big dog appeared in the courtyard and growled and barked at him, baring his sharp teeth.

Armand froze, the taste of fear filling his throat.

The housekeeper ran outside and called the dog. 'Leave Monsieur Armand alone, Beau,' she scolded him. The dog whined but immediately stood down. 'He's a teddy bear,' she said. 'Just likes to pretend he's fierce.'

Armand thought she should keep her dog away from guests, but he didn't want to risk turning her against him before dinner, so he followed her in, still shaken by his encounter with the dog. When he was seated in the picture window overlooking the city, his thoughts soared once more. Soon, if events played out as he envisioned, the old class hierarchy would be destroyed, and he could live in this very château.

He swirled his drink in the expensive, heavy glass and savoured every sip as his imagination grew wings, and his fantasies became ever grander. The housekeeper was amenable, and he might even keep her on to serve him.

But one thing was certain. When he was master of the château, he would shoot that ugly, vicious dog.

CHAPTER 34

Lizzie could barely breathe as she waited for the butler to announce the Gestapo officer's arrival. There hadn't been time to talk to Jack after she drove back with Suzanne from the village. Luc had told her to take his Bugatti, because the villagers would recognise it and welcome them with their charitable offerings.

The rounds had gone smoothly, and people had been grateful for the baskets of produce. Lizzie's tender heart hurt when she saw the conditions the families lived in. One woman who was mother to five young children explained the rations weren't nearly enough to feed her family, and if it weren't for Suzanne's regular visits, they would starve.

They visited ten homes before knocking on the door of the doctor's house. Lizzie and Jack had planned it that way, so the visit didn't attract undue attention. There was a lump in Lizzie's throat as they waited at the front door. Luc had received no response to his note summoning the doctor, and she didn't know what to expect.

A harried looking woman opened the door and ran her hand over her messy hair, grey tendrils spilling from her headscarf. Her eyes looked weary, and her face was deeply grooved with lines. Shouts echoed through the door, and the woman stood aside for them to enter.

Suzanne and the doctor's wife were well acquainted, and the woman made grateful cooing sounds over the food basket. 'This is so generous of you.'

Suzanne introduced Lizzie, and the woman invited them through to the kitchen and asked if they would like something to drink.

A little girl with rosy cheeks clutched at the woman's leg, grizzling for attention. Lizzie's thoughts tumbled around her head. The child surely couldn't be the doctor's daughter, as the woman was too old.

As if reading Lizzie's mind, she tousled the child's hair and said, 'This is my granddaughter, Esther. She's staying with me whilst her parents are away.' A shadow crossed the woman's face, and Lizzie got the impression something bad had happened that she didn't want to talk about in front of the child.

Lizzie's reverie was interrupted when the butler appeared in the dining room entrance and he ushered in the two dinner guests. She stood to welcome them, adrenaline rushing through her veins so violently she felt weak.

It was time for her ultimate performance, and one wrong word could seal their fate. Lizzie squared her shoulders, smoothed out her dress, and steeled herself to face the coming ordeal.

'Herr Walter Von Schneider and the commissaire,' the butler announced.

The Gestapo officer swept in as though he owned the place. Lizzie glanced at Jack, and he threw her a reassuring look that said, 'You can do this.'

Luc welcomed their guests, and they exchanged a few words before turning to Lizzie and Jack.

The commissaire wore his usual police uniform and the Gestapo officer was dressed in a tailored suit, which befitted his role as a member of the Nazi secret police. Lizzie realised the two officials were naturally aligned under the police administration's umbrella. Memories of the reports she had read about the Gestapo caused an icy terror to whip through her body.

Although she'd met Nazi officers on previous missions, she'd not been introduced to a member of the Gestapo. Her heart thudded in her breast as she pasted a smile on her pale face and faked her best attempt at being thrilled to meet the agent of death.

Luc introduced her. 'Meet my charming relative, Madame Dubois from St. Malo.'

'Herr Von Schneider, what an honour,' she said, extending her hand and greeting him with concentrated effort.

The Gestapo officer appraised Lizzie. He took her hand and pressed it to his lips, planting a kiss on her cool skin with his warm mouth. 'The honour is all mine, madame. I hope I shall have the good fortune to sit next to you at dinner, and you shall tell me all about St. Malo. I plan to visit soon.'

It was said more as a command than a request, and Luc nodded subtly to the butler, who glided across the room to switch the place cards at the table without faltering.

Lizzie smiled weakly at her designated dinner companion, whilst slowly reclaiming her hand. 'It shall be my pleasure,' she said, her voice not sounding like her own.

Jack stepped forward to meet the Gestapo officer, shaking his hand, and the moment passed. 'I'm sure my wife will be overjoyed. Thank you for joining us this evening.'

'Please call me Walter,' Von Schneider said, his steely eyes darting from Jack to Lizzie.

Soon they took their seats at the dining table and Von

Schneider praised the decor and art on the walls of the elegant room before turning to the commissaire. 'You were correct in your recommendation, my friend. This château is indeed the most charming place. I hope to return soon as I have business in Toulouse.'

Lizzie struggled to swallow. It was one thing for a Gestapo officer to dine with them for a few hours, but if he was planning on making it a regular occurrence, it would be terribly dangerous. They must rethink their plans for using the château as a base for expanding their collaborative Resistance operations with Lev.

'I'm sure we would all love that,' Jack said, his tone sounding sincere and his face not betraying his feelings.

Despite experience in the field during the past year, Lizzie fought to contain her emotions. She was in awe of Jack's poker face and his ability to trick the enemy.

The butler poured the wine, and Von Schneider made an elaborate fuss. 'The aroma is quite beautiful, and the flavour is an uncommon delight to the palate. I must invite my new team of *Weinführers* over for a tasting. This vintage is perfect for Germany.'

Luc and Jack exchanged a furtive glance at the mention of Nazi appointed wine agents.

Von Schneider shared his intention as if it were a foregone conclusion and an absolute compliment. Lizzie wrestled harder to keep her composure. Every sentence he uttered took them deeper into treacherous territory, and she dare not think about the two British airmen and the Jewish doctor hiding in the cellars at that very moment.

CHAPTER 35

The dinner dragged on for an eternity, as Lizzie did her best to talk to Von Schneider, who asked her about her life in St. Malo. She had no reason to think he suspected her, other than she was guilty and he was a Gestapo officer. Every question felt like an interrogation whilst simultaneously trying to eat the courses the butler served. The dinner was extravagant beyond any she'd eaten at the château, and Lizzie thought Suzanne must have used up their reserves and cashed in all their rations to provide such a lavish meal.

'This is delicious, but I can't eat anymore,' Von Schneider announced after pushing his barely touched dessert plate away, the artistic arrangement of figs and goat's cheese glistening beneath a fruit glaze.

Lizzie struggled to eat because she was tense and needed all her attention to answer the Gestapo officer's stream of questions.

He turned to her once more. 'Do you miss living by the sea, madame? I, myself, was born and raised in Berlin, so have not spent much time on the coast.'

Lizzie answered truthfully. She missed living by the sea a great deal, and a hard knot formed in her chest as she thought of Portelet Bay. How she loved to feel the golden sand between her toes.

The Gestapo officer continued, 'I must say, I am more enthusiastic about my forthcoming visit to St. Malo, after speaking to you.'

Lizzie tried not to panic about the repercussions of him arriving in St. Malo and finding something obviously incorrect from her stories. She'd tried to be as vague as possible. It was a year before the war began when she last visited her cousins. Not that long, but devastating changes may have occurred in the city since the Nazi occupation. How could she possibly know exactly how it looked last month?

Lizzie fumbled through, her nerves tingling as she talked of the beauty of the beach and the old walled city.

'I hope the presence of the *Kriegsmarine* at the port isn't too much of a disruption to your family's tranquil life,' he said.

Lizzie searched her memory for anything she had heard about the German Navy in St. Malo. Her father's voice echoed in her mind, and she remembered a conversation around the table at Regent's Park. He received updates in his job at the War Office and told them that the St. Malo port was being used to transport supplies to the German troops in the Channel Islands.

Lizzie could see Jack glancing at her now and then, in between talking to the commissaire and Luc. They had arranged the table so she would sit on Jack's other side, away from their Gestapo guest. She felt more equipped to hold her own with the commissaire and could steer the conversation to their stay in Toulouse. It wouldn't be strange if she didn't know something because she was still new to the city. This was not how they had planned things at all, and Lizzie was worried that any second she would fall into a trap.

'You must tell me the best places to dine,' Von Schneider said, as though people weren't subject to strict rationing and curfews under his country's occupation.

Tact didn't appear to be one of his qualities. Perhaps he had lost sight of how hard life had been in Germany since the previous world war. They suffered from severe food shortages, massive inflation and unemployment. Lizzie would have thought a person who had lived through those years would be more aware of France's current plight, but he showed no sign of it.

'I'm afraid I haven't dined out much since the war began,' she said carefully, calculating it was better to show discomfort, rather than act as though the occupation wasn't happening.

'Of course, but you must not let the rations overly concern you. Soon this war will be over, and as part of the Third Reich, everything will be plentiful in your beautiful country.' He didn't pause for a response but took a long drink of the wine he had selected for dessert and set his glass down on the table, emitting a burp. 'Excuse me, madame.'

His callous remarks infuriated Lizzie, and she held herself in check. Most French citizens were near starvation unless they were in bed with the Nazis and enjoyed special privileges for their treachery. She thought of her cousins who would struggle to get enough to eat, and her grandparents and friends in Jersey.

The commissaire didn't look like he had missed a meal, and she thought of the Jewish doctor's little granddaughter who had been too sick to travel when her parents were forced to flee Toulouse and escape to Spain. The doctor's wife told them in a hushed tone that they had to get out of France before they were arrested. It had broken her parents' hearts to leave their daughter behind, but her grandparents promised they would take her to them as soon as she was well enough to travel.

'Don't tell us where they are,' Lizzie had warned the doctor's wife. 'The less we know the better, just in case—' Her voice tailed off and the unspoken words hung in the air like a black cloud. It was safer not to share specifics in case the Vichy police captured and interrogated them.

Icy terror ran through her, and she shuddered. There was so much at stake and at moments like this, the responsibility to not put a foot wrong was a heavy load to bear.

'Are you cold, madame?' Von Schneider asked, seeing her shiver.

'Yes, a little,' Lizzie said, somehow mustering a smile as though they were the greatest of friends dining together.

'Your delightful wife is cold, monsieur,' the officer informed Jack, clearly used to people jumping to attention to satisfy his every command.

Jack stood and slipped his jacket around Lizzie's shoulders, and she smiled up at him gratefully.

Von Schneider then proceeded to fire questions at them both about when they were married and how long they had known each other.

'I am a romantic. You can't beat a good love story,' he said.

Prickles of fear coated Lizzie's skin as she listened to Jack's replies. They had practiced their fake marriage cover story and tested each other repeatedly in London but hadn't needed to share it since their arrival. Until now, no one had questioned them about their marriage, but Von Schneider seemed very curious and wished to know all the details.

'Were you married here in Toulouse or in St. Malo?' he asked, his eyes narrowing like a panther's as they flickered from Jack to Lizzie.

Had she failed his test, and he suspected them of lying?

She had already told him they arrived in Toulouse recently and had been married a year. The fact he was now asking Jack the same question when she had already told him the answer, scared her.

She coughed and said with deference. 'Remember, we discussed our arrival was only last month?'

'Oh yes, how silly of me. Too much wine,' he said. 'Perhaps we should take a walk to clear the head.'

Luc stood. 'May I invite you gentlemen out to the terrace for brandy and cigars?'

Sounds of agreement echoed around Lizzie, and she had never been so grateful to be excluded from an invitation.

'Please excuse me,' she said. 'I must leave you esteemed gentlemen to your discussions. It has been a great honour to meet you, Herr Von Schneider.'

Lizzie prayed this would be the last she would see of him. Unfortunately, he wasn't of the same mind.

'But madame, our evening is surely not over so soon?' he glanced at the clock on the wall. 'I was about to say that after brandy, I would very much like a tour of the wine cellars and would be overjoyed if you too, would accompany us. You clearly greatly appreciate wine and besides, a little feminine company only ever improves a tour.'

Panic surged through Lizzie. This was their worst nightmare. How could they take the Gestapo officer and the city's chief of police into the cellars where the airmen and the doctor were hiding?

Jack suggested smoothly that perhaps it would be better to take the tour by daylight another time. 'You would see so much more of the scenery and grounds.'

'Whilst that sounds enticing, I'm unsure how long I will stay in Toulouse. Therefore, I would rather have a quick tour this evening than no tour at all.' His words were spoken in a charming tone but held a determined undercurrent, and it was clear he would not be dissuaded.

Jack gave Lizzie a furtive nod. 'Very well, I'm sure my wife would love to join us for a walk to the cellars, wouldn't you, Isabelle?'

Lizzie smiled and said that, of course, she would join them if that was their wish. They agreed they would meet in the courtyard at nine and catch the last of the daylight.

The men walked out to the terrace and Lizzie left the room sedately, the sound of her heart drumming in her ears. Once in the corridor, she raced downstairs to alert Suzanne.

It was a blessing the housekeeper had discovered them on their recent nighttime sojourn, and after today's visit to the doctor's house, she had made it clear she would assist them in whatever way she could. Lizzie hadn't told her more than she needed to, but it was comforting to know they had another ally in the château.

She entered the kitchen, and several of the staff looked at her, surprised by her sudden arrival, before hastily continuing their duties.

'How may I assist you, madame?' Suzanne asked as she led Lizzie out of the kitchen and into her small private sitting room.

'The Gestapo officer intends to visit the cellars this evening,' Lizzie said.

Suzanne's eyes widened. 'Oh, my God.'

'Did the doctor leave already, do you know?' Lizzie asked, speaking close to the housekeeper's ear.

'I haven't seen him, but then, I wouldn't. It's been such a hectic evening I haven't checked how they are getting on.'

During their drive back from the village, Lizzie had explained that they needed the doctor urgently to treat a wounded man they had hidden in the cellars. Suzanne didn't know more than that, but the little she knew was enough to get them all shot. Lizzie and Jack had agreed they had no choice but to hope Luc was right and they could trust Suzanne.

The doctor had hidden in the back of the car, covered by a blanket, and Lizzie smuggled him into the cellar where Billy was still burning up and had begun hallucinating. She had no choice but to leave the doctor there when she had to rush to dress for dinner.

'Dinner is finished now. The others can clear up. Do you want me to go over?' Suzanne asked, concern etched on her face.

Lizzie's mind raced with potential scenarios. 'Thank you, yes. Go there discreetly, as quickly as you can. Take a different route so the men won't spot you from the terrace. Check if the doctor is still there. If he is, tell him to get away immediately. He can't be seen here.'

At nine on the dot, the men assembled in the courtyard and Lizzie arrived just in time to meet them. Beau left Luc's side and ran to Lizzie, his tail wagging furiously as he nuzzled against her legs.

Von Schneider once again insisted on Lizzie's company, and they walked across the gardens and towards the undulating vineyards.

The sun was still high in the sky, casting a golden glow across the hilltop. 'Isn't the lavender beautiful?' Lizzie pointed into the distance to the swaying purple haze, desperate to steer the conversation away from anything that could endanger them further.

They reached the edge of the vineyards, and Von Schneider admired the glossy grapes on the vines, bathed in the evening sun. 'They look like they are almost ripe.'

Lizzie said she thought the harvest would be in the next few months, and the hard work would begin. She side-stepped more detailed questioning about the vineyards by assuring him she was no expert.

'I understood your husband's family own a wine business in St. Malo?'

Here he was again, prodding and probing. They had modelled Michel Dubois's background on a real Frenchman. They had chosen his name because his family owned a wine business. Val's reasoning was it made a plausible cover in case anyone checked, but it was highly unlikely they would meet someone from St. Malo who knew the real Michel Dubois.

Lizzie raised her chin. She'd had enough of the Gestapo bully's polite insolence. 'Yes, they do, but I'm not involved in the day to day running of the operation. Honestly, I've learnt more about wine since we arrived at the château, and that isn't very much at all.' Lizzie played on the stereotype of a young woman's ignorance, and she giggled prettily as if her head was full only of hot air. 'I confess I don't find business interesting and leave those matters to my husband.'

Von Schneider seemed more than satisfied with her vapid response and applauded her. 'It is rare to find a beautiful and charming woman who truly knows her place. We have a motto, perhaps you have heard it: *Kinder, Küche, Kirche.*'

The memory of the German born Hannah sharing the Nazi motto: *Children, Kitchen and Church*, rose in her mind.

Lizzie nodded and feigned enthusiasm in her green eyes. 'Oh, but yes, of course, I have heard of it. And a fine motto it is—I believe in traditional values myself and can't wait to start a family.'

The Gestapo officer sighed and turned to face Lizzie, his lascivious gaze devouring her. 'It has been a pleasure to meet you, madame. I hope one day to have the good fortune of finding such a fine and obedient wife like you.'

Lizzie fought to keep a pleasant expression on her face

with great effort, but she felt physically sick. What a vile man. Some poor woman would be saddled with him as her future husband.

He continued, blissfully unaware of the effect he was having on Lizzie. 'Ah, these must be the cellars I've heard so much about from the commissaire. He says your wine is the finest in the region.'

'I wouldn't know about that,' Lizzie said demurely.

'Since my time in Paris, I have become quite the connoisseur,' he said, and Lizzie felt a sudden urge to punch him in his arrogant mouth and watch him bleed.

Sometimes, her reactions to the Nazis surprised her. Before the war, it had never crossed her mind that she had such a violent streak.

Luc was leading the way, and at the entrance, he picked up a lantern and the two men followed him down the steps to the cellars. 'Welcome to the Château de Saint-Clair cellars.'

Lizzie's mind raced. Luc knew the doctor had visited earlier, but she hadn't been able to warn him he may still be there. She prayed the doctor had got out in time and he or Suzanne had properly concealed the secret room.

If Von Schneider or the commissaire noticed anything suspicious, it would be the end for them all.

CHAPTER 36

Lizzie hung back, trying to put as much distance between herself and Von Schneider as possible. When he disappeared into the dark cavern with Luc, she turned to Jack, who waited for her. 'What if he suspects something? He asked me so many questions.'

Jack put his arm around Lizzie's shoulders, and his voice was low. 'Remember, the Gestapo are the secret police. They try to trip people up as a matter of routine.'

'Umm,' Lizzie said.

Jack continued, 'Judging by his expressions, I'd say you have a keen admirer, and his questions were just an excuse to keep talking to you.'

'Let's hope you're right. I don't know where the doctor is.'

Jack frowned and said in an urgent whisper, 'You mean he might still be down there?'

Lizzie nodded. 'Suzanne ran to warn him, but only just after dinner.'

Jack said, 'We must stay calm. It will be tricky to see down there at this time of night and the odds are they'll notice nothing. We'd better join them. Did you bring your pill?'

Lizzie nodded solemnly and pointed to her locket. Val had issued them with the usual suicide pills shortly before they left.

Jack reached for her hand. 'If anything out of the ordinary happens, we'll improvise.'

Lizzie entered the stairwell, her heart strumming so hard it reverberated in her chest. They heard the men's voices and soon reached them in the outer wine cellar. Von Schneider held a bottle and was studying the wine label. 'This looks like a very fine vintage.'

'Take that with my blessings,' Luc said.

'That is most kind of you. I will,' Von Schneider replied. 'The Führer instructed us to source only the best for Germany. Earlier, I mentioned my team of specially appointed wine agents. Their mission is to select the top wines to export to the Fatherland. You will, of course, receive a fair price for them.'

'But of course,' Luc said, his face devoid of expression. 'Unfortunately, beyond a small supply for your personal consumption, we won't be able to contribute.'

'Why is that?' Von Schneider asked, a steely current rippling through his voice.

'I'm sure your wine agents will tell you. Last year's harvest was one of the poorest we've had in years, so we haven't much to offer.'

'What about the bottles from previous years? Impressive vineyards such as these must have produced plentiful harvests before the war.'

'Indeed,' Luc said, his voice measured and polite as ever. 'Please forgive me mentioning this if it is in poor taste, but as you are in earnest in your quest to export French wine to Germany, it's important you have the full picture. I wouldn't want you to waste your time. When your troops invaded, much of the wine from our region was taken. After several visits, most of our stock was gone.' Luc avoided saying his cellars had been looted, but the inference was clear.

Von Schneider raised his eyes from studying the label. 'What a shame. I had heard something about wine being seized in the early days. The troops were understandably excited by our victory, but we have corrected the situation now. I confess I hadn't realised you were personally affected. Please accept my apologies for any unruly behaviour.'

Lizzie gritted her teeth. Luc had told them the German soldiers had entered the cellars and informed them they would confiscate cases of their wine immediately. Luc had explained that was partly why the château struggled financially now. Even though they were permitted to sell to Germany and the Axis countries, the currency exchange rate was so poor it was like running a charity. The Nazis made it look as though they were operating a fair market, but when the French wine merchants traded with them, it was more like daylight robbery.

Lizzie hoped Luc's dismal account of wine stocks would end the Gestapo officer's zeal to see more of the cellars, but he was not so easily curtailed.

He held onto the wine bottle and coughed. 'Nevertheless, I should like to continue the tour. I am fascinated by cellars and vineyards and find them quite the most interesting thing about France.'

They resumed walking slowly and neared the entrance to the secret room. Lizzie spoke in a loud voice to warn the airmen and possibly the doctor, they had company. 'Herr Von Schneider, it is a pleasure to have someone so appreciative to show around.'

Please, please do not let them make a sound.

Luc caught on and added to the conversation until they

were all talking. Lizzie held her breath as they approached the secret room.

Lizzie had asked Suzanne to warn them of their visit so they wouldn't think they were coming to see them.

Beau, who had stayed obediently at Luc's heels until then, padded over to the row of barrels positioned near the concealed entrance and whimpered.

'Your dog seems to have a fancy for a glass of wine,' the commissaire said, laughing at his own wit.

The big dog lowered his body onto the cool ground and started scratching and sniffing. Lizzie looked at Jack, fear rocketing through her.

'Come here, Beau. Here,' she said, but Beau's attention was fully on a wine barrel, and he wouldn't be distracted.

'He is certainly fascinated by something,' Von Schneider said, taking a few steps towards the barrel.

Luc snapped at his dog, but Beau didn't obey his master.

Lizzie said, 'It's probably something highly unpleasant, like a rat.'

'My wife is correct. We have terrible problems with rats down here, and they spread disease, you know. I would advise you to proceed with caution.'

Von Schneider stepped back hastily, an expression of distaste on his face.

'Here, boy,' Lizzie said to Beau as he scratched frantically. She moved swiftly towards the barrel, and peered inside, the blood racing to her head.

Lizzie stopped herself from exclaiming and quickly replaced the lid.

'You too, Isabelle. Move away,' said Jack.

'It's nothing,' she said. 'Beau is a hunting dog. It's enough for him to smell the scent of a rodent and he gets very excited.'

Jack was looking at Lizzie strangely, trying to figure out

what was going on. There was a muffled noise, and the commissaire jerked his head up. 'What on earth was that?'

'These cellars are older and creakier than us, my friend! Remember, we are in a medieval maze, and rocks have been known to fall from the ceiling,' Luc said.

Beau was still scratching, and Lizzie wondered how to distract him. 'I'd like to get out of here. It's creepy at night.'

'I couldn't agree more,' Luc said. He ordered Beau to his side, who reluctantly left the barrel and obeyed his master's firm instructions.

'Perhaps it will be better to take the full tour in the daytime, after all,' Von Schneider said. He turned to leave, his distaste for rats and falling rocks evident. 'In my enthusiasm, I seem to have overlooked your experience. I don't wish to endanger you all.'

Lizzie released a ragged breath and moved away from the secret cellar entrance. She exchanged a look with Jack and they both started walking briskly the way they had come.

'You are welcome, any time,' Luc said, as though his preference mattered, and he had a choice about whether to allow a Gestapo officer to plunder his wines on demand.

They reached the top of the steps and Lizzie breathed in the fresh evening air after the musty cellar. Dusk had fallen and the first silvery stars twinkled in the darkening sky.

It would be the most wondrous evening if she hadn't spent it with the devil. As they reached the courtyard, Lizzie counted the seconds until she could excuse herself and planned never to see the Gestapo officer again.

'A wonderful idea has occurred to me,' Von Schneider said, pausing as he scanned the château, admiration burning in his eyes.

Lizzie stared at him, praying his latest idea in no way involved her.

He addressed Luc. 'I find myself not wishing to leave this

evening. Would you be so generous as to offer me accommodation for the night? I'm drawn to this place and would love the opportunity to stay in such a fine château.'

Lizzie gulped, and in her panic, she replied before Luc. 'That sounds lovely, but your driver awaits you, Herr Von Schneider.'

He turned to Lizzie. 'Please call me Walter. I have not forgotten, dear Isabelle. I'm sure in a place as magnificent as this, the staff will find a room for my chauffeur. Is that not so, Luc?'

Luc said smoothly. 'It will be the greatest honour to host you both.'

Lizzie's thoughts collided as she tried to figure out how to handle this latest disaster.

Luc continued, as if he had members of the Gestapo staying at his home regularly. 'Let us move into the library and perhaps I may tempt you with another glass of our finest Armagnac. Our housekeeper will organise rooms for you and your chauffeur immediately.'

Von Schneider, whose mood had been somewhat subdued since the revelation that there was no abundant supply of Château de Saint-Clair wine to loot from the cellars, brightened considerably at the prospect of another drink.

The commissaire thanked them all for a wonderful evening, and excused himself, saying he had an early start.

One down, one to go, thought Lizzie.

Luc led Von Schneider back into the château, with Beau close at his heels.

Lizzie touched Jack's arm, and they stayed outside. His face was a picture of confusion as he waited for an explanation about what had happened in the cellars.

Lizzie leaned closer, 'Suzanne was hiding in the wine barrel!'

Jack gasped. 'So that's why Beau was so excited!'

'Yes, and Luc is going to call her into the library at any minute. What shall we do?'

CHAPTER 37

Armand enjoyed his meal, and after smoking another cigarette, he eased his tired body off the chair and went to look for the housekeeper.

He entered the busy kitchen but couldn't see her. When he enquired where he could find her, no one seemed to know. The butler, who had his hands full, suggested she might be in her private sitting room, taking a break.

Armand tapped on the door, but there was no reply. He tapped again, but still no one responded. His curiosity to see more of the château prevailed and instead of returning to the kitchen to ask someone to find the housekeeper for him, he opened the door and poked his head inside the room. It was small and neat, much as he would expect a housekeeper's room to be.

A hardback register lay on the writing desk, and the temptation proved too great to resist. He shuffled into the room, glancing back over his shoulder to check no one saw him. The hallway was deserted, so he closed the door softly behind him.

He opened the heavy book and thumbed through it, scanning the handwriting, looking for clues. Armand was always searching for clues and fancied himself something of a seasoned detective. After several minutes, he realised it was just a record of mundane housekeeping notes and held no interest for him.

Footsteps approached the door, and he froze, then cast his eyes around for a place to hide. The room was too small, so he decided to pretend he was lost, but the sound of footsteps continued past the door and faded into the distance. The thrill of nearly being caught excited him and he craved more adventure, and wished he could go into the city on one of his surveillance operations.

Armand sighed at the unfairness of his situation and shuffled back out of the room. In the kitchen, there was still no sign of the housekeeper, so he asked the butler how to reach the turret he had seen from the courtyard.

The butler looked surprised until Armand added that he merely wished to admire what must surely be a magnificent view. He gave him directions and pointed him towards a spare lantern, and the disgruntled chauffeur limped out of the kitchens and along the hallway towards the back stairs. The lantern flickered to life reluctantly after several attempts with a match, casting an eerie yellow glow onto the steps.

He dragged his wasted leg up the winding staircase, grunting as he got ever higher, and his chest grew tight as he struggled to breathe. The steps were steep, and he hadn't realised it would be so difficult for him to reach the top after such a hearty meal and several large drinks.

Halfway up, he paused to catch his breath, his muscles burning, and considered turning back. The turret would probably not live up to his expectations, anyway. But he reminded himself he was no quitter and who knew when he'd have the opportunity again? Armand proceeded, slowly but methodically until he reached the top and leant heavily against the stone wall, breathing fast from the exertion.

He let himself rest for a few minutes and after he recovered his strength, pulled himself upright and edged towards the turret room. Armand pushed on the thick wooden door, and it creaked, startling him. The light was insufficient to see properly, and he was regretting going up there at night. His impulsive nature often led him to do things he later wished he hadn't.

Dust floated in the air, and he sneezed loudly as he crossed to the turret window. He pulled back the shutters and was rewarded for his persistence with a breathtaking view of Toulouse and the surrounding countryside. He had made it just in time to see the sun dip below the horizon and the soft cape of dusk coat the skies. The panoramic scene was glorious, and he inhaled deeply. It was the perfect night, and it was so peaceful, he stood there revelling in the experience.

He squinted, trying to work out who was running in the distance. He was surprised to recognise the figure of the housekeeper, obviously in a great rush.

What on earth was she doing at that time of night when her master was entertaining such prestigious guests? Armand watched her run, his mind ticking over as he tried to think of a viable excuse for her strange behaviour.

It made no sense. He concluded it was very odd indeed and couldn't find a reason for it. Armand made a mental note to add the housekeeper—Suzanne—to his list of potential traitors. He would discover her family name easily enough if he made enquiries with his network of informants. They were always keen to please in any way they could, desperate to buy his good favour.

His climb to the turret was proving more stimulating than he had imagined and his juices were flowing again as he thought of uncovering some kind of resistance connection to Suzanne. She might even be the ringleader.

The Resistance was becoming more troublesome, and he had received a fresh set of orders to scale up his investigations into local troublemakers. Recently, a rail track had been destroyed by explosives and the expensive cargo bound for Germany had been ruined and the transport delayed considerably until a new track could be laid. The commissaire was furious and told the Legion they must do better. The police could not handle everything alone and they were relying on them to root out enemies of state before they gained anymore traction.

Nightfall arrived swiftly whilst Armand deliberated about Suzanne and her possible motives for roaming around the château grounds alone at night. He closed the shutters and searched the small turret room to see if there was anything of interest. It occurred to him that this might even be a space the housekeeper used for her treasonous activities, and he regretted not combing her sitting room whilst he had the chance.

Armand pulled the drawers out of the old desk and poked about, but there was nothing inside except for a few dusty Toulousian keepsakes. He explored the room, looking for anywhere incriminating evidence might be hidden. His eyes rested on a shelf which protruded from the rugged stone wall, and his pulse raced at the thought of the imminent discovery that would show his superiors, he was someone to be reckoned with. He reached up to the shelf and sneezed again as a shower of dust tickled his nostrils. His heartbeat picked up pace as he patted the inside of the stone shelf, and his fingers located a large key. He stretched and clutched at it, fumbling to pull it off.

Surely this must be for something significant, or why would a key be stashed away like this? Armand found it most intriguing, and his instincts told him there was more to this château than met the eye. He cast about for a fitting hole for the key but couldn't find one. Then he thought it must be the key for the door and chided himself for missing the obvious, but when he jangled the key in the lock, it didn't fit.

Armand turned the key over in his hands and puzzled what to do. This key must fit something in the little room high in the sky, but what?

The evening brought one disappointment after another. He had still not glimpsed the dashing Michel Dubois, and soon he would have to leave.

Armand made another round of the room, his eyes searching for a lock that could be a receptacle for the key. He stooped down, groaning at the strain as he tried to push the thick heavy rug aside. He scanned the room for any telltale signs of a secret compartment. In his training at Gestapo HQ, they had taught them about the many ways their enemies were caught concealing their spy equipment.

Armand sneezed again, glanced at his watch, and realised Von Schneider might have summoned him already. The Gestapo officer hadn't seemed like a patient man. He must go now but promised himself he would return at the next opportunity and conduct a more comprehensive search. He was weary, and his sore leg throbbed, so he pushed the rug back with his shoe, released a long-laboured sigh, and walked to the door and back down the winding stone steps.

Armand tried to hurry, but it was difficult with his uncooperative leg. Halfway down the spiral staircase, his fingers clasped the cold ornate key in his pocket, and he smiled.

At least he had something tangible to show for his efforts.

CHAPTER 38

Lizzie and Jack lingered in the courtyard. Jack lit a cigarette and inhaled as he searched the sky for answers. 'We must warn Luc and Suzanne.'

'Yes, I wouldn't know the first thing about which rooms to prepare, and the housemaids only follow her instructions.'

They agreed Jack would join the men, and Lizzie would run back to the cellars, check on the sick airman, and tell Suzanne she was needed back at the château urgently.

'I don't like you having to go over there at this time of night alone, but if I don't follow them inside soon, it might look suspicious.'

'It's fine, darling, don't worry. You go in and warn Luc however you can. Make up some excuse about Suzanne needing longer to ready the rooms, and I'll bring her back.'

Jack brushed Lizzie's lips with the lightest of kisses. 'I love you. Be careful.' He turned and strode towards the château, glancing back from the door.

Lizzie blew him a kiss, picked up the hem of her dress and ran as fast as she could across the gardens and towards the vineyards. Her hair flew as she ran, and she was exhilarated by the wind in her face. By the time she reached the cellar entrance, she was panting so hard she had to stop and rest.

Grabbing the lantern, she disappeared into the cellars, almost losing her footing on the rough surface of the steps. The sudden hoot of an owl echoed around the ancient cavern, and her scalp tingled, and her flesh erupted in goosebumps. Jack was right—it was creepy down here at night.

Lizzie arrived in the belly of the dark cellar and held her lantern over the wine barrel where Suzanne had been hiding. Lifting the lid, she found it empty. Then she heard a thud and tapped three times on the wall of the secret room. It was their agreed safety signal. Lizzie opened the door and stood face-to-face with Suzanne.

'What's going on? They need you at the château,' she whispered.

The housekeeper ran her hand over her bun and pushed the loose tendrils off her forehead. 'It's not good news, I'm afraid. Come in and see for yourself.'

Suzanne stepped aside and Lizzie entered the musty room. 'Doctor! I thought you would have gone by now. It's too dangerous to be here.'

The old doctor's face was grey from exhaustion when he raised his eyes to Lizzie's. 'I couldn't leave this poor man in this state.' He stood and moved away from the thrashing airman, whose wound was soaked with fresh blood that had seeped onto the thin makeshift mattress.

Suzanne knelt by the wounded man and cooled his head with a damp towel, soothing him with soft words as though he were a child.

The doctor beckoned Lizzie to the far side of the room and lowered his voice. 'He won't make it through the night if we don't get him to a hospital. I don't have sulfa powder for the infection and without it …' He shook his head, sadness in his eyes.

'But we can't take him to a hospital. That's as good as signing his death warrant,' Lizzie whispered.

'I understand, but what do you suggest? I have tried every trick in the book and can do no more for him here. His temperature is raging, the bleeding has worsened in the past hour, and he is weak from fighting the infection for so long. It has a death grip on him.'

Lizzie looked over at the young airman. He had defended his country and was now slipping away from life in a cold cellar in France, his loved ones far out of reach. She felt inadequate and wished she had a magic wand to restore him to good health.

'I have an idea,' she said.

The doctor looked at her curiously. 'That's good news. I have been out of ideas for some time.'

'It's better I don't tell you the details, but trust me, we will do all we can for him.'

The doctor reluctantly agreed to leave after checking on his patient one more time and changing the bandages on the wound.

'Do you know your way home through the woods?' Lizzie asked, as he stood at the exit with his doctor's bag.

'I was born in the village, madame, you need not worry about me. I will make my way home through the woods and stay out of sight.'

Lizzie thanked him again and said she would be in touch.

'Good luck,' he said. 'I will pray for Billy and for your plan's success.'

After the doctor left, Lizzie talked to the other airman. 'Get some rest. It must be difficult, but we will try to get you out of here tomorrow.'

'Billy won't make it across the mountains like that,' he said, desperation in his voice.

Lizzie patted his shoulder. 'Don't worry. I'll return in the morning and will know more about how we'll get him to safety then.'

Lizzie told Suzanne about Von Schneider and his driver staying over as they hurried back through the shadowy vineyards illuminated only by the moonlit sky, and towards the château.

Suzanne frowned. 'I couldn't have picked a worse time to leave.'

'My husband went to warn Monsieur Luc and distract Von Schneider.'

Suzanne said she knew which rooms to give the guests, but they needed freshening up. When they let themselves in quietly through the staff entrance, only the butler remained in the kitchen, reading a newspaper.

'The others have retired for the night. Where did you disappear to?' he asked, looking at Suzanne, clearly surprised to see them enter together.

'Apologies. I lost my wedding ring on an errand in the vineyards this afternoon and went in search of it. Madame Isabelle saw I was distressed and was kind enough to help me look for it.'

'Did you find it?' he asked.

'I'm afraid not,' Suzanne said, sniffing dramatically as though she may break down in floods of tears at any second.

'How unfortunate,' he said.

'It's the only thing I have left of my dear departed husband.'

The butler looked uncomfortable and fell silent.

Lizzie lay her hand on Suzanne's arm. 'Never fear. These things have a way of turning up. I shall help you search again in the morning when we can see what we're looking for.'

Suzanne thanked Lizzie, and they scuttled off together to the housekeeping stores to prepare rooms for their unwanted guests.

That night, Von Schneider slept in the château's largest guest suite. In its heyday it was the grandest but was now shabbily elegant. Lizzie had requested Suzanne put him as far away from her rooms as possible, and despite the ominous situation, their spirits were giddy as they made up the beds.

Being in terrible danger sharpened the senses. She had noticed it on her first mission, and realised she was addicted to the thrill of working undercover. For a fleeting moment, she wondered whether life after the war would seem dull. It was difficult to imagine being married to Jack and living in London with no war raging. If the SOE didn't need them anymore, what would they do? She shook herself back to the present and Suzanne thanked her.

'It's so kind of you to help like you do. I shall miss you when you leave.'

The housekeeper's words touched Lizzie, and she wondered how long they would stay. They had barely established the Resistance network, but their cover could be compromised at any moment, so she never knew.

'I wish I had a scorpion to hide in his sheets,' Lizzie muttered, and they both dissolved into laughter at the thought of the entitled Gestapo officer stung by a scorpion in the middle of the night.

When Lizzie finally climbed into her giant bed, she was bone weary, but her mind raced as she waited for Jack to return.

It seemed ages until he quietly let himself in and sat heavily on the bed next to her. 'Are you awake?'

'Yes, of course. Did you do it?' Lizzie asked, turning to face him.

Jack ran his fingers over the bearded shadow on his face. 'Yes. It's late, but Val should get my message first thing.'

'Do you think they'll send a plane to pick up the airmen tomorrow?' Lizzie couldn't get Billy's haunted cries out of her mind. 'You should have seen him tonight. He's in a desperate way.'

'All going to plan, he'll be in a hospital in Blighty by tomorrow night.'

'Let's hope it's not too late,' Lizzie said, holding onto Jack's hand like a life raft.

The state of the wounded airman had reminded her how fortunate they were, and how dreadful it was when she was in London waiting for Jack when he was away on an operation.

'I can't believe we had to send a message when there's Gestapo in the château!'

'I know, it's far from ideal, but I don't see how else we can get the airman to a hospital. You were right, he wouldn't make the journey to the border, never mind across the mountains in that condition.'

When Jack eased his large frame onto the mattress next to her, she nestled in his arms and was grateful for his warm, solid presence. They drifted off to sleep together on one side of the giant bed.

That night, even though Lizzie's body ached from sheer physical exhaustion, she slept only fitfully, and images of the wounded airman and the doctor's granddaughter permeated her consciousness each time she awoke.

As dawn broke over the valley and the soft light of a new summer's day filtered through the shutters and spun patterns on the white walls, Lizzie's eyes flickered open and all she could see was Billy's ashen face. Her soul was filled with melancholy, and she had a horrible sense of doom that something terrible was on the horizon.

CHAPTER 39

Breakfast was a strange affair with Von Schneider present. When the plates had been cleared away, Suzanne served more coffee, and he didn't seem in any rush to leave. Lizzie was on edge, waiting for the opportunity to check on the airman.

Von Schneider made little grunts as he leafed through Luc's newspaper. Raising his head and moving the paper aside, he announced with a look of great satisfaction, 'Operation Barbarossa is a dazzling success. The Soviet Union is now under Nazi rule, and we are exterminating those filthy Jews. Of course, we'd have to kill all the Russians to rid them of communism, but we must start somewhere.'

Fury gripped Lizzie, but she willed herself to stay silent, pretending to be absorbed in drinking the remains of her coffee. He wasn't addressing her, anyway. In his view, she was but a mere woman and understood nothing of warfare. It was true that she knew little about traditional war tactics, but she knew a great deal about underground resistance and espionage.

Lizzie decided she would add this Gestapo monster's

name to the SOE list of Nazis who committed heinous crimes. He had talked at length with Luc the previous evening about the Third Reich and how much he admired the Führer's grand plan.

The desire for vengeance burned in Lizzie's chest like a raging fire, but she sat at the table as though it were just another regular morning in the château.

Luc engaged with Von Schneider with all the skill of a seasoned diplomat. He agreed the invasion of the Soviet Union was a success and spoke a lot without saying much at all. Lizzie realised she had a lot to learn from Luc.

Her eyes moved to Jack as the Gestapo officer addressed him. 'And what do you think of the progress we're making?' he asked.

Jack didn't hesitate and applauded the German forces as though he were their biggest fan. 'The skill with which the Wehrmacht, the Kriegsmarine and the Luftwaffe worked in synergy and caught the Soviets off-guard will be written about in the history books for future generations to study. It was a masterful operation.'

'You are a wise man, monsieur.' Von Schneider looked gratified by Jack's praise and resumed reading the newspaper and drinking his coffee.

Lizzie tapped her foot beneath the table and glanced at the clock repeatedly. The morning was passing, and their guest still showed no signs of leaving. Eventually, he lay the crumpled newspaper on the table and fixed his gaze on Luc. 'I should be most obliged if we could take another tour this morning. You were quite right that it was a mistake to go last night. I barely saw anything of the vineyards and the commissaire tells me your grounds are extensive.'

Luc replied if that was his wish, he would be honoured to give him a tour. His face betrayed no emotion, and Lizzie had to work hard not to show the tension she felt at the thought of the Nazi poking around the château grounds in daylight. Even if he didn't insist on revisiting the cellars, they were in the vineyards, and she wouldn't be able to check on the airmen whilst he was liable to appear at any moment. Lizzie glanced at Jack, who lit a cigarette after offering one to Von Schneider, who declined.

'Shall we begin our tour?' the Gestapo officer said.

They stood, Lizzie too, but just as they were about to leave the table, Suzanne entered and whispered something to Luc, who turned to Von Schneider to tell him he had a telephone call. He strode after Suzanne, his figure a tall blur of grey green, to take his call.

A few minutes later, he returned. 'I'm afraid I will have to cut my delightful visit short.'

Lizzie exhaled slowly, trying not to show the relief that spiralled through her. She hadn't realised just how tense she was until that moment.

'Oh dear, that is a terrible shame,' Luc said. 'Duty calls, I presume.'

Von Schneider said he was needed urgently in Paris and would cut short his trip, but he would be back.

'I am most disappointed to have to say farewell so soon after we have become acquainted.' His steely eyes searched Lizzie's. 'The good news is I shall be able to visit St. Malo sooner than I had planned. I am so looking forward to seeing your beautiful city, madame. And I shall endeavour to return to visit you here as soon as my schedule permits.'

Lizzie conjured an amiable smile and said she was sorry he must go and wished him a pleasant trip back to Paris.

The men shook hands, and Von Schneider crossed to Lizzie's side. 'Believe me when I say, madame, our conversation was the highlight of my time in Toulouse.' He fixed his gaze on Jack's face. 'You are a lucky man, indeed.'

Jack gallantly agreed that he was, but Lizzie saw a muscle

twitch in his jaw, and she guessed he had the same overwhelming urge to punch the smarmy smile off the Nazi's face that she had experienced the previous night.

They gathered in the courtyard to see Von Schneider off and say their last goodbyes, as his driver appeared, dressed smartly in uniform. Lizzie had noticed the French veterans working in the Vichy administration still wore military garb. He had slept in a small room in the staff quarters below stairs. Lizzie watched him stare at Jack as he limped to the car.

The driver moved the vehicle and struggled to get out quickly to open the door for his esteemed passenger to enter.

Von Schneider eyed him with unconcealed distaste, saluted and snapped, '*Heil Hitler.*'

The chauffeur raised his right arm and repeated the chant.

The Gestapo officer turned to face them, raised his arm again, and looked at them expectantly.

The hateful words stuck in Lizzie's throat, but she forced the infamous salutation through her lips. She didn't dare look at Jack or Luc, but heard the low rumble as they, too, paid homage to the devil.

A memory of seeing the driver before surfaced. His face was vaguely familiar, and she recalled a similar looking military man with a limp. Lizzie sifted through the images in her mind as though watching a movie and trying to place him.

In her training, she had learnt that the ability to recognise faces and connect them to past situations and events could mean the difference between life and death.

Finally, the car edged away, and they watched it turn out of the gates and onto the road.

Lizzie exhaled. 'My God, I thought he would never leave.'

They agreed he was the most ominous guest any of them had ever had the ill-fortune to endure. Luc asked for an update on the airman and whether the doctor had treated him. His expression was grave when Lizzie told him he was fighting for his life the previous evening.

Jack told Luc he had requested an urgent pickup by plane for that night, and he would contact London again for confirmation shortly.

After collecting a basket prepared by Suzanne, Lizzie once again raced through the gardens and whizzed along the track through the vineyards. The grape-laden vines undulated to a lazy rhythm in the soft breeze, and the scorching sun beat down on her forehead.

All the way, she prayed the airman had stabilised, but the sinking feeling she had felt throughout the night remained with her as she entered the cellar and tapped three times on the wall.

CHAPTER 40

Lizzie left the cellars and emerged into the heat, her mood subdued as she made her way back through the vineyards and towards the château. She sat in the shade in her favourite spot beneath an apple tree in the orchard and waited.

Her mind jostled with conflicting thoughts, and she was impatient for Jack to appear so they could talk through the events of the past day. So much had happened during Von Schneider's visit, and Lizzie was worried circumstances were spinning out of control.

Jack waved as he approached, and sat down in the shade next to her, his legs outstretched on the grass. 'What a lovely orchard this is. I think I shall look back and miss our time here.'

Lizzie jerked her head up. 'Why, are we leaving?'

'We have no instructions to leave yet. I was just appreciating the beauty of the château.'

'Yes, and I appreciate it even more now the bloody Boche has left us in peace.'

'Quite,' Jack said, an amused expression on his face as he gazed at her. 'I was afraid he was planning to move in.'

'You haven't asked about Billy.'

Jack's eyes were full of sadness as they met hers. 'I feared the worst after what you said last night. Tell me, darling, did he make it?'

Lizzie reached for Jack's hand. 'He's hanging in there, but the fever hasn't passed, and his wound is still bleeding. I feel so sorry for the other airman too, holed up in there. Do you think we could let him out for some fresh air? I was tempted but with the vineyard labourers milling about, I didn't dare risk it.'

'I feel for him too, but no, you did right. It would endanger everyone here. If the authorities get wind of us harbouring British airmen, retribution will be swift. They will make an example of us. You heard the commissaire talking at dinner about quashing the Resistance and anyone who assists them?'

Lizzie nodded. She had heard him even though she had tried not to. Luc turned pale during the conversation, and, for the first time, she fully appreciated what he was risking to help them with their mission.

'What did Val say?'

'They are sending a plane tonight. She told me to send a separate message with the coordinates of the pickup for extra security, so I'll go back later.'

'Thank goodness Von Schneider didn't ask to stay another night, or we would have had no choice but to cancel it.'

Lizzie perked up at the news. 'I'm so pleased we can get the airmen home. I can only imagine how awful it must be for their families, if they've been advised they are missing in action.'

Lizzie thought of her brother Archie, and Oliver, Juliet's

fiancé, who were both fighting. She shook her head. It didn't help to dwell on her loved ones in danger. Lizzie had learnt soon after the SOE recruited her to use her anguish to fuel her motivation. She didn't want to look back in years to come and regret not doing all she could when she was in a position to make a real difference.

Jack interrupted Lizzie's thoughts. 'Me too. As a plane is coming, I asked for weapons and supplies. We must do all we can to prepare Lev and Marguerite to run an organised Resistance network after we leave.'

'Do you think they are up to the job?' she asked.

Jack lit a cigarette. 'He's obviously a strong character. I'd put money on him being a good leader.'

'And what about Marguerite?'

'Everything she's done so far has been helpful. She's gone out of her way to arrange our meetings with Lev. Without her, we wouldn't have even met him.'

Lizzie agreed with Jack's analysis, but wanted to hear his calculations. 'Why Lev? Could she not be the leader? She is committed, and they have already carried out extensive Resistance activities collaborating with her contact at the border.'

'Yes, that's true. They're a good team. Marguerite is well positioned to gather intelligence at her job at the café, whereas Lev can no longer work as an artisan and is doing his best to avoid forced labour.'

'I didn't know he was an artisan.'

Jack dropped his voice even lower. 'He was before the statutes. I believe he's better positioned to be the official network leader, but Marguerite is a key player, too. We were lucky to find them so soon after we arrived.'

Lizzie frowned. 'I have to say it. What if it's not luck? Even after all this, it may still be a trap. Lev—and even Marguerite—might not be who they say they are. Have you thought of that?' Lizzie asked. 'They could be double agents working with the Vichy regime.'

Jack nodded. 'I considered the risk, of course. It's almost impossible to know for sure who to trust in this melting pot, so I must go with my gut.'

'And your gut still says we can trust them?'

'It does, but logic backs up the feeling. In my experience, you can't fake the pain in Lev's eyes. And meeting Marguerite like we did couldn't have been a setup because even we didn't know which café we would choose on our first visit to the city.'

Lizzie searched Jack's face. 'It's so difficult when every decision is a matter of life and death.'

'Which is why most people aren't cut out for this line of work.'

Lizzie sighed. They would just have to pray they had made the right decision. 'What shall we call the network?'

'I haven't given it any thought. They should name it,' Jack said. 'Our job is to give them the resources to scale up operations so they can get more airmen out and sabotage the Vichy infrastructure that feeds the Nazi war machine.'

Lizzie said, 'I promised the doctor's wife we would help them get out of France. Their granddaughter is well enough to travel now. Could they leave on the plane with the airmen? There are only two adults. It would be tight but doable.'

Jack looked downcast. 'No, I'm afraid not. London would never agree to it, darling.'

'I was afraid you'd say that, but after we took Hannah back with us last time, I thought perhaps we could bend the rules for a good cause.'

'We must apply our resources to prepare the way for the

Allied invasion. Our orders don't include helping Jews escape.'

Lizzie was momentarily taken aback by the harshness of his statement, but then she realised she shouldn't be shocked. Jews, even some who were British born, were routinely interned in Britain and classed as enemy aliens. The British government was paranoid about German spies and no one with any potential connection to Axis powers was safe.

Lizzie didn't approve of the situation, and neither would Hannah, although she wouldn't be surprised. In the past, Val had turned a blind eye to Hannah using British resources to help Jews escape as long as she was an asset to the SOE operations. It was a fair deal, and one Val didn't report upline to their boss, who wasn't as understanding.

As if reading Lizzie's mind, Jack said, 'Val is sympathetic to the plight of the Jews, but the SOE is tangled up in bureaucracy and we can't always act how we might wish. The government hasn't allowed Jewish immigration into Britain since early in the war.'

Lizzie, who thought of Hannah like a sister since their time together in Paris, raged inwardly. 'I understand we must follow our orders, but how will we live with ourselves if we don't do all we can to save everyone who is fleeing from Nazi persecution, not just the lucky few?'

Jack sighed. 'I wish I knew, but war is like a savage game of chess. We can't move all the pieces, or we'll lose focus on winning.'

Lizzie wasn't satisfied with his answer and stared into the distance, wondering what more she could do. It was so long since she'd seen Hannah, and she missed her.

Jack reached for her hand. 'We took a significant number of Jewish children on the Kindertransport programme, who managed to flee Nazi-controlled territories in time.'

Lizzie managed a watery smile. 'Yes, I remember seeing

their lost little faces in the newspapers when they arrived alone in a foreign country without their families. Thank goodness they escaped.'

The figure of a man came into view through the trees, and Jack reached for the gun he kept strapped to his ankle beneath his trousers.

'Do you know him?' Lizzie said, her hand over her eyes, squinting in the sunshine.

The man came closer, and Lizzie saw Jack relax his grip and she looked at him expectantly.

'Look closer,' he said.

'Ah, now I recognise him.'

A thin man wearing a cap set at a jaunty angle and braces over his shirt approached them, the ghost of a smile on his face.

Jack stood, brushing leaves from his trousers, and Lizzie jumped to her feet.

'Lev,' Jack said, shaking his hand vigorously. 'Good to see you. Everything alright?'

Lev enquired about the airmen, and told them their contact was on their way to Toulouse.

They walked through the orchard, and Lizzie and Jack updated Lev on the grave condition of the wounded airman and how they planned to evacuate him that night.

'I see, so it's a wasted journey for our contact to come all the way here.'

'I'm afraid so,' Jack said.

Lizzie said it wouldn't be a wasted journey if they smuggled the Jewish doctor and his family to the border in place of the airmen. She explained they were waiting for a chance to escape, and Lev said he would pass on the message.

'Have you met the St. Girons contact before?' Jack asked.

Lev replied this would be the first time. Marguerite had handled the communications side of things.

'I've requested equipment like we discussed,' Jack continued.

'That is good news. If we're to make our operations more effective, we're going to need regular supplies.'

They talked about future potential targets and Lev said perhaps it was for the best the agent was coming. 'Shall I arrange a meeting with you, and we can plan a smoother passage for future escapees? The airman probably wouldn't have been wounded if we had more safe houses along the way and they hadn't been forced to rest in someone's barn.'

Lizzie could see Jack was pondering whether it was wise to meet with another unknown contact. It could be a trap. Undercover work was draining in that one never knew who to trust.

Jack looked at Lizzie. He was her commanding officer, but he often conferred with her. She gave a slight nod.

'Yes, let's do it. Anything that will build a strong foundation for the network is worth the risk. What time shall we meet?'

Lev said he would get a message to them if the contact arrived before nightfall, and they agreed he would come back that night to help move the wounded airman to the pickup spot and hide the equipment.

CHAPTER 41

Von Schneider had left for Paris and Armand breathed a sigh of relief at the station. On the drive back to the Legion, he kept turning over the details of his night at the château. The sense that all wasn't quite what it seemed hit him again after his visit to the turret. The housekeeper racing around outside at night, the young couple who had arrived at the château out of the blue in wartime, and the mysterious key.

What were they up to?

Armand turned over the events in his mind as he drove, and his thoughts predictably circled back to Michel Dubois. Much to his disappointment, he had only seen him briefly that morning. His French was exquisite, and he was Luc's relative from Brittany, so why did he have the nagging feeling he was missing something?

His preoccupation with Michel Dubois had become an obsession, and he had meant to begin surveillance of the couple, but unfortunately was too busy with official duties to follow them. Now he would begin in earnest. Even if the couple were innocent, the housekeeper was definitely up to no good.

He eased the vehicle into the Legion car park and patted his pocket for the key he had stolen from the turret room. Stolen was such an ugly word, he reasoned. Confiscated was more fitting. It was, after all, his duty to be vigilant in all matters concerning potential enemies of the state, and he took the commitment seriously.

Armand raised his head as he walked as if marching in an imaginary honours' parade, where he would be commended for his service. As he turned the corner and approached the door, he saw a woman hovering outside.

She rushed forward at the sight of him. 'Good morning, Monsieur Abadie, I have important information for you.'

'You bother me on a Sunday? It must be urgent,' he said, huffing. Armand had fallen into the habit of coming into his office on Sundays because he had the place to himself. The others were with their families and not being a family man and not having close friends, he found Sundays dull. Instead of sitting at home alone, he would come in and study his suspect notebook and check out the informer notes he had collated during the week. Now this woman had interrupted his reflection time, and it irritated him.

'Forgive the intrusion, I would not have come if it wasn't important,' she said, touching the brim of her hat with a nervous gesture.

'Very well, you'd better come in,' Armand said, and she followed him inside. It was a sultry morning and his office was humid.

'Take a seat, madame.' Armand waved at the chair on the other side of his desk. He extracted his notebook, and with the solemnity of a detective, he opened it and located the page marked with the informant's name. 'Here you are. Last time we spoke, you agreed to bring me information about anyone suspicious frequenting your shop in the village.'

The woman nodded.

'What do you wish to tell me?' Armand waited, his pen poised, hoping it was something worthwhile and not the usual dreary nonsense people came to him with, hoping in exchange to get preferential treatment and extra rations.

'It's about the man you asked me to keep an eye out for.'

Armand's head snapped up. Now she had his full attention. 'Go on,' he said, his tone commanding.

'I knew I'd seen him before and was trying to think where I recognised him from,' said the woman slowly, relishing the telling of her tale.

Armand clicked his tongued. 'Yes, and presumably now you know?'

She raised her face to the ceiling as she spoke, as though acting out the revelation. 'It came to me in the middle of the night.'

'Yes, yes,' said Armand. 'I don't have all day, madame, please get to the point.'

The woman's lips pursed, and lines of annoyance creased her brow. 'Well, you see, the man is the spitting image of Monsieur Saint-Clair's nephew, who used to spend summers at the château. It must be at least twenty years since I saw him last. He and his brother used to buy sweets in our shop. Well, it was my father's shop then, God rest his soul.

Anyway, a few days ago, he came in for cigarettes. It took me ages to place him, but I'd know his eyes anywhere. They're so dark, they're almost black. He's grown into such a handsome man. Mind you, they were good-looking boys then too. Us village girls used to trail about after them. Quite a stir they caused, but they kept themselves to themselves. You know what those posh types are like.'

Armand sighed. The woman was determined to draw the story out. 'I fail to see why this concerns me. A handsome boy with dark eyes visited every summer aeons ago, so presumably dark eyes run in the family. But the man I want information about isn't Monsieur Saint-Clair's nephew. He's a distant relative from St. Malo.'

'I haven't got to the best bit yet,' the woman said, clutching her handbag and staring at him with her chin thrust out. 'What do I get when I tell you what you want to know?'

These informants were all the same. All they cared about were their own selfish desires. Armand couldn't resist taunting her. 'But madame, is being of service to France and a thank you from the government not enough to satisfy you?'

She shook her head. 'No, monsieur. A thank you, whilst pleasant, won't put food in my belly.'

'Very well, so it's food you want?'

'Triple rations and increased supplies for my shop,' she said, a cunning expression on her face, as though she knew she'd got him.

Armand reined his irritation in, eager to hear what information she had about Luc's relative she deemed so important that he would reward her so generously.

'Done. As long as the information pertains to the man in question and is not just village gossip from when you were a girl. There is, after all, nothing sinister in Luc Saint-Clair having hosted his nephews for the summer.'

'I haven't made myself clear,' she said, her eyes gleaming.

'Now is your moment, madame. Please reveal what you know and let us both get on with our day.'

'A glass of something strong might help me recall the details in sharper focus,' she said.

Armand groaned, before turning to a tray on the sideboard where he kept a bottle of brandy. He poured the amber liquid into two glasses and passed one to the informant.

She drained it in one shot and resumed talking. 'The boys were Monsieur Luc's sister's sons. To my knowledge, the family would travel from England every summer to stay at the château. She and her husband had emigrated there, you see, and the boys were born in London and grew up there.' Now the woman leaned back in the chair, looking pleased with herself.

'I still don't see how this applies to the distant relative and his wife. Are you saying he is directly related to the English boys?'

The woman licked her lips and pushed her glass forward on the desk for a top up. When Armand followed her cue, she took a sip and then paused dramatically.

'What I'm saying is he is not a distant relative from St. Malo. He is Monsieur Luc's nephew.'

Armand blinked as his thoughts whirled and the significance of this detail shifted his chess pieces around the board until he could see how he would move to a checkmate. 'If this is true, it changes everything, madame.'

'It's true,' she said, sounding smug. 'The father had some kind of factory in London, but I remember hearing he died quite young. There was gossip in the village, and if my memory serves me correctly, that's around the time when they stopped visiting.'

Armand slugged down the rest of his brandy, his heart beating fast with the thrill of victory in his sights. Finally, his initiative would pay off handsomely.

'And you are quite certain this man, Michel Dubois, is Luc's nephew?'

'I am. As I said, it's those eyes. I would know them anywhere.'

'Then, madame, we have British spies lording it up at the château, right under our noses!'

Now the woman looked jubilant. 'I'm happy I could be of service. Is there anything else you would like me to do?'

Armand thought for a minute. Von Schneider was well on his way to Paris by now. The commissaire would spend the day with his family. Soon Armand's delusions of grandeur gripped him as he imagined the glory of orchestrating this great arrest himself.

He could imagine the newspaper headlines now: *British spies captured single handedly by Armand Abadie, a distinguished war veteran.*

There was a glow in his chest as he fantasised about the promotion and recognition that would surely be his. He would be a hero in France, and everyone would know his name.

He pictured the mortification on the commissaire and the Gestapo officer's faces when they learnt they had been so easily fooled by British spies. The commissaire had dinner with the couple twice and presumably didn't suspect a thing! What an embarrassment for the Vichy police. And the Gestapo, the infamous political police force whose speciality it was to spot signs of opposition and resistance to Nazi rule.

A beatific smile spread across Armand's face as he contemplated the extent of his superiors' failure. If he pulled off the capture of the British spies, this would be proof for all to see that he deserved a promotion to the top of the Legion. Once there, it was just a few stepping stones to being recognised by the Reich.

'Monsieur,' the woman interrupted his thoughts, snapping him back to reality. 'What would you have me do next?'

Armand lit a cigarette and inhaled deeply. 'Nothing. Don't tell anyone what you told me. And I mean *anyone.* This must remain a secret just between you and me, or we will lose the element of surprise. You have done well and will be rewarded appropriately. Thank you, madame.'

The woman insisted on his authorising her reward on the spot, and he did so quickly to get rid of her. Once she had left, he put his feet up on the desk, poured himself another large brandy, and began planning exactly how he would capture the British spies in action.

CHAPTER 42

The hands on the clock crawled by as Lizzie and Jack waited for the pickup that night. Lizzie was always uptight when she had a rendezvous with a British plane, whether to take her home at the end of a mission or drop in equipment. There was so much that could go wrong and the implications of being caught were terrifying for all involved. The responsibility of knowing their actions affected Luc and all the residents of the château and perhaps even the village, weighed heavily on her conscience.

Lizzie's nerves were on edge as they waited for news of Marguerite's contact. There would not be time to go into the city to meet them if they didn't receive a note soon.

Jack had been to the cellars and checked on the airmen. He returned an hour later, and Lizzie could see by his expression that the situation had not improved.

'He's hanging on by a thread,' Jack told Lizzie when he found her sitting on the sofa, reading a book from Luc's extensive library, with all the windows wide open.

'It's a miracle he's made it this long.'

'Any word from Marguerite?' he asked.

'Nothing yet,' she said. 'I feel so impotent, waiting around like this when so much is at stake.'

'By dawn, this should all be over. The airman will be on his way to hospital, the doctor and his family on their way to St. Girons, and we can make plans to escalate operations. I've been thinking we only need a couple more weeks to get Lev up to speed, and we can go home.'

'That makes me happy and sad simultaneously,' Lizzie said. 'I love it here. I love living with you as my husband, but I also miss my family. Hopefully, they received a postcard by now to let them know I'm well.'

Jack stroked Lizzie's cheek. 'They will have done. Val takes keeping agents' families updated very seriously.'

'What am I supposed to be doing again?' Lizzie pulled a comical face. 'Oh yes, I remember. I'm working in Oxford.'

'My darling wife. I dread living apart from you. I've grown so used to being with you almost every minute of the day, and us falling asleep and waking up together.'

'Me too,' Lizzie said, moving to sit on his knee and running her fingers through his hair. 'Being demoted to plain old Lizzie Beaumont instead of your wife, Isabelle Dubois, won't suit me at all.'

'There's nothing plain about you, whatever name you use. Did you notice how infatuated that bloody Nazi was with you? I thought he was going to claim you as the property of the Reich!'

Lizzie rolled her eyes. 'He did seem rather smitten, which is odd when I did everything I could to discourage him.'

'That probably only added to the attraction.' Jack trailed his fingers along the sensitive skin of her arm, and her body responded instantly to his touch. Their lips touched and the heat between them ignited into a blaze as their kiss deepened and they were lost in each other. Their urgent need chased away all worries of airmen, Jewish escapees, and Resistance operations.

There was a light tap at the door. Lizzie jumped guiltily out of habit from their stolen moments in London. 'Who can that be?'

'I'll find out.' Jack slid Lizzie gently back onto the sofa and crossed the room. After a few muttered words Lizzie couldn't decipher, he returned and handed her an envelope. 'From Marguerite?'

Lizzie tore the envelope open and extracted the folded note. She read aloud in a hushed tone:

My dearest Isabelle,

My good friend wishes to have the pleasure of meeting you. I shall bring him for drinks tonight.

Sincerely,

Marguerite

'Sounds like they mean to bring the contact to meet us at the pickup,' Jack said.

Lizzie sighed. 'I suppose that's the end of our leisurely afternoon. We'd better think through our plans for later.'

Jack smiled wryly. 'I did warn you being involved with another agent was off-limits for this very reason …'

'You did. I'm not involved with *another* agent, though. I'm involved with you! And, Captain King, let me assure you, I have no regrets.'

'That's good to hear, Seagrove. I wouldn't have it any other way.'

'I admit, when you told me we'd undertake this mission together and stay in a château in the South of France, I harboured a romantic vision of us wandering through the vineyards hand in hand and making love on a blanket every afternoon, sipping the latest château vintage.'

Jack's laugh rumbled across the large room. 'Well, we managed a few romantic picnics before things started kicking off. Since then, it's been impossible to grab a quiet moment, what with the head of police and the Gestapo in the house and fugitives in the cellars.'

Lizzie reached on tiptoe to kiss him. 'You're right, though. Things should quieten down after tonight and we will have some time alone in between training our recruits and getting the network running smoothly.'

'I hope so. By the way, there was something odd about the turret room yesterday,' said Jack.

'What?'

'There was a smell, like someone had been up there.'

Lizzie whispered, 'You don't think they found our equipment?'

'The radio was untouched. I always leave a thread across the top when I put it away. It hadn't fallen, but the rug had changed position slightly.'

'Why didn't you say something?'

'I didn't see any point in worrying you last night. I thought a housemaid probably moved the rug, and the fragrance was theirs, or perhaps the scent of lavender wafted in the window. But this morning I swear it was the same scent on Von Schneider's driver. His cologne smelled just like it. You know that angry looking little man with the limp?'

'Yes, but why would he have been in the turret room?' Lizzie asked.

'My guess is he was poking around for his Gestapo paymaster.'

'Makes sense. He might have had orders to take advantage of the opportunity. Von Schneider is from the secret police.

But if the driver had found anything, surely, we wouldn't have had such an amiable farewell and would have been marched off for questioning.'

'My thoughts exactly. We're safe, darling, for now. But if that little snitch comes over again, let's make sure we have eyes on him.'

'I saw him looking at you. It was weird. I can't put my finger on why.'

They agreed to watch out for him and then launched into fine-tuning plans for the pickup. It had a lot of moving parts, and one wrong decision could be fatal.

Dinner was a quiet affair. Luc, Jack and Lizzie were pleased to be alone again. They discussed the night's plans in coded language and muted tones on the terrace, and in an unexpected sentimental moment, Luc hugged each of them tightly when it was time to retire to their rooms.

'Good luck,' he said, his eyes glistening. 'Both of you are a credit to the family, and to France. When I see my sister again, I shall tell her so.'

'We will see you at breakfast, Luc,' Lizzie said, patting his hand, emotion swelling in her chest. He was such a dear man and had welcomed her into the family from the moment they arrived. She would miss him when it came time to leave.

They only ever talked about after the war, as if winning was a foregone conclusion. Jack had taught her that in the early days. He said there was no room for doubt. They must hold the vision of winning in their minds at all times, or they may as well give up now.

It was clear Luc understood the great danger they would be in that night, taking the airmen to the British aircraft. If they were caught, they would be shot as traitors, probably in the Place du Capitole, but only after they were interrogated and tortured to extract their secrets.

Luc had volunteered repeatedly to come along and assist

them, but Jack told him he would be the most useful staying in the château. If things went wrong, he should deny all knowledge of their activities. That way, there was a chance the residents of the château wouldn't be accused of being complicit.

If Luc were caught red-handed with them, it would be the end of the Saint-Clair family legacy.

CHAPTER 43

Lizzie tied her yellow silk scarf around her neck and examined her reflection in the mirror. If they ever needed good luck, it would be tonight. Lizzie saw her cheeks were flushed, and her green eyes shone, giving her a slightly manic look.

Jack's tall reflection appeared in the mirror beside her, and he rested his hands on her shoulders. 'Ready, Seagrove?'

She nodded. 'Ready, Raven.'

Using their official code names helped them click into mission mode. Tonight was their most dangerous operation since arriving in Toulouse. They must lay the foundation for the new network, and tonight's events would serve many purposes.

They would receive the first drop from the SOE, the airmen would vanish from right under the noses of the Vichy regime, and they would work hand in hand with the nominated new leader, Lev, and his key people, Marguerite and the contact from St. Girons.

The château was in darkness and all the shutters firmly

closed when Lizzie and Jack crept out of the kitchen door into the warm night. Lizzie wore an old dress and scruffy sandals she'd borrowed from Suzanne, and Jack wore the clothes of a labourer with braces and a cap on his head, Lev style. That way, if they were spotted after curfew, they could pretend they were casual summer labourers sleeping in the vineyards.

The waxing grey moon floated in the black sky, which was decorated by a smattering of glowing stars. Jack lit their way with his torch, and they took careful steps across the uneven ground, and Lizzie felt her chest thud in time with her feet.

'It's not an ideal night for a pickup.' Jack glanced up at the sky.

'I wondered about landing in conditions like these. They usually come on a full moon.'

'That's ideal, but as you see, solar movements don't always correspond with the urgency on the ground.'

When they entered the shadowy vineyards, Lizzie said, 'It's spooky with the vines swaying like that.'

Jack shone his torch in front of her so she could see more clearly.

'Ouch!' Lizzie squealed.

Jack reached for his gun and spun around, ready to pounce into action. 'What?'

'Oh, sorry, it's nothing. A branch grazed my arm, that's all.'

'Take a deep breath and stay calm. It's all okay. No one knows we're here,' Jack said.

Lizzie breathed deeply. On previous missions, she'd been out every day on undercover work, and it had built up her endurance. This time, she'd become too relaxed at the château, waiting to respond to events. Living amongst enemies and integrating in the local community was a different kind of spycraft. Another time, on this type of mission, she would know what to expect.

Dry twigs snapped beneath their feet as they walked, and Lizzie's senses were heightened as they approached the cellars. There were so many pieces to the operation. First, they must extract the wounded airman from the cellar and get him to the meadow on the other side of the vineyards.

As they reached the cellar entrance, three hazy figures stepped out from the shadows of a copse of olive trees. Lizzie recognised Lev and Marguerite, and presumed the third was from St. Girons.

In the pale, ghostly light, Lizzie squinted and saw a man with black hair, dressed similarly to Lev. He was about Marguerite's height, a good head shorter than Lev and Jack.

Marguerite moved towards them and said in a hushed voice. 'Meet my friend, Angel, who has been helping us get our people out.'

Lizzie's jaw hung open as she stared. She saw the recognition dawn in the new arrival's eyes.

'I should have known it would be you!' Lizzie gasped.

Then they flew into each other's arms, squeezing so hard they took their breath away.

'Me too!'

Jack stared at them, his mouth curving into a smile. 'Angel!'

Then Jack put his arms around them both and they all hugged, overjoyed to be reunited.

'It's so good to see you. What a surprise. It didn't even cross my mind it would be you two,' Hannah said.

Lizzie noticed Lev and Marguerite looked baffled.

Marguerite said. 'What are we missing? How do you three know each other?'

'Let's just say we are old friends. You couldn't have recruited anyone better,' Lizzie said.

Lev, who had been silent until now, stepped closer. 'It was more the other way around. Angel recruited us.'

'None of us can do this alone,' Hannah said.

Lev replied, 'It seems your reputation precedes you.'

They huddled together talking in whispers, Lizzie elated to see Hannah again so unexpectedly.

Jack said, 'Sorry to be a killjoy, but we must press on. There will be plenty of time to catch up properly in the morning when this is all over.'

They entered the pitch-black cellar with only a lantern. It wouldn't do for a trace of light to filter into the valley at this hour.

Lizzie and Hannah held hands, which spoke volumes in the silence. Jack and Lev uncovered the entrance to the concealed room, and they slipped inside one by one. The small room was dimly lit, and a sniffle met their ears. A silhouette hunched on an upside-down crate next to a mattress, his head in his hands, making whimpering sounds of quiet desperation.

'Oh my God, what happened?' Lizzie asked.

The airman raised his tear-stained face. 'Poor Billy was in a terrible state all day. I tried to get him to hang on for tonight. I promised we would get him home to his family, but just before eleven he slipped away.'

Jack bent over the deceased airman and gently touched his forehead and closed his eyes. 'May he rest in peace.'

'I failed him,' his friend said, his voice breaking. 'His wife recently gave birth to a new baby, you know. He never even got to see his son.'

Lizzie moved towards the distraught airman, who was a hero in the Battle of Britain, but was crushed by the death of his brother in arms.

'It's not your fault. You did all you could,' Lizzie said, soothing him. 'He lost too much blood; you heard the doctor.'

It was hard to watch a grown man, especially a war hero, weep, but she understood the impersonal nature of war. Eliminating the enemy was something they did by rote, without feeling. If they let themselves feel every time they killed an opponent, they wouldn't be able to function. But to lose a dear friend made it all too real.

Lizzie prayed for the airman's soul, and for his friend, and she prayed she would never witness one of her loved ones die in such a wretched way, unable to save them because they couldn't get the care they needed.

So far, she had been lucky, and Lizzie touched her yellow scarf. It was best not to think about it. Most SOE agents who had been recruited since she joined at the inception of the organisation created on Churchill's orders to wreak havoc on the enemy didn't survive more than six weeks. Lizzie read the reports in London, and although she and Jack rarely talked about the high mortality rate, it was ever-present in their thoughts. They were both fully aware of the price on their heads every time either of them went undercover.

'Where shall we bury him?' Hannah asked. Her voice belied her formidable male disguise. Lizzie stared at her. Her blonde hair and eyebrows were dyed black. And her breasts were invisible beneath her shirt. Lizzie remembered how she had bound her chest during their mission in Paris when she first saw her pretend to be a man. Hannah was an expert at disguise and Lizzie learnt a lot from her.

The airman's voice interrupted Lizzie's thoughts. 'We must take him home. That's the only thing we can do to honour his and his family's sacrifice.'

Jack said, 'Absolutely, but he will not be easy to carry and the plane is due in around thirty minutes. We'd better get going.'

A heavy silence fell as they wrapped the fallen airman in a blanket and between them lifted his deadweight. They carried him out of the dark cellar which had served as his tomb, and into the watery moonlight. The only sounds were the buzzing of insects and rustling of creatures who came to life at night.

It was fortunate they were many hands because they were all breathing hard as they navigated the craggy path through the sloping vineyards. Holding their solemn burden, they trudged into the meadow Luc had advised them to use for the assignation with the British plane.

They laid the body down carefully on the grass and waited for the pickup, as they caught their breath. Lizzie thought of the pilot and navigator who would find themselves transporting the fallen airman home, instead of rescuing two heroes. Lizzie sighed. Such was war. There was no escaping tragedy, and it found them at every turn, usually when they least expected it.

CHAPTER 44

Armand crouched by the hedge on the road by the lavender field, all his senses alert as he watched and waited in the darkness. The road looped around the outskirts of the château grounds and, after poring over maps and intercepting a coded message, he had discovered this was the designated pickup spot for the British spies.

It wasn't certain the rendezvous was scheduled for tonight, but he would return every night until they appeared. He had dragged a Vichy radio specialist away from dining with his family and ordered him to make sense of the coordinates and decode the message.

By cross-referencing the coordinates with the map, the disgruntled Legion member had presented him with this location. Armand refused to enlighten him when he asked for more details and, fortunately, the man was keen to return home and didn't press.

Armand was determined to claim the hard-won victory for himself. When his colleague parasites were taking it easy, he was working around the clock to save his country.

His leg throbbed in the uncomfortable position, but the pain was merely a niggle in the grand scheme of things. His thoughts were firmly set on the success that was now within his grasp. Thank goodness the informant had told him about the British spies when she did, or he would have missed his time to shine.

The first thing he did when he discovered spies were operating in his backyard was grab a wireless set from the Legion and hole up at home.

Living at the top of his apartment building was finally to his advantage. Armand had brewed a fresh pot of coffee and organised a space at the table in the kitchen. The experts at Gestapo HQ on his course in Paris had taught him how to operate a radio and to intercept enemy messages. All afternoon he listened and by early evening he was growing weary and discouraged.

What if the spies had a secure line he couldn't tune into with any of his Gestapo tricks? He continued fiddling with the radio and found various channels. Armand was not a man who gave up easily. He heard snippets of German army talk, channels with crackling and hissing on the airwaves, and a British news broadcast that almost sent him to sleep. But still, he didn't give up. He had a feeling something was going to happen.

The static caused interference, but when a transmission that met the criteria of a spy message started coming through, Armand was ready. He scrawled down all he could. It was a brief message and most of it went over his head. All he could deduce was a set of numbers and a few words.

He knew from his training, in such messages, a contact in England would give a Tommy spy coordinates to meet a plane, or the spy would instruct his handler where to land.

By now, Armand's face was almost purple, and he was breathless with excitement as he overlooked the meadow, waiting to catch his prey. The rendezvous was planned for 1 a.m., but the radio expert couldn't confirm on which night from the limited information.

Armand heard murmurs in the distance. Tonight was the night. He drew his gun, and his pulse raced.

Perhaps the couple planned to return to England, but they had not bargained on an opponent of his calibre. Armand had considered bringing backup, but he estimated he could overcome the husband with the element of surprise, and his silly wife would be no match for his military prowess.

He was surprised when he saw several of them approach, but rather than leave because he was outnumbered, his vision only grew more grandiose. He couldn't make out the figures clearly, but he heard female voices. The sound of a plane hummed overhead, and he remained motionless, like a tiger waiting to pounce.

He realised he had infiltrated a full-scale Resistance cell, not just stumbled on a couple during a mission, as he had assumed. Armand quickly adjusted his plan, which had been to capture and present the couple to the police with their hands bound, ready for interrogation.

Instead, he would dismantle the cell and if a few of the traitors must die, so be it. As long as some remained alive, they could extract the information they needed to lead them to others in their treasonous network. What a prize he would give his country—he would be celebrated throughout all of France.

CHAPTER 45

Lizzie and Hannah stood side by side, heads together, whispering as they crammed in as many words as they could until they must inevitably part again.

'When will you set off?' Lizzie asked.

'There's no time to waste. Marguerite told me about the doctor and his family. We'll leave tomorrow as soon as we can get them out of the village without arousing suspicion.'

'I'm so glad. They are good people. The doctor did everything he could for the airman.' Lizzie shook her head and smiled. 'I still can't believe we didn't guess it was you creating an escape route across the Pyrenees. A daring operation like that has your name written all over it!'

'I couldn't use Paris as a base after our last operation, so I got organised to help Jews who had fled south. And others who wanted to escape.'

'Why the male disguise?' Lizzie asked.

'I've found it simpler in this line of work. I sneak across the demarcation lines into occupied territory regularly, passing as a labourer.'

Lizzie glanced at Jack and saw he was in deep conversation with the airman, who was more composed now.

'So, you know our man from St. Girons,' Lev said, approaching them, a smile reaching his eyes.

Lizzie laughed.

'Today was the first time we met,' he said, gazing at Hannah. 'Michel asked me to name our network. Angel is joining forces with us officially and we decided to call it the Lavender Network.'

Lizzie looked from one to the other and got the peculiar feeling this was the start of something monumental.

There was a distant hum on the breeze, and they looked upwards.

'Here they come,' Jack said. 'Everyone in position.'

They retrieved their torches and stood in formation so the approaching plane could see the lights and know where to land.

The hum of the plane grew louder, and Lizzie prayed the château residents couldn't hear it, or they would have some explaining to do in the morning. Packages tumbled from the sky in quick succession, thumping the ground, and soon the Lysander was flying low, until its wheels skimmed the grass and bounced to a standstill near the Lavender Network's first reception committee.

Lizzie held her breath. The navigator appeared at the rear door and Jack ran over with Lev to greet him and explain the situation. Jack was training Lev on the job so he would be ready to organise the drops once they returned to London.

They went back to get Billy's lifeless body and carried him towards the tiny plane. Once the two airmen were aboard, the navigator signalled they would take off shortly. British planes only touched down in emergencies such as this, and never stayed more than a few minutes because it was far too risky.

Just as the navigator was about to close the hatch, a bullet whistled past Lizzie.

'Get down,' Jack said, his voice sounding odd.

As if in slow motion, Lizzie watched Jack return fire into the shadows. She drew her gun and threw herself down on the grass as she searched for their attacker. 'What's going on?' she hissed.

By now, Hannah, Lev and Marguerite were all in position, weapons poised, searching for the invisible target.

Another volley of bullets ricocheted off the plane as the engine thrummed for lift off.

'Hold fire,' Jack commanded.

Lizzie guessed he didn't want them all shooting because they would make so much noise. They didn't have silencers on their guns.

She moved closer to Jack. 'Were you hit?'

'It's nothing,' he whispered.

Lizzie saw blood seeping through his shirt and fear shook her. 'It's not nothing.'

Jack didn't move from his position out in front.

'Signal the navigator to wait, so you can board the plane and return home,' Lizzie said, dread clutching at every fibre of her being. 'You need treatment, and you can't get it here.'

'Cover me,' Jack said, his voice strangled as he moved towards the bushes where the shots had come from. 'Stay back with the others, Seagrove. That's an order.'

Lizzie was conflicted. She was terrified Jack had received a mortal wound, but disobeying orders and displaying erratic behaviour in the heat of battle could endanger them all.

More shots rang out. Jack stumbled and he released a groan that turned her nerves to ice.

Lizzie made a snap decision. 'Get down, Raven. I'm taking over as second in command.'

A hazy figure holding a gun appeared at the edge of the

meadow. A cold fury swept over Lizzie, and she strode towards Jack's attacker, firing at him with every step. Suddenly, the assailant was in front of her, his face shrouded in darkness, and she emptied bullets into him with no hesitation. It was as if someone else had taken over Lizzie's body and was doing the shooting.

Lizzie watched the man lurch and then tumble to the ground, clutching his chest. His head lay at an unnatural angle on the ground as blood trickled from his lips.

The metallic song of the Lysander's propellers caught Lizzie's attention, and she signalled to the plane. With every passing second, staying on enemy soil grew more dangerous, but things had already gone sour. She was determined Jack would be on the plane and not end up like poor Billy.

The navigator waved to confirm he'd understood, and the propellers and the engine noise lessened slightly.

Lizzie's gun was still trained on the edge of the meadow, but no one else emerged. After several moments, she calculated the assailant had been a lone shooter or they would be surrounded by now. She issued orders to the others to check no one was lying in wait, ready to attack, when they turned their backs.

She kneeled next to the man, who was wheezing and whining like a dying animal.

Jack approached, his shirt dripping with blood. 'Good job, Seagrove.'

'Is it your shoulder?' Lizzie took a sharp intake of breath to calm herself. Her voice was strained and his praise barely registered as she prayed silently that the shooter hadn't hit a vital organ.

'I'll be fine. It's a flesh wound, that's all.'

Lizzie breathed properly for the first time since he'd been shot.

'Who have we here?' Jack said.

When they leaned over and saw the assailant's face, in the light of the torch, Lizzie and Jack recognised him instantly as Von Schneider's driver, his features now distorted in agony.

Lizzie pulled off her yellow scarf in one sharp movement and tied it around Jack's shoulder over the torn, blood-stained shirt. 'Press this to it until you board the plane, and they can bandage you properly.'

'Yes, miss,' Jack replied, a sardonic smile on his lips.

Lizzie rifled through the pockets of the man's military tunic and withdrew a wad of money, a large ornate key, a gold pocket watch and a slim notebook. She shone the torch onto the pages and scanned the text as she read aloud. 'It looks like a list of names of informants and notes.'

Jack peered over her shoulder as she ran her finger down the names until it hovered over Michel and Isabelle Dubois, which was the most recent entry. Beside it were the scrawled words: *Luc Saint-Clair's nephew visited every summer. From London.*

There was a woman's name next to theirs, listed as the informant.

Jack let out a low whistle.

'He was well and truly onto us,' Lizzie said.

The man shifted on the ground and mouthed something. Lizzie leaned over to catch his laboured words.

'You've lost the war,' he gasped.

Armand released one final ragged breath as the life shuddered from his body. Then his eyes glazed over like a curtain closing after the last encore.

A vision of Abraham, the Jewish soldier he had executed in a trench in the Great War, before stealing his gold pocket watch, haunted him in his last second of consciousness and accompanied him straight to the gates of hell.

CHAPTER 46

Jack turned to Lizzie as the navigator waved again. 'We can't make them wait any longer.'

'You're injured and need treatment,' Lizzie said. 'Please go with them.'

'I'm not leaving you here,' Jack replied, his tone resolute.

'But if I leave with you, who will clean up this mess? There are too many loose ends that point to Luc.'

Lev and Hannah reappeared and walked towards them. 'We've searched the area, and it's all clear. He must have acted as a lone wolf.'

Hannah pointed to the blood on Jack's shirt. 'How are you holding up, Raven?'

Jack said he was fine, but his skin had a sickly pallor, and Lizzie's panic grew as she studied his face.

'He should leave on the plane and get treatment. He's been hit in the shoulder,' she said.

Hannah nodded and exchanged a meaningful look with Lev.

Lev said, 'You two have done what you needed to do. Get out whilst you can, and we'll finish up here.'

Lizzie said, 'I will stay, but Raven must leave.'

The sound of the Lysander's engine whirred louder and Lizzie knew time was running out. They must decide now.

'Let's both go. They can clean up without us if we give them proper instructions,' Jack said.

Lizzie considered leaving with him. What he said about the network made sense. Hannah was there and they could handle it, but she wasn't certain she could get Jack to leave if she didn't go too. She nodded.

Jack stepped forward and clapped Lev on the back with his good arm. 'We will both leave. You are the leader of the network and you're right. Our time is up here.'

They agreed on the steps they must take immediately to keep Luc and the château residents safe. Lev, Hannah, and Marguerite nodded as Jack listed what they had to do.

Lizzie said, 'There's also a radio set hidden in a secret compartment in the floor of the turret room at the château. Tell Luc we said you should take it. Oh, and please give him our love.'

Lizzie and Hannah hugged fiercely, and their eyes were wet as they parted. The familiar scent of lavender pervaded the cool night air as they all said goodbye and wished each other good luck, knowing they may never see one another again.

Lev said, 'Thank you for all you've done. And to think I nearly didn't trust you.'

Emotion bubbled in Lizzie's chest when she saw Lev was deeply moved.

Jack said, 'We all had to take a chance on each other. And thank goodness we did.' He patted Lev on the shoulder. 'Message as soon as it's done.'

'We will,' Lev said.

As the plane took off, bouncing across the grass, Lizzie

waved to the members of the Lavender Network until they disappeared from view.

Then she doused Jack's wound with alcohol and bandaged his shoulder with firm movements.

He winced. 'Ouch. That hurts like hell.'

'Oh, don't be a baby,' Lizzie scolded. 'It's better than bleeding to death.'

'I can't argue with that, but your bedside manner could do with some work,' he said, raising one eyebrow.

Lizzie laughed and relief spiralled through her. If Jack had that much attitude, he couldn't be in too bad a state.

'Looks like your scarf has seen its last outing. That blood won't come out,' Jack said. 'Sorry about that.'

'Never mind. That's what lucky scarves are for.'

They sat in silence as the plane climbed higher into French skies and only when they crossed the Channel did Lizzie relax.

Jack said, 'If there was more space, we could have brought the driver's body with us and disposed of the evidence that way.'

It was a tight squeeze already, with the airman's body wrapped in the blanket on a shelf at the rear and the other airman perched next to him like a guardian angel. Lizzie and Jack were wedged on the hard bench.

'There literally isn't room for another soul!' Lizzie said. 'How will they hide his body, though?'

'Lev will handle it. They'll bury him somewhere out of the way. He said he knows the woods well.'

'And what about the informant? She will be a threat when she realises he has disappeared.'

'The network will eliminate her. There's no other way to protect Luc, and it's dangerous to leave informants in play, anyway.'

Lizzie nodded. 'The network is being baptised by fire.'

'It's the best way to learn. They have Hannah with them for now and she knows what to do.'

'It was incredible seeing her. I'm sorry we won't wake up at the château tomorrow. Dear Luc will expect us at breakfast. And our sudden disappearance will be suspicious,' Lizzie said, sadness ringing in her voice.

'It's a shame, but Marguerite promised to get a message to him to let him know we're safe but had to leave. Luc is quick-witted. He'll say we were called away on urgent family business.'

'I wish we could have said a proper goodbye. The last thing I expected was to be leaving tonight. It's just as well we hugged after dinner.'

'Yes, it was almost as if he had a premonition.'

The plane whirred through the sky towards its destination. Lizzie was exhausted but too on edge to fall asleep. Jack dozed on her shoulder after a swig of whisky from the navigator's flask. She glanced out the window as first light broke and gasped in awe when the dome of St. Paul's Cathedral etched against the pink dawn sky like a welcoming talisman came into view.

Jack winced and opened his eyes. 'Where are we?'

'Look,' Lizzie said, pointing to the skyline. 'We're flying over London.'

'Welcome home to Blighty, darling,' Jack said, taking Lizzie's hand.

Lizzie looked over at the airman, who had nodded off, his head bumping against the panel. 'We had a successful mission, but my heart hurts for them.'

Jack's gaze followed hers. 'It could have been even worse. At least one of them is alive and will go home to his family.'

'What about Billy? Who will break the news to his poor wife?'

'The RAF will notify her and arrange the funeral. He'll be

buried with full military honours after being missing in action for weeks. We are bringing his body home, and she can mourn him. Too many of our boys have fallen in foreign fields and lie in unmarked graves. Billy's death is a tragic loss of life, but at least they can have a proper burial.'

They reverted to silence, immersed in their own thoughts of the horrific price of war and another grieving widow and fatherless child.

CHAPTER 47

London, June 1941

Jack cursed under his breath as he shifted against the pillows on the hospital bed. When he settled, he said to Lizzie, 'Do you think it will be a smooth collaboration between Lev and Hannah?'

'I'd say so. Did you not notice how mesmerised he was by her?'

'No, I can't say I did, but I hope they will make a good team.'

Lizzie laughed. 'Everyone's mesmerised by Hannah.'

'That's true,' Jack said. 'Although you thought I was besotted with her when we first met. Lev might just, like me, be impressed by her ability to get the job done. Angel has become a legend in the Resistance.'

'I have a feeling there's more to it than that. He usually barely smiles, but he was bewitched. And that's with her dressed as a man! Goodness knows what effect she'll have on him, when he sees how gorgeous she is.'

'Poor Henry,' Jack said, his voice glum. 'It would destroy my brother if he lost her.'

'Emotions run high in wartime, and it's easy to understand why people snatch whatever happiness they can in the moment, but Hannah is focused on getting people out of France. She loves Henry, and I doubt she has time for romantic liaisons, anyway. The poor love is always on the run. Imagine what it's like to be permanently undercover in France, not in and out for short periods like us.'

'It's madness. I've tried to get her out, but you know how stubborn she is.'

'She's the most courageous person I've ever met,' Lizzie said. 'And she won't be stopped. The Lavender Network will be a force of nature.'

'I hope her bond with Henry is enough to sustain them through these years of barely seeing each other,' Jack said, still thinking of his brother flying with the RAF.

A red-headed, cheerful nurse with freckles appeared, reminding Lizzie of her sister, Evie.

'Will I live?' Jack asked the nurse with a cheeky smile.

'I daresay, although that's a nasty wound. You're going to have to take it easy for quite some time. And I'll not ask how you got it!'

'Mum's the word. Loose tongues cost lives,' Jack said, tapping his nose.

'Who knows how I'll keep busy when this war is over,' she said, and bustled off with a smile, promising to return with tea and biscuits.

A FANY driver dropped Lizzie outside her house at Regent's Park after she had changed into her uniform and been debriefed at Baker Street. She raised her hand to knock, excited but a little nervous to see her family.

Violet, their housekeeper, opened the door, and a delighted smile spread across her face. 'Your mother is going to be over the moon,' she said, ushering Lizzie inside. 'No case?'

Lizzie shook her head. 'It was in the other vehicle.'

Violet didn't seem suspicious, but the innocent question reminded Lizzie how easy it was to slip up. They left Toulouse so suddenly they couldn't take their cases, so it would be up to Luc to hide them.

'Lizzie, darling! Why do you never give us any notice?' Rose ran to her daughter and almost squeezed the air out of her with her tight hug.

Lizzie laughed. 'I can go and come back later if you'd prefer.'

'You know I didn't mean that. It's just unnerving how you pop up out of nowhere, but I'm delighted you're home.'

'How are you, Ma?' Lizzie asked.

'I'm fine. How about a cup of tea and a piece of Violet's new war cake? It's just out of the oven.'

'I haven't heard of war cake, but I'll definitely give it a go,' Lizzie said, following her mother into the drawing room.

'The rations make it almost impossible to make a good cake, but Violet is so clever with the ingredients, she always produces something tasty.'

Violet brought them tea and cake and Lizzie marvelled at how quickly she had transformed from being Isabelle Dubois to Lizzie Beaumont.

Lizzie ate the cake and enjoyed a cup of English tea, whilst she did her best to answer her mother's questions about her time away, without revealing the truth.

'Evie is training to be a nurse, and says she's found her

vocation. She should be home any minute,' Rose said, glancing at the clock.

Lizzie breathed a cautious sigh of relief that she'd passed her mother's interrogation. Soon the other family members trickled in and there were hugs all round.

When Lizzie's father entered the room and saw her sitting there, he dropped his briefcase and scooped her up in his arms.

'Anyone would think she'd been fighting on the Western Front, the way you carry on when she comes home,' Rose said, smiling.

Lizzie and her father exchanged a discreet look. He was the only member of her family who knew she had been on a mission. Lizzie thought it must be hardest on him when she was away.

Rose continued, 'A few days ago, I had a nightmare that something bad happened to you. Your captain was with you, but then I woke up.'

Lizzie said, 'Just as well, but I don't know why you insist on calling him my captain! He's my commanding officer, Ma.'

Rose looked at her in that discerning way all her children were familiar with, as if she could read their minds. 'Anyway, you're home now, thank God. I shall say no more about it.'

'Over dinner that evening, the chatter was boisterous and incessant. Evie and Juliette found nothing strange about Lizzie being away for extended periods. They plied her with their latest news as if she'd been away on holiday, not undercover on a deadly mission, dining with the Gestapo.

Lizzie longed to tell Evie about the red-haired nurse who seemed like a good omen for her nursing career, but she stopped herself just in time. There was no reasonable excuse for her to have been in a hospital with Jack, waiting for him to be released. As far as her family knew, she'd been working with the FANYs, and had come straight home.

So much of her life must remain secret, and her transition from Michel Dubois's wife to Lizzie Beaumont was brutal in its speed. She wondered how Jack was feeling and wished she could see him at his flat. Lizzie sighed. If she went out again this evening, they would find it odd, and her mother was already suspicious enough about her relationship with Jack.

She would have to wait until tomorrow. His wound wasn't serious, but he needed to rest. He would be fine, but she missed him so much. Lizzie told herself she was being dramatic and suggested to her sisters they play board games. Soon they were laughing and shouting like old times, until tears of laughter streamed from her eyes.

It was good to be home.

At Baker Street a few days later, Lizzie was working at her desk when Val entered.

'We received a message from your new agent, Heart.'

That was Lev's chosen codename. He had told her his name meant Heart in Hebrew.

'What did he say?' Lizzie asked, praying it was good news.

'He used Angel's codes, so she must have trained him.'

'Yes, they received the radio in the supply drop, but we had no time to set up a system with him. Thank goodness Hannah was there.'

The message said the driver and the informant will not be a problem, and they will monitor names from the notebook. All other loose ends are tied. Angel delivered the package to St. Girons. Whatever that means,' she said, fixing a hard stare on Lizzie.

'What a relief. There was so much to clean up after we had to fly out unexpectedly like that.'

'And what was the package?' Val asked.

'Hannah came to drive the airmen to the border, but

obviously plans changed by the time she arrived. It would have been a wasted journey, so she smuggled out the doctor who treated the airman.'

Val's expression was glum. 'Jewish?'

Lizzie nodded. 'The statutes are just as oppressive under the Vichy regime as they are in Nazi occupied territory.'

Val didn't reply. Later that day, when Lizzie filed the copy of her superior's report, she noticed there was no mention of Angel's extracurricular activities.

Some things were better left unsaid.

Lizzie let herself into Jack's flat with her key and shook her umbrella in the hall. The rain was coming down hard, and it reminded her of the storm at the château. It was a shame she'd had to leave her reversible raincoat behind. Perhaps it would be waiting for her one day when they visited Luc after the war.

Jack heard her enter and called out from the bedroom.

She ran to the bed and leaned down to hug him. He groaned.

'Oh sorry, darling, does it still hurt? I'll have to remember to be gentle with you whilst you recuperate.'

'I'll be good as new soon. Sore, that's all.'

Lizzie said she'd brought him a piece of war cake from home to cheer him up. 'My mother calls you *my captain*, you know.'

Jack rolled his eyes. 'She's not wrong. I am lost when you're gone. It's strange without you beside me at night.'

'For me too. Takes me ages to fall asleep. Still, at least there were no bloody air raids to deal with.'

'Yes, the Boche seem to have laid off London. The Blitz stopped whilst we were away.'

'All okay with your mother?' Lizzie asked.

A shadow crossed Jack's face. 'I called her, and she sounded fine.'

'Will you tell her you saw Luc?'

Jack lit a cigarette. 'I wish I could, but I'd be breaking the Official Secrets Act.'

Lizzie sat beside Jack on the bed and studied his face as her emotions collided. His muscled bare chest was bronzed from working in the vineyards, and his shoulder was bound. 'You look like a wounded soldier.'

'I'm fine. How are you?'

'The end of the mission was a whirlwind. It could have gone very differently. I keep thinking about how I could have lost you.'

'I think he intended only to wound me so he could take me alive. British spies posing as French citizens and related to Luc Saint-Clair. We would have been a big catch for the Vichy regime. More valuable alive than dead.'

'Ah, that makes sense. He wanted to be the hero and impress the commissaire and the Gestapo bully.'

A vision of the dying veteran flashed in front of her eyes.

'I know that look. What's troubling you, darling?' Jack said as he studied her face.

'Did I kill him for nothing?' she asked.

'No, of course not. He was a nasty piece of work. If you hadn't shot him, Lev or Hannah would have finished him off seeing as I was out of action. You saw his notebook with all the names of innocent people his informants were spying on.'

'True,' Lizzie said.

'I haven't told you how incredible you were taking charge like that, Seagrove. I pity your opponents.'

'Something came over me when he shot at you.'

'The way he was shooting, it would have been easy to miss his target in the dark, even if he only meant to wound me. The chances are you saved my life.'

'I like that version of events,' Lizzie said. 'Makes a change me saving you instead of you saving me.'

'When they debrief me, that's what I'll tell them, then. Off the record, though, don't disobey my orders like that again!'

They both laughed, knowing that was another order she was unlikely to follow.

Jack reached over to tuck a stray lock of Lizzie's hair behind her ear. 'That was an abrupt end to our mission. I thought we'd have more time together.'

Lizzie glanced at the two gold wedding bands that lay on Jack's bedside table. They needed returning to the SOE prop room.

Her voice was soft. 'It was weird going back to being Lizzie Beaumont with no warning. I loved being your wife. We must do it again soon.'

Jack held her hand, and his eyes shone. 'Oh, we will, darling. Have no doubt about that. As soon as this damned war is over, you will be Mrs Elizabeth King. And if I have my way, I'll never let you out of my sight again.'

THE END

For more Lizzie and Jack, download the exclusive reader-bonus Seagrove & Raven exclusive chapter: *"Until Tonight, My Love"* straight to your inbox:

www.RachelHenke.com/seagrovebonus

Not read Book 1 or 2 yet? Read the full story so far:

Summer Of Fire

Shadows In Paris

Continue the adventure with Book 4 in the series on Amazon worldwide: *Tides Of Resistance*

. . .

If you enjoyed *Whispers At Dawn*, please leave a review. Thank you.

Read *Twin Flames* Excerpt - From the gripping historical adventure romance series also by Rachel Henke

"According to Greek mythology, humans were originally created with four arms, four legs and a head with two faces. Fearing their power, Zeus split them into two separate parts, condemning them to spend their lives in search of their other halves." Plato

York, present day

Cara Bailey arrived at the entrance of *The Olde York Bookstore*, her favourite antiquarian bookshop in York. The shop, situated in a half-timbered Tudor building, meandered across three floors. It could do with a new coat of paint, yet despite the shabby exterior, the shop emitted a welcoming glow.

Cara stepped inside, out of the bright morning sunshine and the chime of a ceremonious bell announced her arrival.

'Hello Cara,' called the proprietor with a big smile.

There weren't many traditional bookshops around anymore, and she'd been a loyal customer since her student days. Cara had come to collect a copy of a rare textbook she'd ordered for her latest project.

'Good morning, John. How are you?'

'Very well, thank you. I believe we have something for you.'

'Yes. That's right. I'll have a wander upstairs first.'

'No problem.'

'It's such a treasure trove in here; there'll be something I can't resist.'

She walked up the spiral staircase and then scanned the shiny shelves looking for something special to jump out at her. There was typically at least one book in the history section she was compelled to buy, and she fancied a new historical novel too. Cara took care not to confuse fact with fiction in her work because the lines could so easily blur. There was always an intriguing thread to follow; a detail or an idea she'd not come across before. Widely recognised as a pre-eminent authority on the Tudor period, Cara loved her job.

A quiet contentment washed over her, and she exhaled slowly, enjoying the moment. If there was such a thing as a happy place, this bookshop was hers. She had poignant childhood memories of trailing from bookcase to bookcase, after her father.

It was unusual to meet anyone in the history section at this time of day. She spotted a dark-haired man in the far corner who was engrossed in a book. She didn't give him any further thought; he appeared lost in his own world.

Cara studied the shelves. A glossy gold and rich burgundy tome on the top shelf caught her eye. She stretched on tiptoe to try to extract it. It was no good. Her height wasn't sufficient to hook the edge of the book with her fingertips. She scanned the area and noticed a thick wooden stepladder, which she dragged across the carpet. Cara climbed the steps, and her fingers touched the book as the toe of her shoe snagged the hem of her skirt. Losing her balance, she cried out. Unable to regain her footing, she tumbled off the steps. She landed in a heap on the thick red pile carpet and banged her head on the bottom of the stepladder. Cara lay still, temporarily oblivious to her fate.

A moment passed before she opened her eyes to see the dark-haired man hovering over her.

'What happened?' she said, as she searched his handsome face.

She pulled herself up on to her elbows and winced at the sharp pain that pumped through her skull.

'I don't know. One minute you were on the ladder, and the next, boom—I heard you cry out and saw you lose your footing, but I couldn't make it over in time to catch you. Are you okay? You hit the ground with such a thump. You gave me quite a fright,' he said.

Lines of concern creased the delicate skin around his liquid brown eyes, and for no apparent reason, Cara's heart lurched. Why was his face familiar?

Although fuzzy headed, she experienced a flash of recognition, as if she knew him. She'd known something similar before, but only with places, not people. Perhaps she was concussed.

Then came a whooshing sound; at first soft, but gradually building into a piercing crescendo. It was an eerie high-pitched noise which haunted her ears. The man's face grew hazy and then disappeared. The floor tilted, she had a sensation of falling and reached out to try and grab something.

Was it an earthquake? She dismissed the notion. She tried to steady herself and clutched at a pillar as the bookshelves whizzed around her.

What the...

She stared into a misty vortex as chilled air strangled her throat. She coughed and gasped for breath.

And then she was gone.

Newgate Prison, London, 1536

. . .

Cara saw two candles glowing on a wooden chest in the corner of the dingy room. She was surprised to find herself sitting on a hard, cold floor. Her last memory was of bookshelves and a handsome face. She stared about her in dismay.

A grubby, short man with unkempt grey hair, called out in a rasping voice, 'Now, now ladies and gents, keep the noise down, please. We've had quite enough rabbiting for one day. We'll see what His Majesty's service has planned for you tomorrow shall we, on your day in court? You'd better get yourselves a good night's sleep because it might be your last before your necks meet the noose.'

His sinister laugh echoed around the freezing cell as the door slammed and his keys jangled in the lock. Cara shivered and ran her hands up and down her arms in an attempt to warm her chilled skin.

Her eyes adjusted to the meagre light and she was surprised to find the man from the bookshop sitting alongside her on the floor. Her hand lay casually across his thigh. It was an intimate gesture, and he seemed at ease as if it was the most normal arrangement. The disconcerting thing was that it felt normal to her too.

'Don't worry my darling wife. We'll figure this out. It's simply an unfortunate misunderstanding. At least the children will be fine at Willow Manor with my parents, and they won't know any different.'

Wife, children, Willow Manor...

He turned and pulled her slim body against his and stroked her tangled hair. Her eyelids grew heavy, and a wave of exhaustion hit her as she slumped on his shoulder and took solace in his embrace.

George savoured the comforting tickle of his wife's breath on his neck as she dozed. He didn't want to move for fear of disturbing her. They'd been apart for too long; he'd yearned to have her close and had been terrified he would never see her again after the recent tumultuous days at King Henry's court.

Unlike most marriages between nobles, theirs was a love match. Cara had been Anne Boleyn's favourite lady-in-waiting right up until the end. How could they have known the threat of the executioner would be the outcome of Cara's royal appointment to the queen? And even if they had known when Cara received the summons to join George at court, they had no choice but to obey the royal edict.

George grew weary and lost track of time; it could have been five or forty minutes later. He removed his jacket, taking care not to wake Cara. She stirred as he folded the material into a makeshift pillow and eased her head down on to it so she could sleep undisturbed. He had work to do, and he wanted her to gather her strength. She had endured a terrible few days, not knowing what had become of him after he was arrested. He must find a way to get them out of here before the trial tomorrow. They were accused of treason and Cara faced an additional charge of witchcraft. If they went before Henry VIII's court, the odds would be stacked against them, and they would have little chance of escaping the hangman.

George wouldn't permit anything to happen to Cara. What would become of their boy, Thomas, and their daughter, May, if they were both executed? Besides, he'd rather die than lose her. Life would be unbearable without Cara in his world.

Failure was not an option. He must find a way to save his family, and he must act now, or it would be too late.

'May I serve you, my lord?' asked an impish looking lad emerging from the shadows. He was scrawny, but George guessed he must be at least nine years of age. He had wise eyes which belied his years.

George was startled. 'How do you know who I am?'

'My eldest brother is in your service in York, Sir: he's a stable boy. Never seen him so content. He sings your praises. He said you run a fine household and treat your servants fair.'

The boy doffed his cap and inclined his head towards him.

Possible plans flitted about George's tired brain, but options were limited with the trial due to take place early tomorrow morning.

'That's very kind of you. I may need your help. What's your name, boy?'

'Everyone calls me Swifty on account of my being so quick.'

'I see,' said George, smiling at the boy and instantly liking him.

He sensed he could trust him.

'I can help you to escape, my lord. I've been locked in here before and escaped through the secret cellar. The night guard is a drunk and sleeps like the dead once he's down. I'm planning to make a run for it tonight.'

'If you truly can help us to escape before the trial, we'll take you with us, and you will be well rewarded for your efforts. Now tell me, how on earth do we get out of this hellhole?'

Swifty held up one grubby finger and pressed it tightly against his lips, urging George to be quiet. He turned and beckoned George to follow him and then darted towards the other side of the long, dimly lit cell.

'Here, my lord, do you see over there?' the boy pointed to the bottom section of the filthy wall. 'If it's the same as last time I was in the clink, we can squeeze through. It's stinky and dangerous though. I don't know if my lady will be able to get down there. It ain't no place for a lady.'

'Don't worry about that. She's no ordinary lady. Show me exactly what you mean.'

They knelt next to the wall, and George saw what the boy meant. He could hear a gurgle below and the stench accosted his nostrils as he lowered his head. It was a long shot, but he believed they could squeeze through the narrow opening and enter the putrid underworld of Newgate. From there, Swifty assured him, they would be able to make a dash for it before daylight.

'There's something I haven't told you though, my lord.'

'Oh dear, I thought it sounded too simple. What may that be then?'

'Others have tried to escape this way and been ambushed by prison guards as they came out. It all depends who's on duty at the exit.'

George ran his hand through his hair and shot a rueful look at the boy. 'We take the risk of being slaughtered by crossbow or being hauled before the court with a high probability of facing the hangman by dusk tomorrow. I fancy our chances against the crossbow.'

George and Swifty huddled in the corner and began planning the details of their escape from Newgate Prison.

York, present day

Cara opened her eyes and realised she was back in the bookshop. She didn't understand what had just happened. One thing was for sure; the prison had seemed so real that she could still smell the damp cell. The vision must have been caused by blacking out. She tried to recall the details, but they were fading fast.

She gawped at the man who towered above her.

Confusion engulfed her normally rational mind as their eyes locked. A jolt ran through her like a current of electricity.

'I'm George Cavendish.'

She accepted his outstretched hand, and he helped her up. Cara's heart pounded, and she feared he must surely hear it.

'May I get you something? Let me see if I can bring you a glass of water. Perhaps you're dehydrated; it's a hot morning.'

He dashed off before she could reply. Cara stared after him and patted her messy hair.

What a state she must look.

She stood in the same spot, feeling awkward, uncertain what to do. She contemplated dashing downstairs, but it would be rude to leave without saying thank you, and she would probably bump into him on the way out, anyway. A few minutes later, he reappeared, smiling as he walked towards her.

As she sipped the water, she attempted to come up with something sensible to say.

'I wish I'd been able to catch you,' he said, 'I just missed you as you toppled off the stepladder.'

'Oh no, really, it was all my fault. I was clumsy.'

Her cheeks flushed, and she shuffled from one foot to the other.

'How's your head?'

He seemed truly concerned and in no hurry to leave.

'It's fine. I must get going. Thanks for the water. I'm so sorry for the inconvenience.'

Cara was reluctant to tear herself away, but she couldn't think of a good reason to stay. She tried not to stare at him, but she was mesmerised. A force beyond her had taken over her senses, and she was drawn to him.

'Are you sure your head's okay? May I call someone for you, or drop you home? I could get my car.'

His smile caused her stomach to flutter.

'No really, thank you, I'm absolutely fine. I was only out for a second. I can drive home, no problem.'

Cara looked towards the stairs, torn between making a quick exit and an ominous foreboding that she might never see him again.

'Well, it was lovely to meet you,' he said, looking into her eyes.

She stared back at him: neither of them broke eye contact.

'How about I take your number? That way, I can check in to make sure you're okay. It's the least I can do if you won't let me drive you home.'

His charm was irresistible. She rummaged through her handbag for a business card but couldn't find one, so she scribbled her number on to the back of a crumpled receipt and passed it to him. As he held out his hand, their fingers brushed. His skin was smooth and warm. Cara's hand tingled, and a fierce sensation surged through her. She had trouble breathing and maintaining an appearance of normalcy. Her lips moved in an unsuccessful attempt at a smile, she croaked a quick goodbye, rushed towards the stairs and then turned to give him a quick wave.

To her relief, the proprietor was nowhere in sight, and she spotted her textbook on the counter. An assistant took her payment and didn't try to engage her in conversation other than a brief, perfunctory exchange.

What a fool she'd made of herself.

She made her way along the cobbled street towards the car park. She couldn't have handled the situation with less grace.

Cara pulled a face as she turned the key in the ignition and joined the lane of heavy traffic moving in the direction of her cottage in the suburbs of York.

She drove straight home; she'd suffered enough turmoil for one day and had lost her enthusiasm to go to the office and tackle her project. Her head was still spinning from the encounter with the enigmatic man in the bookshop. She needed some time alone to make sense of events.

Cara pushed the cottage door open, relieved to be home. How could an ordinary visit to the bookshop have such a monumental effect? Nothing much had happened. She'd banged her head, briefly lost consciousness, and then met a gorgeous stranger. What was the big deal? The thought that her life had been turned upside down and would never be the same again flashed through her mind.

She sipped her tea and tapped her nails rhythmically on the pale china cup. Physically she was present at the oak table in her favourite room; the cosy kitchen in the old Tudor cottage. Mentally she was miles away. Anxious thoughts collided into one another and jostled for attention. Cara's brain yearned for a logical explanation for the morning's events so that she could move on. It seemed like nonsense, but she knew in her bones she'd experienced something pivotal. She flipped open her laptop and typed 'love at first sight' into the search engine. A long thread of results appeared. She clicked on one at random and scanned the article.

"Love at first sight is a rare experience of instantly recognising someone on a soul level. You feel as though you already know this person, even though you've never met them before in this lifetime. It's a feeling of deja-vu: like coming home."

Cara scrolled down, trying to make sense of the words. Irritated and tired, she pushed her cup across the table.

Dr Cara Bailey PhD, award-winning Tudor expert, researching love at first sight. Whatever next?

The phone rang and interrupted her reverie. She

recounted a severely edited version of the morning to her fiancé, Daniel, carefully avoiding any mention of George. Daniel would think she'd lost her mind if she told him what had happened.

'Are you sure you're okay, darling? I don't like the sound of you blacking out. How about I give Doctor Fitzgerald a call to see if he can fit you in for a quick check-up this afternoon?'

'No, really. Thank you. I'm absolutely fine. I was probably dehydrated. I'll stay at home and take it easy for the rest of the day.'

'Well, if you're certain. I know better than to try to push you, so I'll give you a call later to check in. Promise you'll call me if you need anything or you feel unwell. I'm worried about you.'

The phone rang again almost immediately. It was an unknown number.

'Cara? This is George, from the bookshop,' she heard the warmth in his voice.

'Oh, hello. How are you?'

'You've been on my mind, the way you blacked out like that. I couldn't stop thinking about you. . .' His words trailed off.

Cara melted. There was something magnetic about their connection.

After a moment, she replied, 'I'm fine. Thank you. I don't know what came over me. I'm sorry for causing such a fuss.'

'I'm so relieved to hear you're feeling better.'

'It's thoughtful of you to call to check up on me.'

'Perhaps we'll bump into each other again in the city without such dramatic consequences,' said George.

'Yes, that would be nice.' Cara paused but couldn't think of anything to say to prolong the conversation. 'Bye for now, then.'

'Bye, Cara. It was lovely meeting you.'

Violent feelings of loss flooded through her and snatched at her breath.

She stood for a moment, as she clutched her phone, surprised at the intense emotions that gripped her.

Cara didn't move for several minutes. Then she rose abruptly, shook her head and resolved to put George out of her mind. Hoping for a good night's sleep, she muted her phone and went upstairs to bed.

At three in the morning, she awoke. Her heart beat fast and a sob caught in her throat. Her nightshirt clung to her sweat-drenched body. It had been an awful dream; as vivid as the vision in the bookshop. She was with George. Again. This time he'd been arrested. In the dream, she had looked on as one of the soldiers charged him with treason, by order of King Henry VIII.

What were these terrifying visions?

One thought crashed into the next until her head throbbed.

Cara walked into the kitchen and poured herself a glass of water. Her hand shook. She plucked a fresh T-shirt from a pile of neatly folded clothes in the airing cupboard and threw the drenched nightshirt into the wicker laundry basket. Her pale face stared back at her in the mirror; she looked as if she'd seen Anne Boleyn herself.

She sank down on to her bed and within moments, sleep mercifully transported her far away.

. . .

“Really enjoyed this book I couldn't put it down. Brilliant storyline and loved the characters would definitely recommend this book.”

“I enjoyed reading this book the timelines were very vivid and I could imagine myself being in that time.”

“Love this time travel book! It is so good that I couldn’t put it down !Such an interesting story and gives you so much detail on the history of our monarchs. Now reading the second book in this journey and loving it.”

SEAGROVE & RAVEN SERIES

Book 1: *Summer Of Fire*

Book 2: *Shadows In Paris*

Book 3: *Whispers At Dawn*

Book 4: *Tides Of Resistance*

ALSO BY RACHEL HENKE

***Twin Flames* - Historical Adventure Romance Series**

Twin Flames

The Uprising

The Runner

The Covenant

ACKNOWLEDGEMENTS

Special thanks to Russell Cooper, my inspiration in life, love, and writing. 🩶

Thanks to my amazing team of advance readers: Greta Cooper, Anita Davis, Ella Henke and Clare Horrocks.

And to my loyal readers around the world who read every book I write! Thank you for your continued support and enthusiasm.

ABOUT THE AUTHOR

Rachel Henke's novels are historical romantic adventures about strong women and tortured heroes, destined to be together against all odds.

She dreamt of being a novelist since she was seven years old.

Rachel lives with her real-life romantic hero in the beautiful Surrey town of Weybridge, where the Rivers Wey and Thames meet. She spends her days drinking excellent coffee, telling tales, and meeting the incessant demands of their bossy toy poodle.

facebook.com/rachelhenkeauthor

instagram.com/therachelhenke

tiktok.com/@rachelhenke

Printed in Dunstable, United Kingdom

65377672R00194